I0831143

A Chance to Remember

Other books by Ramona Louise Wheeler:

Starship for Hire
Have Starship, Will Travel
Walk Like an Egyptian

A Chance to Remember

Ramona Louise Wheeler

BETANCOURT
& COMPANY
Doylestown, Pennsylvania

This Betancourt & Company edition
copyright © 2004 by Ramona Louise Wheeler.
All rights reserved.

First Betancourt & Company edition: January 2004

A Chance to Remember
A publication of
Betancourt & Company, Publishers
P.O. Box 301
Holicong, PA 18928-0301

www.wildsidepress.com

FIRST EDITION

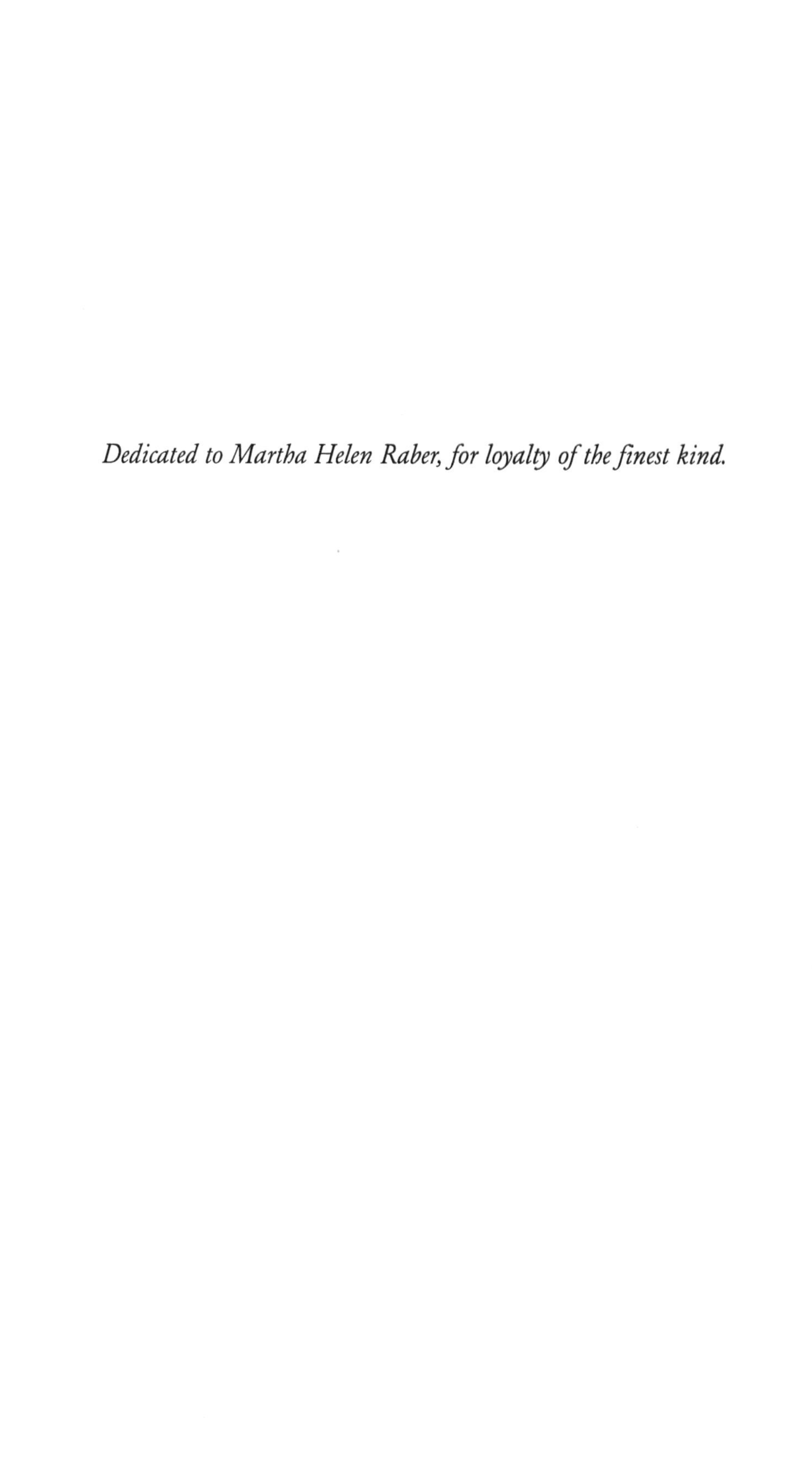

Dedicated to Martha Helen Raber, for loyalty of the finest kind.

For the Want of a Coat

Ray and Rokey flung themselves headlong into the ditch at the edge of the landing field just as barrage of laser-guided sonic blasts raised a wave of steaming mud behind them. Stunbolts screamed past, slicing through the rain. Rokey shoved Ray deeper into the rain-slicked mud at bottom of the ditch, howling at him.

"I've got my head down!" Ray shouted back at the Wozurn. Storm-driven winds tore his words away into the night.

Mud exploded above the ditch with sloppy percussion, and the spray of hot splatters was lit like fireworks by flashes of lightning. Ray and Rokey scrambled up the opposite side of the ditch and sprinted across the field. Bolts slammed into the mud behind them, driving them on.

"You said the guards had orders not to shoot!" Rokey shouted at Ray as they reached the ramp of their starship, *Yankee Shadow.* "You said they had orders!"

"I said they were idiots!" Ray shouted back at him as they raced up the ramp. "Do you remember that I said they were idiots!"

They both leaped for the airlock controls in the same gesture. Rokey let Ray punch in the commands. The panel would not open.

"Open it!" Rokey screamed at Ray over the sonics rattling the ramp at their heels.

"It's locked!"

"It can't be locked!"

"The keys are in my coat," Ray said, his voice suddenly cold and even.

Both men knew why his coat had been left behind with Colonel van Zandt.

Rokey raised locked fists and smashed open the airlock control-panel. Ray leaped aside with a curse to avoid the shards of flying plastic, then hastily signed in at the security link. The hatch slid open and they threw themselves into the airlock. Rokey slapped at the inner hatch controls and they ran inside to the safety of their starship.

Once they were on the bridge, Ray and Rokey slid into their seats at the controls. They had the ignition sequences fired up before the safety webbing had fully buckled around them. Lasers from ground-fire units poked up at the *Yankee Shadow's* underbelly in a dazzling spray of lights as she lifted away. The fierce winds grabbed at an open cargo hatch and twisted the *Shadow's* flight.

"Fix that!" Ray ordered sharply.

Rokey grunted as he began rapidly punching in shield commands. The unsteady pitch of the *Shadow's* flight smoothed. "How'd that hatch get opened?" he said angrily. "Scubb! Did they get our cargo, too?"

"We'll ask them when we're in orbit."

The *Yankee Shadow* soared away.

Rokey suddenly began frantically resetting controls and jabbing at screens, his copper-colored eyes red with shock. "Holy Grid, Ray!" he whispered. "They took our fuel-cells! We don't have anything left but batteries!" His panicked words dissolved into guttural, polyglot cursing as he felt the stomach-wrenching lurch of the artificial gravity going offline, replaced by the ragged pull of acceleration.

"Can we make orbit?"

Rokey shook his head. With a finger-touch to a screen, he fed the data to Ray's console.

Ray read it, understood, looked out to the storm-clouded night racing past the shield.

"I can't go back there, Rokey." Ray's voice was so quiet that the fear rang clearly in every syllable.

Rokey sighed, rubbing his palm over the rain-soaked fur on his head and flicking mud from his whiskers. "You're the captain, Ray, and you know the options."

"I can't go back there," Ray whispered, unable to look

Rokey in the eye. "You know what will happen to me."

Rokey nodded. "Not to mention that, 'Kill the Wozurn,' line," he said. "I've heard that from van Zandt before and that's twice too many times."

"We can still make the other side of the planet." Ray turned to his control panel.

"It's just as muddy on that side."

"At least we can put a planet between us and them. Give us some room to maneuver when we fight," Ray said. "You just find us someplace to land – and we'll need someplace big and flat."

Ray set the Sperry holo-globe to higher resolution, and settled into the task of flying.

Rokey busied himself with images they had taken from orbit when they arrived. His face muscles began twitching as he contemplated the meager choice of landing sites on the planet's other hemisphere. "Pretty sketchy," he muttered. "I can't tell how solid any of this is."

"Fake it. I need a vector *now!*"

Ray swung the starship up and out of the atmosphere. Pale stars shivered into sight as they briefly nosed into the edges of space, but the *Yankee Shadow* could not reach escape velocity. Momentum carried the starship one stage higher before she arched downward, surrendering to the planet.

Eventually her belly slapped the top of the sky. Ray slowed her powerless descent the way primitive astronauts had done, cushioning horrendous speed on a pillow as big as the horizon. The starship bounced and shuddered, skipping across the top of the sky, sinking deeper with each bounce. Heat-shield signals flashed.

Rokey flattened his ears and held on. He was accustomed to Ray's dare-devil piloting, aware that he was alive because his captain could fly this way.

Ray did not look up from his controls, straining to maintain control of his starship's meteoric descent. The shields glowed, filling the bridge with fiery brilliance. The orange-hot light set Ray's green eyes into deep shadows, outlining his hard features.

After a long, terrible time of burning silence, Ray said, "Landing gear down. Extend the skids."

Rokey slapped at his controls. "Gear down."

"Hang on."

Rokey braced himself.

The big starship skipped like a floundering duck across the ice-crusted surface of the giant lake that Rokey had mistakenly scanned as a flat, snowy plain. Thick layers of ice vaporized on contact with the *Shadow's* superheated shields. The lake boiled around her. The *Shadow* plowed forward, throwing up a roiling atmosphere of steam. She almost made the shore, sliding to a stop with a hiss of steam in the shallows at the shoreline. Her nose settled onto the jagged teeth of rock along the beach. Steam billowed around her, condensing to thick rain that splashed the shield and obscured what little there was to see. The night outside was incredibly dark beyond the ship's lights.

Ray's sigh of relief was loud in the hissing silence. He dropped his head onto the back of his gloved hands and focused on calming his ragged breathing. Rokey mumbled reassurance in Wozurn.

"Thanks, old man." Ray raised his head at last to look around. Warning lights buzzed on every monitor. He sat up straighter, flexing his fingers stiffly, and peeled off his muddy gloves to fling them on the deck.

"Holy Grid!" Ray said, looking up at the splattered drops on the shield outside. His hands were shaking badly as he smoothed his wet hair.

A final wave smacked the *Shadow's* tail fins. She lifted lazily in the water, pressing her nose more tightly against the rocks of the shoreline. Rokey yelped, but it was gentle swell. The starship settled more securely and evenly into the rocks.

Rokey made a cynical suggestion.

Ray grimaced. "Sure. Find me a phone booth and I'll call the Coast Guard. I'm sure I've got the Gold Card in my other pants."

The Sunny Side of the Street

Morning did not improve the look of things.

Ray leaned against the frame of the airlock hatch, glumly surveying the bleak landscape. The nothingness surrounding them was cold and gray, a monotonous stretch of beach relieved only by the brilliant contrast of the *Yankee Shadow's* white hull gleaming against the mud. The sky was low with featureless clouds. The *Yankee Shadow* tilted drunkenly onto the rocky shore, half-in and half-out of the lake-ice frozen in wave shapes around her tail.

A freezing wind whipped Ray's blond hair painfully about his face and stung through his flight jacket, chilling his face even with the protection of the filter-mask. He pulled the collar up higher, hugging the jacket to himself, scowling as he remembered the coat left behind in van Zandt's room.

Ice creaked against the ship's hull.

Ray closed the airlock and turned back inside, pulling off the facemask in the same gesture. He rubbed his hands briskly on his thighs and stamped his feet to warm up once he stood in the corridor. His green eyes were as bleak as the gray clouded skies.

Rokey looked up from his work when Ray came into engineering. "Is the sun up?"

Ray nodded.

Rokey returned to his work, but he only fussed over it, brushing contacts with his fingertips and rearranging the arranged lead ends. "Forget it, Ray," he said. "We're alive."

Ray stood studying Rokey a long moment. "I'll make hot cocoa." He went out to the galley.

Rokey came in later to find Ray seated at the galley table, hunched over and staring down unseeing into his cup. Rokey poured cocoa for himself and slid into the seat opposite Ray.

Ray did not look up when Rokey nudged him gently under the table with his foot. Rokey waited, then nudged him again. Ray glanced up only to frown and look away. "Cut it out, Rokey."

"Quit sulking, Captain," Rokey said. "We got away clean, and there's few what can say that about van Zandt."

Ray did not answer, staring down into his cup.

"At least be flattered that such a fortune was spent in the pursuit of love." Rokey stopped at the sight of Ray's fierce eyes.

"No," Ray said carefully. "I am *not* flattered, and that was *not* love."

Rokey shifted in his seat and swallowed hot cocoa. "I've got the broadcast systems back online. We can signal for help if we can figure out whom we can ask."

The planet was artificially terraformed, a likely spot seeded a thousand years before with specialized, planet-chewing bacteria. These hard-working bacteria had already evolved algae beds and pond scum pouring oxygen into the pristine air. Ray and Rokey could breathe with the filter-masks, but there was nothing else in this star system except van Zandt's HQ. There was no one else to hear their broadcast.

"This would be a lot easier if you would get mad and yell," Ray admitted to Rokey after a time. "It is my fault, and I know it."

"Captain, I send you my sympathy for the loneliness of command, but I am just glad that we both got out of that building alive."

"We'll think of something," Ray said quietly.

Rokey nodded. "We'll think of something."

Ray sat staring into his cup.

Rokey scratched his chin fur thoughtfully, looking at Ray through half-lidded eyes. He downed his cocoa in a single gulp and left without a word.

Ray glanced up after Rokey left, and he sighed, appalled at his own poverty of inspiration and at his poverty in general. What a wealth of unusable possibilities, he thought to himself bitterly – a million dollar starship, a hold full of priceless cargo, with a dealers' market out in the stars just begging for every piece of it. A full hold, empty tanks, limited supplies, and one very tired captain. Getting out of Johann van Zandt's trap had taken a lot out of him.

Ray looked down to the slight cant to the *Yankee Shadow's* decks from her uneven perch in the lake. Maybe it had taken everything.

"I hate planets," Ray muttered. He left the cup on the table and went up to the bridge.

Rokey had an idea.

"We have a hold full of photon-converters, remember?" he said to Ray, much too cheerfully.

Ray scowled at him. "We have a hold full of photon-collecting *satellites,*" he corrected carefully. "You want to launch them with handmade balloons? I do have some silk underwear."

"I read the manuals, Ray. This can work."

"You've gone space happy, old man," Ray spoke in low growl. "Those things only work in orbit."

"You can't let prejudice blind you, son," Rokey said. "They work *faster* in orbit. There is a difference."

Ray studied Rokey's face with narrowed eyes, gauging how serious the Wozurn was. "How much difference – in time?" Suspicion was clear in his tone.

Rokey shrugged, drawing his whiskers flat to his face despite an impulse for all his follicles to flare. "We can power the batteries up to window-leap demands in about two years."

Ray kept his breathing even, but his face paled. "OK." He made himself take another slow gulp of air. "OK, nice work, old man. Two years beats eternity in anybody's exchange rates."

"That's two years without your games machine." Rokey braced himself for Ray's rage in response to this bad news.

Ray looked at his partner with shock. He had braced himself for annihilation. Boredom was just a slower kind of hell. Ray swallowed hard against the curses rising up. "Do we have enough for some movies?" he said quietly. He knew what Rokey's priorities were.

Rokey looked down at his toes. "Now and then."

Ray turned away from Rokey to the dash controls in front of him. "I'll, uh – I'll get to work on a manual inventory of current supplies, and a, uh – a schedule on what we can recycle."

"Good idea, son," Rokey said. "Get the tanks out for testing the algae in this lake."

"We should name it," Ray called to his partner as he went out, knowing Rokey could hear him almost anywhere in the ship. "How about Fake It Lake?"

"Works for me," Rokey called back.

Ray began to study panel readouts in earnest, lapsing into military training he ordinarily hated himself for knowing.

Ray liked even less the inevitable conclusion that he was the one most suited to dragging the satellite crates out onto the frozen muck of the lake shore. Rokey was caught up in the desperate realization that he had forgotten one crucial, irrevocable question to ask the computers when designing this compromise to their energy crisis. The flow from the photon-collectors was degraded enough by the atmosphere that he would have to use a direct, shielded line-feed in order to get the power into the *Shadow's* batteries.

The problem was a tiny one, but could well sabotage their meager hopes: the output plugs of the black market satellites and the input of the *Shadow's* battery adapters were incompatible.

That was the price for the convenience and discount service of black-market materials. Anyone might build unlicensed or illegal hardware, but *no one* messed with the signal input/output adapters. The union on that deeply rooted necessity was millennia-strong, and rivaled the interstellar government for the reach of its enforcement. Those wonderful little hardware interface-devices that linked the various and many-faceted technologies of the galaxy were as mystically, fanatically and ritualistically protected as the Vestal Virgins. No one plugged into a board or power unit not his own without the permission of local deities or at least the legal representative of said deities – and never, *ever* without a jack that matched its particular jill.

Rokey had set himself a complex task, wading through the encryption programs assigned to the drivers of each and every satellite photon collector in their cargo of black market goods. These were the finest that illegal money could buy. Anything of lesser quality would have doomed them to a cold and dismal fate. Ray's insistence on carrying only top-of-the-line goods was their salvation – a slow, boring salvation, nevertheless one that beat the hell out of a frigid starvation onto death.

They both knew that this was the best alternative to anything they could work out. This knowledge kept voices calm despite hysteria. It gave each man a gentle patience with the other's panic that was a comfort in the long, chilling nights of this pseudo-place.

Ray swung the last crate into place on the frozen beach and unlatched it. He was shivering and his fingers were stiff with cold despite his gloves. He sprinted back to the loading ramp, glancing once at the stacks of opened crates piled around the ship. He was grateful that the last one was out. The clouds never seemed to lift here, and he had to trust to computer readouts that the filtered light would work. A sharp wind keened through him and drove him into his ship. Ray ripped off the filter-mask with a sigh of relief as the airlock closed behind him, leaving him in the relative warmth inside.

In just one week, Ray had come to hate this planet more than any jail he had ever slept in.

Radio, Radio

Rokey reached under the tangled quilts and yanked Ray up by his shoulder, pulling him into the light with an excited gesture. "Ray!" Rokey was almost shouting. "The radio! They're on the radio!"

Rokey released Ray and ran out.

Ray could hear him racing to the bridge. Ray sat up in his bed, rubbing grit from his eyes. He had been sleeping too much over the last few months. Had he just dreamed Rokey's excited intrusion?

The clear sound of radio static from the bridge made his glass-green eyes flash with sudden, tropical lightning. Ray leaped to his feet and felt about for his terry robe. As he raced out of his quarters, he thrust his hands into the sleeves, struggling to get inside-out from outside-in. He found Rokey hunched over the radio, ears thrust forward, every gesture of him focused on the faint, static-ripped voice in the speaker. Ray froze.

The distant voice was Wozurn, speaking in the throat-ripping growls and snorts of the native Wozurn tongue. Although Ray was unable to speak a word of Wozurn other than pronouncing Rokey's full name and titles correctly, he did understand the language. He had difficulty with this Wozurn voice, however. The accent was thick and the radio signal was weak and distorted. Ray stood still, keeping his excited breathing as quiet as he could, waiting.

Rokey signed off with their rescuers, grinning happily. His copper-colored eyes were shining. "Captain Briggs and the *Tzipory* are on their way!!" he said to Ray. "We are saved, saved,

saved!!"

Rokey leaped up to grab Ray in a giant, rib-crunching hug. Both men were whooping and shouting, months of repressed fear and hysteria burned away by the voice in the radio.

The next morning, they began packing up and reloading their sprawl of satellites, returning them to the hold. Rokey helped. Their lagging, half-starved strength was buoyed by the energy of anticipation. The job went quickly. Ray had come to see this place as staring out at his own grave. Six months here felt like entombment. He wondered if he could have survived another eighteen. He had begun to lose faith, even in luck.

That faint Wozurn voice in the radio static restored a great deal of Ray's belief in himself. Captain Briggs and her copilot, Nolsey, were in a flightgun armed with photon repeaters and, therefore, loaded to the nines with spare fuel-cells, more than enough to put the *Yankee Shadow* back into space and through the intraspace window that was the final exit from this dreary place. Ray really was lucky enough to draw rescuers down out of the heavens, even lucky enough to draw Wozurn rescuers Rokey could talk to. Ray trusted Wozurn. He trusted them enough not to ask why they were jumping through remote intradimensional windows armed like cyberspace dream-warriors. Luck could not stand up to questions like that.

Four days later they had everything packed up and stored away. In their months of being marooned, they had groomed, polished, repaired and refurbished every piece of the *Yankee Shadow* they could reach. Twice. She gleamed. Everything worked to manual specs and better. They were ready for guests.

"Captain Briggs is a lady," Rokey kept saying to Ray.

He said it often enough, with just enough of a nervous twitch to his whiskers that Ray caught on to how powerfully affected Rokey was by their rescue, and by their rescuer. Rokey talked with her often as she approached. Her ship was old-fashioned, she explained to them. Deceleration from window-jump speeds was awkward without the aid of modern enhanced inertial dampers. Ray did not mind the wait. He used some hoarded power for his games machines. He was appalled at how rusty he was, at the same time totally thrilled by the sudden newness of once-familiar routines.

Patient Spider by the Door

However good Ray's good luck might be, there was a dark side.

Captain Briggs' last frantic radio call was barely audible even to Rokey, ripped with static and interrupted by bursts of incoherent swearing. Ray could not understand a word. Rokey's shocked stance and flared mane made it clear something had gone terribly wrong.

Rokey finally turned to face Ray with the news, his eyes bright red with anger. "That bastard van Zandt has been sitting on the other side of the planet all this time, cozy warm and well-fed, waiting for you to call him for help!" Rokey was shouting. "He shot Briggs' ship! He shot her!"

Ray had a lot of rage stored up at Johann van Zandt's destructive effect on his life. Ray had always responded with the simple desire to get as far away from van Zandt as the galaxy made possible. For the first time, Ray began to think about revenge and murder.

"He's still out there?" He spoke in even, clipped tones. His face was as cold as the heated passion storming in Rokey. "Was she coming here to see him, then?"

Rokey drew a deep breath, trying to find words. His own outrage was for Briggs' safety. He did not have the guilt that was driving Ray. "Briggs' people were the ultimate buyers of those satellites," he explained. "She was sent to investigate why they hadn't arrived. But van Zandt doesn't want you rescued. He wants you to have to ask him for help."

"How badly is she hit?" Ray could not meet Rokey's eyes.

Rokey shrugged. "I can't tell from what little I could hear.

She said she would call again once she had landed."

"Do you think she should land? Shouldn't she try to get out the window again?"

"They shot out her drive engines." Rokey could hardly believe this himself. Briggs' had spat the words out with painful clarity. "Van Zandt told her that no one gets to rescue Captain Harris but him."

"So now we have to go rescue her?"

Rokey nodded. "If she survives the landing, yes. We have to rescue her."

"I'll go unpack my heavy boots again," Ray said as he went out.

Rokey looked out to the bleak, cold landscape and the frozen lake. "I guess I better finally unpack mine, too."

Captain Briggs was a good pilot, as good as Ray Harris, good enough to land despite the serious damage to her little starship. The *Tzipory* actually made it to the Fake It Lake, but on the opposite shore, two thousand kilometers from the *Shadow.* Ray and Rokey tracked her in their scopes. The last moments of her flaming descent were visible in the clouded night, a meteoric flash streaking the sky with fire and vanishing into the dark horizon.

Neither man said a word. There was nothing they could do but wait for the radio call, or to decide, at last, that it would not come.

After a long, silent three hours, Ray leaned forward to the control panel, touched it uncertainly, then looked over at his partner. "If enough of her fuel-cells survived, they could get us out."

"And there's someone out there who will take very effective revenge on van Zandt once he learns what happened to Captain Briggs. We owe it to her." Rokey had been saving a somewhat awkward piece of information about Captain Briggs. Rokey knew how Ray felt about the kind of people Briggs had called "family."

"Who might that be?" Ray knew from Rokey's drop in volume that he was reluctant to say. "Someone else in van

Zandt's grubby little kingdom?"

Rokey winced. "No, not quite as bad as that. Ever hear of a Free Trader ship name of the *Tamaroan?*"

"Oh, Rokey, please!" Ray groaned. "Not pirates! Please, say it ain't so!"

"Don't call them pirates."

"They live like pirates!" Ray protested.

"But they call themselves Free Traders."

"I can call myself a Wozurn pup, but I still won't grow points on my ears! You live like a pirate, you're a pirate!"

"You'd look ridiculous with pointed ears."

Ray caught himself on his response to that, remembering why they were here and what had just happened. "I'll wear my hat," he said.

"You'll wear the whole damn suit," Rokey was staring out to the black, cold night. "These people are used to respect."

Ray shrugged. "Like I have a choice. Rescue by a pirate beats having to ask van Zandt. I don't think he will shoot at the *Tamaroan* if they come here looking for Briggs."

"That's a fact."

Ray put a hand on Rokey's furred shoulder. "I am sorry, old man. I know she was important to you."

Rokey did not answer.

Their grief was premature. Briggs' radio signal was clear when she called them. She told them that she had put out the onboard fires, and buried her copilot. They would have to come get her and the precious fuel-cells. The cells were intact and could get the *Yankee Shadow* out of this star system. Her ship would keep her alive until they got there, but she had a broken leg and internal injuries. She would have to wait for them to come to her.

"I will sleep now," were her closing words. "I will call you when I wake up."

Once Ray and Rokey had recovered, they went up to the galley and began some serious planning. They had been chipping the ice away from the Shadow, taking what time at it that they could stand in the cold. She was almost clear. They had collected enough power in the seven months here to melt them free of the rest. How far it would carry the *Shadow* after that was a guess. They argued out the possibilities, then made themselves get a night's sleep.

Ray and Rokey went out at dawn with the heaviest tools they had and shattered, by hand, the final layers of ice around the tail and landing gear. The work was grueling and monotonous. They quickly gave up conversation in the bitter cold, smashing grimly at the ice. Ray directed his white-hot anger and outrage at the lake as though he could melt it with sheer intensity.

At noon time, Rokey called a halt. "That's it," he declared shakily. "This is about the warmest this day will get."

They went inside and stripped off their wintry gear. Each had a cup of hot cocoa, quickly, before going on to the final work of freeing their starship. Nothing seemed certain now. The last details were down to Ray's skill and luck. Ray knew he had to be calm. It would be a long, cold walk to the *Tzipory* if he couldn't get his starship free with battery reserves.

They used the *Shadow's* outer speakers to set up a sonic resonance within the last of the ice, building this frequency until the mechanical energy shattered the ice. Ray had to be ready to switch power to antigravity control and lift free before it could resettle.

The starship was released with a wild, abrupt surge and vibration that flung them both hard into their safety straps as they soared upwards in a shower of sparkling ice-crystals.

Rokey whooped with surprised delight.

Ray's attention was full on his controls. He aimed the floating ship toward the horizon where the *Tzipory* had crashed.

Loading Briggs' surviving gear and effects aboard the *Shadow* and refueling from her fuel-cell supply was the best fun Ray had had in many long months. Rokey and Briggs cast each other curious glances at Ray's gleeful tunes and high spirits as he shouldered boxes and crates, tapping out brief flashes of drum roll beats against the hull. Every time Ray looked at the *Yankee Shadow,* he fell in love with his starship all over again. What a wonderful starship, he thought to himself. What a wonderful place to be.

Briggs herself came onboard last, leaning against Rokey. Her flame-orange fur was ragged, with scorched patches on her hands, arms and back. Her long, black cheek whiskers had been burned back to stubs and one ear tip was missing, but her brilliantly orange eyes, outlined by black stripes, were calm. She paused at the airlock entry to look over her shoulder once at the *Tzipory.* Rokey waited patiently, supporting her with one arm around her waist.

Ray curbed his delight, realizing how high a price Captain Briggs had paid for his happiness. He helped to settle her surviving gear into the guest quarters on the *Shadow* with a deliberately gallant air while Rokey took her below to the automated hospital unit in sickbay.

"He is charming, your little captain," she observed to Rokey as he helped her into the hospital cradle.

"You'll get used to him."

"He is the first Terran I have ever seen – he seems quite insubstantial to be such a formidable pilot."

"We both lost a lot substance over the last few months, ma'am. He'll beef up as we go."

"He has earned your respect even though he is as naked as a child?"

"I've been lucky. This ship attracts a peculiar kind of metal in her captains. She wears away everything else."

"You are very fond of this ship, Rokey. More than I am of the *Tzipory.*"

"I designed the *Yankee Shadow,* ma'am," Rokey explained. Pride showed in his voice, and the tilt of his whiskers. "She's seen me through many a storm."

Briggs reached out and gently smoothed the fur along Rokey's forearm. "You make me glad that I was able to save you and your *Shadow* from this awful place."

Rokey laughed, but he did not ask if she meant the starship or his captain.

She grinned up at him, showing white fangs in her fiery face. "I'm young yet, Lord Rokhmyr. I can afford a little inconvenience." She winked at him. "Just think how glad old

Jak will be to see me. Won't this teach him not to take me for granted?"

Rokey smiled her, more politely than genuine. He had not convinced her yet to call him "Rokey" and not "Lord Rokhmyr."

"If he's fool enough for that, my dear," Rokey said, covering the sting of concern he felt, "he won't last very long."

They laughed together. Rokey went out to help Ray get the fuel-cells installed.

Ray was flattered that Briggs called him charming. Rokey omitted the "little captain" part. Ray would have forfeited his gentlemanly status on finding out he was referred to as "Lord Rokhmyr's Little Captain." Raymond Harris was not called 'Captain' because he owned a starship. He had earned that rank on a battlefield in cold space. It had a lot to do with his opinion of himself.

Ray did not buzz van Zandt's field before leaving the planet. He just burned out of orbit as fast as the *Yankee Shadow* would go.

Once through the window and in the safety of intraspace, Ray paced the *Shadow's* decks with all the solemn appreciation of a man in a museum. Every surface gleamed. Every fitting was up to specs and better. Everywhere the emotion of starting out brand new burned through him.

Happy Jak and My Lady's Pirates

Ray was wakened by the double alarm of his bedside comlink frantically buzzing and the shudder of a blast shaking his starship. Ray landed on the deck, wide awake. The blast hit again. Ray leaped to his feet and ran out. He stopped in the corridor abruptly, spun around and ran back into his quarters to grab his dressing robe and throw it on as he ran out again. Their guest, Captain Briggs, was a lady.

Ray raced to the bridge. His partner, Rokey, was already in his copilot's seat, snarling into the radio in Wozurn. The black ruff of fur around his face was raised up like an angry mane, and his long white whiskers were flat to his face.

The *Yankee Shadow* had been floating for the last ten days in a sparkling cloud of interstellar dust at Captain Briggs' requested rendezvous point. Briggs was waiting for her husband, Lord Jak, onboard his giant tradeship, the *Tamaroan.* Evidently, Lord Jak had, at last, arrived. The *Tamaroan's* flightgun armada was closing around the *Yankee Shadow* with daring speed and precision. That many flightguns were well able to destroy the *Shadow* and all trace of her.

Ray slid into his seat at the dash and scanned readouts. There was nothing he could do. They were surrounded.

Rokey continued his throaty explanation into the radio mike. The radio snarled back at him. There was a burst of light outside the ship, a dazzling side-swipe.

Ray at last unraveled Rokey's end of the Wozurn conversation. "She is not a hostage!" he shouted at Rokey. "Tell them she's our *guest!*"

"I *am* telling them that!" Rokey returned angrily. "Get Briggs up here – fast!"

Ray leaped up to obey.

Captain Briggs, however, was soundly asleep, snoring in the noisy Wozurn way. The alarm on the desk buzzed unheeded – and inaudible – through her snores. Ray was not amused. He had stopped speculating about Wozurn physiology after just a few nights of trying to sleep through the noise of *two* Wozurns onboard snoring. He had to shout to hear himself above the lion-sized noise.

Ray shook Briggs roughly. She only curled up tighter, her snore shifting to a higher pitch. He shook her again. She growled under the snore. Another blast to the *Shadow* tossed him on top of her. Inspired, Ray shrugged to whatever fate or hallucination was watching, and kissed her.

Briggs' golden eyes flew open. One great arm lashed out and wrapped around Ray, pinning him against her furred chest. Ray grinned into her fanged snarl, trying to explain. He took a deep breath and made an attempt at Lord Jak's Wozurn name. Ray's pronunciation was backed by another blast slapping at the ship. Briggs gave Ray a return kiss, sweeter than even Ray Harris would have guessed, then pushed him aside as she leaped to her feet. Their hospital unit had healed her injuries thoroughly during the trip here, restoring her ragged fur to its flaming glory. She raced ahead of Ray to the bridge.

Briggs began shouting at Lord Jak on the radio. The flightguns surrounding the *Shadow* flipped end-over-end and withdrew.

Rokey sat back in his seat, sweeping down his ruffled mane with one hand. Ray noticed, at last, the wistful look on his partner's furred and usually impassive face. There was a tilt to ear and whisker Ray had never seen before, making Ray think about how long it had been since Rokey had even seen a woman of his own kind, much less become friends. Now Briggs was returning to her husband. Ray pictured himself in a similar spot, and that wistful look made a lot of sense. Even Ray had come to like Captain Briggs.

"I'll get dressed while you and Briggs dock us with the

Tamaroan," he said quietly to Rokey as the snarling conversation via radio continued. He thought it best to leave Rokey alone with Briggs just then.

"Put your uniform on, son," Rokey said without looking at him.

"Rokey!" Ray began a protest.

"Yes, I know," Rokey cut him off. "But these people have never seen an Earthman before, and you're going to look like a Wozurn child to them. Don't forget that we Wozurn don't get a coat of fur until adolescence, and other than our fur, we don't look that different from Earthlings."

"Ears," Ray said with dignity. "I have small ears. And no whiskers."

"You're still going to look like a child to them. The fact of your homeworld being under marshal law *because* you have that uniform is what will impress this crowd the most. Trust me."

Ray grumbled as he went out to his own quarters. He knew perfectly well that if he truly intended never to wear his old uniform again he would have destroyed it before now. Glory, dishonor, victory and despair, wrapped up together in a few meters of gold-colored permaweave. Bounty hunters could get twice the price on his head if they brought him in wearing it. He had already killed three men to save himself from dying in it. Rokey would not have asked him to wear it without good reason, but Ray did not like to think what those reasons might be. He cued the security lock to the secret panel at the back of his closet and waited while the passcode cycled through.

He hesitated before taking out the garment bag it was stored in. When he held the drape of fabric over his arm, with its soft sheen, bronze shoulder stripe and insignia, he felt the same troubling exhilaration he had felt the first time he saw it, indeed, every time he saw it. The charge it carried now was almost unbearable because it was the last one left. Of the entire Auruma Space Fleet Special Fighters Squadron, this was the last uniform. Captain Raymond Harris was the lone survivor.

Ray did not dare go down that alley of dark memory. He set his mind firmly on the problem ahead, and began to get himself dressed and ready to meet Lord Jak and his pirates – correcting himself every time he thought of them that way. Lord Jak and the *Tamaroan* crew did not think of themselves as pirates. They talked like pirates, lived like pirates and fought like pirates, but they called themselves "Free Traders." They were likely to kill anyone who said otherwise.

Rokey had warned Ray to keep his mouth shut. Rokey warned him of that often. Just this once, Ray was ready to obey.

Lord Jak met them in the corridor of the docking bay, eager to see his wife after months of separation and anxiety. Jak was a big Wozurn, a clear head taller than Rokey and more. He wore a fancy red weapons harness strapped across his back instead of a collar of rank. He was striped in blue and gray, with such elaborate patterns that the deep, crisscrossed scars on his chest almost did not show. One ear tip was lopped off, unnecessary in an era when anything biological could be repaired. Clearly, it was an honor scar. Dignity warred with menace in his carriage, stately and heavy footed until he swept Briggs up in his powerful arms, swirling her around with a happy howl. For the briefest of moments they were just lovers met again after a terrible ordeal.

Jak's lieutenants stood behind him, dour, impassive, enormous. One had black fur, one white, and the third the color of smoke and ashes. Ray decided to let them set the tone. He stood silently behind Rokey in as menacing a stance as he could manage while remaining elegant. The uniform had reminded Ray of the way a suit could change things. He had to stay aware of that, and not get carried away with it in a crowd of people who wore honor scars and weapon harnesses.

"Come to the party!" Lord Jak said in SpeakEZ, beaming around at everyone. His voice was as enormous as his presence. "The whole fleet is partying to welcome home my Lady Briggs! You will be guests of honor! You bring her home to me!"

Jak paused then, as though searching his memory, aided by a nudge in the ribcage from his wife, clasped in his arms. "Lord Rokhmyr," he said awkwardly, meeting Rokey's eye. "It is an honor." He bowed his head gruffly and swung about. "Come!" he called loudly, covering his discomfort with volume. "We party!"

Rokey was wearing the collar of his Wozurn aristocratic rank. It accentuated, somehow, the sleek, elegant lines of his features. Ray had seen that collar before only in old news holos of Rokey's past career. It was dark red, edged in gold, with a white metal radiolarian emblem under Rokey's chin. Wozurn glyphs in the same white metal ran in narrow lines, like flowing raindrops around the collar. It was Rokey's only tie to his aristocratic past, as dangerous as Ray's golden uniform.

Ray had never before stood this close to Rokey's Wozurn, overly-civilized culture. He had never fully grasped the tapestry of galactic history that was the backdrop of his friend's here-and-now life. The crew of the *Tamaroan* were as cut off from "respectable society" on Wozur as Rokey was himself, yet they nonetheless respected his past titles. He was not "Rokey" to them, a drunken insomniac. He was the legendary "Lord Rokhmyr," Earl of Rokherton Keep, firstborn of the fourth-eldest first-family of Wozur, eighth in line for the seat of galactic leadership, and president of the biggest university in all civilization.

Ray decided it was his obligation to be certain he did nothing to tarnish that reputation. He stood straighter in his uniform and tried to look grim.

Pirates on Parade

The common room on the *Tamaroan* was as enormous as everything else on the enormous starship. Ray could have parked the *Shadow* on the dance floor without disturbing anyone. Most of the crew were Wozurn, but there was a fair percentage of other aliens as well: Phridyan, Defton-Hoyt and a group of enormous Argglyddian off to themselves around a fountain of lights. Ray was the only Earthling here, one-of-a-kind in an alien crowd.

The common room was packed, literally, to the rafters. The space was organized with artificial gravity fields so that the tables and bars as well as the dancers, drinkers and idlers were scattered about casually in the air, layered between sliding airwalks and blocks of sculpted light. At first glance, the dance floor was an explosion in slow motion.

Ray stood at Rokey's side until he had oriented himself and located the exit signs. He stood a while longer because the place was too big and too busy, with an army's worth of people.

At the central point of the cathedral ceiling was a holo-display of flight log sequences of the *Tamaroan* in battle, with close-ups of Captain Briggs' lost flightgun starship, the *Tzipory,* skimming and darting around the giant ship in silent battle. Ray was impressed. The *Tamaroan's* automatic flight recorders were remarkably well directed, capturing the precision space battle with loving detail. Ray watched the holo-display carefully.

Captain Briggs was a skillful pilot, as daring as Raymond Harris, seasoned by a good many more years of practice. He began watching out of respect and found himself watching with excitement. Apparently, being eighty years old in Wozurn age did not mean she was old, rather that she had had time to get good at what she did. Briggs was obviously aware of the flight log eyecams following her every action in battle. She flew and fought like a movie star, using the ship's minimal, antique inertial dampers as high-class ballet slippers. The magnesium sizzle raged in 3D silence over the party. The whole room was exploding with excited noise and music.

Ray also began to take stock of the nature of the *Tamaroan's* enemies. His father had raised him to believe that pirates attacked the weak and flailing. Space pirates were sharks in very deep water, yet Ray did not see a single vessel the *Tamaroan* attacked that was not either galactic federal issue or else minions of one of the many megalopolis corporations that kept the price of living in the galaxy so desperately high. If Ray had not been taught to hate pirates, he would have been proud of them, reminding himself for the hundredth time that they were *not* pirates. They just lived that way.

Ray stayed at Rokey's elbow, looking grim and thinking about that while he watched the *Tzipory* flash and dip. Careful editing, perhaps? He wondered.

Ray turned to the bar, tuning in to the growls and snarls of the Wozurn conversation there. Toasts were going around to the *Tzipory's* co-pilot, Nolsey, and his brave efforts to help keep her flying amidst van Zandt's attack. Oaths against Johann Mohammed van Zandt were shouted out with great gusto, washed down with something that sizzled amidst its foam. Ray began to feel considerably improved in spirit. van Zandt had put Ray and Rokey through a long, cold, muddy stay in hell. He had nearly killed Captain Briggs for rescuing them. Finding new friends who would be new enemies for van Zandt was satisfying, especially since these new enemies had such a big army for exacting revenge.

Briggs ordered a round of toasts to Lord Rokhmyr. The cheers were deafening, as though everyone wanted to impress him individually. After a few more such raucous rounds, a pair of twin Wozurn women, slight in form and matched in bright orange fur patterns, cuddled up against him at the bar. They had very perky ears and whiskers, and they seemed to move in unison, dancing sinuously around Rokey's bulky form. After a half dozen more of these tumultuous toasts to Lord Rokhmyr, these two whispered simultaneous somethings into Rokey's broad ears that made him roll his eyes in delight. They led him away, and Ray found himself on his own at the bar.

The lights and extravagant warmth were wonderful after the months of dim despair and desperate energy conservation he and Rokey had been through before the *Tzipory* had found them. They had named the lost planet where they were marooned "Mudball" and both had expected to die there. Instead, the *Tzipory* had died there, almost taking the lovely Captain Briggs with her. Nolsey, the co-pilot, was buried back there. The *Tzipory's* salvaged fuel-cells had gotten the *Yankee Shadow* free of Mudball and Johann Mohammed van Zandt, and it looked like the light and energy of the *Tamaroan* might get Ray and Rokey free of the mud that van Zandt had ground into their souls.

The *Tamaroan* was big enough to have inertial-sink hardware that could draw energy from the intraspace dimension, like a boat drawing hydrogen as fuel from the water pushed aside by its bow. There was no rationing, no limit, no need even to consider the energy used or the need for fuel. Energy was here for the demands of life, for the empowerment of all, for sheer entertainment. Ray was happy to see so much light and color, even the wild extravagance of dancing in microgravity.

At the far end of the hall was an arena-size zero-gravity tank, outlined by racing stimlights. The brightly lit ZG was ringed with targets and swirling with colored fog. At this distance, the figures inside looked like flashing birds or fish. Ray saluted Briggs and Lord Jak, then drifted away through the fields and slidewalks and crowded aisles to the rim of the tank.

He stood in the air at the rim, leaning against the stimlight railing to watch. The tank was big enough for fifty or more to play at once. About three dozen or so were playing at the moment, mostly Phridyan.

Ray was familiar with Phrid, a planet even newer to the galactic community than Earth. He and Rokey had visited their world once, on a most lucrative and pleasant cargo run not too many years earlier. The Phridyan language was fresh in his mind. This group were southerners, taller, leaner and more distinctly lizardlike than the heavyset race of the northern continent the *Shadow* had visited. The men had ivory-white scales, with eyes the color of fire-lit brass. The women were scaled in rainbow colors that shifted with micro-etching sheen. They were appealingly humanoid in sleekly fitting deck uniforms that left their long, restless, whiplike tails free.

A group of such girls waved and giggled at Ray with musical bird-voices, so he drifted over to join them watching the game.

Three Defton-Hoyts also standing there smiled up at him with angelic, green faces and sky-blue eyes hypnotically bright. Ray grinned down at them, careful to keep his boots clear of their massive, clawed toes and kangaroo tails. He had once seen a Defton-Hoyt slash a man's brains out with those claws, lashing out like meat grinders while balanced on that thick, powerful tail. He had a lot of respect for those claws.

These Defton-Hoyt, however, just giggled when they caught his eye, whispering together excitedly when he looked away.

As Rokey predicted, everyone was fascinated by Ray's uniform and his soft, unfurred and unscaled skin. Earthlings were known here only by reputation. They spoke with him in SpeakEZ, teasing and flirting. The girls did not know that he could also understand the Phridyan chatter among themselves. He kept the secret, warming a little at their remarks to one another about his physique, enjoying the sheer femaleness of their conversation. Women were women wherever he found them, and Ray enjoyed women whenever he found them.

This group was a lovely, bright contrast to the gray past he had grown used to seeing. He had been stuck in the mud for a long time, he realized standing there. He relaxed, at last, letting the many intoxicants warm him more, listening, talking, flirting, looking at the life suddenly bright, energetic and excited around him.

"Will you play?"

Ray grinned at the question and said, "Yes," but the girls meant the game in the ZG.

He had not done anything like their ZG playing since his days of military training. He knew his training gave him considerable advantage despite his lack of practice. ZG was a target game originally designed for training soldiers for hand-to-hand combat in space. Elaboration of game technique had turned it into a popular sport. Local variations were in vogue, nothing too complex. He had picked up most of the rules already just by watching. Ray had a moment of reluctance when he learned he had to surrender his gunbelt in exchange for the harmless target pistol. He decided it would have been suspicious to insist on playing armed, or to refuse to play unarmed, so he added his own to the unguarded pile of weapons beside the tank entrance.

Once he dropped into the zero-gravity field and felt the sensation of freedom stretching and twisting there, Ray's spirits lifted. He turned his attention from suspicion to the players and to the game.

The teams were fairly evenly matched for Wozurn and Phridyan players. Their ornaments, flashy in the bright lights, looked merely gaudy up close. There were eight Defton-Hoyts floating in a ring at the corner of the tank, their great, thick tails dangling loosely behind them. Each had jeweled caps over each thick claw, blunting them; nevertheless, they could still deliver a stinging blow. The leader of the opposing team was a tall, well muscled Phridyan youth wearing intricate chest armor, with arm-guards over his deck suit. The armor looked to be carved of some dark wood, with fancy cut-amber scales set in careful patterns. These were arranged so that they clicked when he moved, a cheerful, pleasant sound. The honor scar across his face, smearing the scale pattern into a downward arch, gave him an otherwise unpleasant look. His grin was even less pleasant. He was not pleased that Ray was playing, particularly that he was playing with that particular group of Phridyan women. He did not say that in so many words. His displeasure was clear in his eyes.

"I am Azimond, Captain Harris. I know who you are. You should think twice before playing here with no practice. Would you prefer that we played the first round with a handicap?"

"You already are," Ray replied quietly.

The girls flashed around Ray like brilliantly colored birds, laughing and trilling, calling out to Azimond that he was afraid to play with the great lord Rokhmyr's alien squire. Ray had a moment to wonder if these women had not perhaps had a less pleasant reason for asking him to play on their team.

Azimond leaped out into the center of the arena, giving the command for the game's start. The target globe darted into the field. Ray sprang after it, launching himself from the starter ring, first to touch it with his hand, thus winning the right to first-fire for his team. Azimond maneuvered his team to intercept it. Ray let him. He preferred the game when both teams were firing.

His teammates used the game as an excuse to tease him with their tails and to bump against him in passing. They played well, accurately hitting the whirling globe as it flashed through the swirling, colored fog in the tank and flickering in and out of sight. Ray kept a steady line of laser fire aimed at the globe and never let it slip, leashing it to him on a lead-line of light. Members of Azimond's team tried to block his aim or tackle him. Ray evaded them with skilled ease. He enjoyed the envious glares of the players even though he knew it was not fair. They had learned to play this as a game. Ray had trained to fight for his life this way. The pace picked up. The score for Ray's team climbed steadily. The crowd at the rim of the tank got larger as word spread of his performance. Bets began to go around. Ray leaned into the game, happy with the foolishness of it and content to stretch and to dash through the air, surrendering to the freedom. The sparkling lights of the target globe, luring him around, were burning away, point by point, the mud in his soul from van Zandt's trap on Mudball.

Ray found himself defending the team position more and more directly against Azimond. The Phridyan dove at him steadily, lashing Ray's face with his tail once as he flashed by. Ray made himself ignore the razor cut on his cheek that hard-scaled lizard tail made on one such strike. On another, Azimond fired close enough that the target pistol scorched his gun hand. Ray wheeled smoothly in the weightless field, facing the lean Phridyan squarely, weaving a steady laser net around Azimond like a cage, a dazzling display of target-laser skill. Ray had won many a bar bet in the service with this little trick of the wrist. Ray bore in, noting with satisfaction the uncertainty striking the reptilian eyes.

Ray tightened the net of laser lines, lithely dodging Azimond's return fire. They swirled past each other in the colored fog. Ray tightened the light net into a figure eight across the jewels on Azimond's chest armor as he spun about. Amber-colored sparks flashed around the arena.

Ray braked himself in the catch-zone at the edge of the tank, arched gracefully across the restraining wall, firing steadily at Azimond. Ray was breathing harder than he liked for such simple zero-g acrobatics, but the kid was panting.

The gong for the end of the round sounded. Ray's team had won. Azimond shrugged inside his armor, glaring hotly yet unable to challenge Ray further against he laughter of his team-mates. "It's only a game." He turned and kick off toward to his friends at the other end of the tank. Another round started but Ray declined.

He climbed out of the tank, feeling better about many things. The blaze of life and challenge here was just what his human soul needed. He had been lost in space long enough. He exchanged the target pistol for his own gun, grinning to himself, and began to look around for the next game.

A table full of Wozurns caught his eye and called him over. "Quality manufacture," one of them observed in SpeakEZ as he pointed to Ray's gun.

Ray grinned crookedly and patted the handle as he sat down. "I've got quality friends."

Ray dimly remembered the grizzled blue scar on the old man's forehead. This was Two Knife, Lord Jak's second-in-command. Two Knife chuckled, and raised a toast to Ray's victory in the ZG tank. Ray sat down with them, grateful for the chair and a semblance of gravity.

"You've got some quality enemies as well," the Wozurn said to him with a congratulatory wink. "We're all looking forward to taking out van Zandt."

Ray grinned, feeling a surge of drunken camaraderie. "It's gonna look great on TV."

Laughter went around the table. A pair of Defton-Hoyts

flipped into the seats on either side, asking him to foot wrestle. They waved their thick tails behind their heads. Their dark, angelic faces smiled at him, giggling with feminine grace. Ray declined, so they suggested a drinking-song match instead. Ray said he had not had enough to drink yet for that kind of fun. The pair giggled even more, drifting away under the pressure of Two Knife's glare.

Ray nodded thanks to Two Knife and sat back with a sigh of contentment.

A few minutes later, a Wozurn woman with iridescent white fur sat down at the table.

"I've been looking forward to meeting you, Captain Harris," she said to him in a voice as rich as an operatic singer. There was a strange, unpleasant light in her coppery eyes, despite her smile. "I am Zabor."

"How do, ma'am," Ray said politely. She was staring at him with unnerving intensity.

"Zabor here is our chief cargo master." Two Knife leaned forward at the table to be heard above the noise. "She's the lady who sent Briggs and Nolsey out looking for those missing solar cells," he added. "She's the reason you're here."

Ray saluted her politely. "Thanks for the rescue, ma'am."

Zabor did not take her eyes from him. She was small and slender, with long, silky fur that seemed almost curly it was so luxurious. She had diamond studs in her ears, several in a line along the outer edges. They flashed with sullen heat in the lights as she moved. "It is unfortunate that things worked out so badly," she said after a moment.

"Yes, ma'am," Ray said. "My private fight was not supposed to cost anyone else."

She nodded. "So often that is how it works out, isn't it?"

"I am sorry about Nolsey," Ray said, puzzled by her intensity. "Was he a friend of yours?"

Zabor shook her head, frowning slightly. "There are many men on this ship. I cannot know them all. I wanted to meet you, Captain."

"Why is that, ma'am?"

"Briggs brings home interesting prizes," she replied. "She has the most astonishing luck."

"Yes, ma'am, she does," Ray agreed. "Better than Nolsey's,

though, it would seem."

The others at the table agreed solemnly. A round of toasts to Nolsey was made. Zabor continued to stare at Ray, her eyes metallic and hard over the rim of her glass as she sipped.

Rokey returned, twins in tow. Ray went over to stand beside him at the bar.

Rounds of the house special were served. Ray foolishly downed his in two gulps. He spun around slow-motion on his heel and managed to set the glass down safely on the mirror-finish bartop while he leaned on his elbows. Two Knife's reflection in the mirror top winked at Ray atop a grin. Ray winked back. Someone ordered another round of house specials. Ray just hung there on his elbows, listening to the wild music backdrop Rokey's rumbling conversation. Ray got dizzy trying to keep up with who was saying what, so he just looked down to his own reflection in the mirrored glass, and kept nodding.

Through blurred vision, Ray was yet able to determine that he was having a good time, a very good time, indeed. In a moment of clarity, someone with warm, rainbow-bright scales led him away to a much quieter, even nicer place. Ray had occasion to think to himself that pirate parties could be a lot of fun, if you got out of them alive. He even forgot to remind himself that they were *not* pirates.

Yo, Ho, Ho, and a Dead Man's Thumbprint

Several days later, Ray looked up and noticed that he was on the bridge of the *Yankee Shadow.* He had apparently been sitting there for several hours, staring out glumly at the huge arc of the *Tamaroan's* bulk hanging against the stars, much too close to the *Shadow.*

Something about the closeness of the *Tamaroan* in that vast zone of star-swept space depressed Ray terribly. At the moment, however, he could not put his finger on the problem. Ray could not feel his fingers or his toes, for that matter. His hair hurt. His hair hurt all the way down to his neck, and his eyes were doing unspeakable things to his brain.

Staring at the *Tamaroan* was definitely getting him downhearted. He had been having such a wonderful time over there on that pirate ship with those pirates at their pirate party.

That must be it, Ray thought painfully to himself. He tried to breathe with less noise. More fun than human beings can stand. Something else, however, had happened at that pirate party, something Ray needed to remember, something important, something awful.

"I was having such a good time," Ray protested aloud, wincing at the noise. Of course he was. He dragged himself to his feet and stumbled out to look for Rokey.

Ray found him at last down in sickbay, floating asleep and happy in hospital. The *Yankee Shadow,* being privately designed, had medical technology of an advanced and expensive kind. Rokey had overseen the design and installation himself.

Other degrees of private luxury had been passed up in order to have onboard a sickbay as well equipped as a medcenter trauma unit. Rokey was an educated man and he had his priorities in place. Curing hangovers was the machine's specialty, fine-tuned to Rokey's chemistry. Ray checked all the biocomp readouts, determining that Rokey had only checked in for his hangover and was not injured. Ray woke him up.

"It's my turn," Ray mumbled once Rokey was awake and sitting up.

Rokey, fully recovered, was disgustingly cheerful. Ray just glowered at him as he hoisted himself up to the rim of the hospital cradle and swung his lean legs over into the zero-gravity field inside the cradle. "Don't wake me 'til it's over," he said as Rokey lowered the breathing mask over his face.

Something about the grin on Rokey's furred face gave Ray a sudden chill. Just before the sleep-field swept his brain off to dreamland, Ray realized what Rokey was smiling about.

When Rokey woke him out of hospital a few hours later, Ray awoke with the same awful memory revived. He sat up with a groan, his earlier physical distress converted now entirely to emotional angst. "Tell me I was dreaming, Rokey, please!" he said.

Rokey shook his head.

"It was just a *party*, Rokey!" Ray protested. "I couldn't have done something that *stupid* at a party!"

"If I could do something that stupid at a party, son, why not you?" Rokey said, followed by a heavy sigh and a shrug as he turned away.

"Rokey! Tell me we did *not* sign up with Lord Jak's crew!" Ray had to keep a shrill note of hysteria out of his voice.

Rokey just moaned quietly as he went out. He was still moaning as he went up the stairwell to the galley.

"I'm a pirate now," Ray said to himself. The words sounded as awful as they felt. Hospital had repaired his body from the effects of the pirate party, nonetheless it would take more than magnetic fields to save his soul from what he had just done. "I'm a pirate."

He was shaking his head as he went out to follow Rokey to the galley. His career options had just taken a drastic turn – whether they called themselves pirates, or not.

Welcome to the Family

The bridge of the *Tamaroan* was as outsized and overly stylish as everything else onboard. The command-seat at the center was on a raised dais of ornately carved wood, a curious anachronism in the midst of the control panels and digital screens. Ambient light was low and warm, for the ease of reading backlit displays, making the rich, dark of the wood look alive.

Rokey wondered how close the situation actually was to out-of-hand. He certainly did not feel that he had any control over events anymore. He kept his movements slow and deliberate. His royal collar was already chafing the fur underneath, and he knew he was going to be wearing it for some time. These people did not want to be called pirates, yet there were a lot of guns everywhere. Even the maintenance crew went around armed.

Lord Jak did not leave Lord Rokhmyr standing The nearest crew member surrendered her seat to that the two men could talk face to face.

"I wanted to talk to you without having to explain to your squire as we went along," Lord Jak said to him in Wozurn.

Rokey had not thought Jak would consider Ray as anything more than an oddity. Perhaps this was a courtesy being shown to Lord Rokhmyr and not to Captain Harris. Rokey just nodded.

"Your Honor, there is a rumor going around the crew that your squire is actually your illegitimate child, with surgically altered ears and features. Is there any truth to this?"

Rokey had to laugh, laughing louder and more heartily as

he thought about this. Earthlings truly were a mystery to these people.

"He pleases me as much as any son of my flesh," Rokey said finally, brushing his whiskers back with his fingers and suppressing more laughter. "I've worked hard to teach him some manners, but he is a fully grown Earthling male, and as competent as he seems."

Lord Jak took this news solemnly, nodding. A calculating look drifted across his scarred countenance.

Rokey chuckled. "He did do well in the ZG, didn't he? I've seen him do stuff, but that was new even to me."

"It was new to all of us."

Rokey realized that this backed up Ray's assessment that these people pretended to a military-inspired lifestyle more than they actually practiced it. Ray had been trained by a real military. The difference showed. Rokey looked calmly at Lord Jak, who sat brooding in his oversized command seat.

Jak leaned closer to Rokey, switching to SpeakEZ as though to prevent his crew from following their conversation. SpeakEZ was not a common lingo among these people. Wozurn was the language by which the ship herself was run.

"I do *not* consider your contract with the *Tamaroan* to be as permanently binding as the wording might suggest, Your Honor," Jak said. "I do realize you and your squire signed on under unusual circumstances."

"We were drunk out of our minds," Rokey suggested helpfully, also keeping his voice low.

"It was a good party." Jak grinned.

"And a good reason to celebrate," Rokey said.

"I missed her a lot," Jak confided. "It is difficult to run this ship without her. She has the most organized mind I have ever encountered. She seems to know where everything and everyone is, at any time you need them."

"She certainly knew how to find us."

"Which brings us to the cargo of solar cells you are carrying, and your contracts, Your Honor."

Rokey tilted an ear toward Jak.

"I need those cells."

Rokey gestured around, taking in the gigantic starship. "This ship sucks power out of intraspace, Jak. What do you need solar cells for? And satellite arrays at that?"

"Not for this ship." Jak hesitated, looking down to his hands resting across his command console. "It is for my children – our children, the children of the *Tamaroan.*"

He was speaking so quietly that Rokey almost could not follow his words. "Children?" Rokey also whispered.

"This is so difficult," Jak murmured.

Rokey rose to his feet, and Jak looked up with startled dismay. "Join me on the *Yankee Shadow,* Jak," Rokey said. "We can talk there more comfortably."

Lord Jak followed Rokey out gratefully, pacing beside him in silence through the corridors to the docking bay where the *Shadow* sat. He curtly ordered his bodyguards to wait at the bottom of the ramp, then went onboard alone with Rokey.

Rokey knew Ray was asleep as soon as he stepped onboard. He took Jak up to the galley and waved him to a seat. Rokey padded over to set up a carafe of hot chocolate and two mugs. "Now, tell me all about this," Rokey said, in Wozurn. He set the mug in front of Jak, and sat down himself.

The big Wozurn sniffed at the mug, clearly unfamiliar with the aroma. "What is this? It smells like *loranai,* but different."

"Cocoa," Rokey said. "It's from Earth. We have analogs on Wozur. L*oranai* is one of them. But this travels better and keeps longer in storage."

Jak picked up the hot mug and sniffed it again, more deeply, concentrating on the flavors. "Yes, I have often wanted to start a trade business with *loranai,* but we have found, as you say, that it does not travel well. This is from Earth, you say?"

Rokey nodded. "But you can get it in a lot of places, these days. It's been catching on as the Earthlings spread through the star lanes."

Jak sipped, wincing a little at the heat, and smacked his lips, tasting the cocoa on his tongue thoughtfully. He drank again, more deeply. "I will have Briggs look into this. Perhaps we can get a cargo of this for trade in the Hinterlands."

"Briggs loves cocoa. You'll want to find some just for her. Is that where we're headed? The Hinterlands?"

Jak shook his head and set the mug down on the table, looking at it instead of Rokey as he spoke. "The *Tamaroan* is going to the Hinterlands, eventually. We have one important stop to make along the way."

"Oh?"

"You will be pleased. We are going back to the system where Briggs found you, and we will deliver some justice to this Colonel van Zandt."

"Oh?" Rokey's whiskers flicked up.

Jak nodded. "We will destroy his fleet completely and leave him stranded in his lair. I think that is the kind of justice your squire will best appreciate."

Rokey chuckled, enjoying the dark humor. "I think you got that right."

Jak nodded again. "We must also retrieve Lieutenant Nolsey's remains, so that he can have proper funeral ceremonies and his place in the ship's crypt. We will return his ashes to Wozur." Jak's voice faltered. "Eventually."

"Then we go to the Hinterlands?"

"No."

Jak could not meet Rokey's eye as he said that, turning his face aside, which seemed strange. Rokey wondered what the bad news would be.

"Where are we going?"

"You, the *Yankee Shadow* and her cargo, are going somewhere else entirely, and when next we meet, we will be even. My Briggs rescued you, and you will repay her by bringing those solar satellites to our children."

Rokey said nothing to this as Jak swallowed more of his cocoa. "This is good," Jak said. "I will find this for Briggs."

"I'll make sure the *Shadow's* manifest-computer gives you a list of all the distributors and their systems." Rokey waited for Jak to tell him why the *Tamaroan* could not make the solar-cell delivery herself.

Jak sat back into the cushions of the galley bench. He sighed. "I wish we could take them there ourselves. I miss little Wennofar and the boys." Memory brought a sudden smile. "Especially the boys. They will be in fur soon."

"Now that Briggs is back and safe, shouldn't you take her to see them, let them know their mother's not lost?"

"My children are not born of Briggs, but of Zabor. Briggs feels that she is still too young for motherhood."

Rokey began to get a hint of why Jak did not want this conversation to be overheard by his crew. "Briggs never once mentioned Zabor or children, Jak, not in time we traveled with her. She talked about you incessantly." Rokey paused, not wanting his irritation at that be heard in his voice. "She never mentioned them. Is that why you can't make the delivery yourself, and visit them?"

"No," Jak said unhappily. His eyes tilted downward at the outer corners, and his whiskers twitched. "I wish it were as simple as that. Briggs is quite fond of the children, so much so that she would do anything to protect them, even though they are not her own. It is enough for her that they are *my* children."

Lord Jak said that so matter-of-factly, almost distractedly, that it did not sound like bragging. "Zabor is far more jealous of Briggs than she of Zabor. But that is another squabble. We cannot visit the children because we dare not lead anyone to them. She told you nothing about them simply because, as much as she came to like you and your squire, she was not going to trust you with knowledge of the children, not without being far more certain of you."

"She is a smart lady."

Jak smiled up at Rokey, daring to meet his eye for a flash. "Smartest I ever met. That's why I had to bind her to me with every contract I could find."

"You mentioned something earlier about *my* contract?" Rokey said.

"Yes, Your Honor. The children are in a resort-school we put together on an uncharted, unregistered world far enough off the major lanes that we have some hope of keeping them safe. Briggs is terrified we will lead someone to them if we go there ourselves."

"Who is it you might lead there?"

"That is another domestic squabble entirely, Your Honor. Let me elaborate it only enough to say that the kidnapping, torture and ransom of children is not an uncommon means of persuading parents to do or say or pay something that they might not otherwise."

Rokey noticed that Lord Jak was more eloquent in Wozurn than in SpeakEZ. "It does happen, yes," he said. "Who wants what from you enough to threaten your children?"

"The same people who chased you into exile, Your Honor."

A tense silence fell between them as the two Wozurn met each other eye to eye over this statement.

"Independent tradeships such as the *Tamaroan* are no longer popular at home, Your Honor," Jak went on. "The net that failed to catch you when you fled Wozur caught a great many others. The governing of Wozur is no longer truly in Wozurn hands."

He reached out and gently touched the radiolarian emblem on the collar at Rokey's throat. "We had the choice of letting a leash be attached to our own collars of rank and status, or leaving them behind and declaring independence."

"It's treason to abandon your collar status." That was the only reason Rokey had fetched his along with him when he fled. He was not going to add the very real crime of treason to his exile, because it was not his loyalty to Wozur that was in question.

Lord Jak nodded. He touched the spot on his own throat with lingering fingertips, as though missing the feel of it there. He shrugged. "I wear that weapons harness now, instead, and it is status of a rank I have created for myself, the assurance of my authority in that rank. I do not need the collar of Wozur anymore." He did not sound convinced.

"I miss my own sons," Rokey said softly. "And I *did* get to watch them grow up."

Jak looked away, putting his hands flat on the galley table between them. "Briggs is *right.* The women are *right.* A starship with full armaments is *no place for children.* But I miss my sons. I miss little Wennofar, and I am not getting to watch her grow up."

"This resort where your children are is in need of photon collectors?"

"Everything helps."

"How many children are there?"

Jak looked pained. "Every crew member who has family has an investment in the place. There are two hundred and eighty-three unfurred children, and forty-two newly-furred, mostly boys, as well as twenty-eight Phridyan young, together with a staff of about a thousand. We equipped the place with the best of everything."

"Which, of course, requires a lot of energy to keep using."

"Yes."

"What are we supposed to do after we deliver the satellites?" Rokey said.

Rokey could see the gratitude clear in Jak's eyes as he realized Lord Rokhmyr was agreeing to the deal. "As long as you do nothing that will draw anyone's attention to that location, or connect them with the *Tamaroan,* you may do what you please," Jak said. "When you have completed the delivery, wait at Club Sargasso. Everyone goes there, so you can come and go unnoticed. I will send an agent to meet you, and you can pass along any news," – Jak's voice caught. He took a deep breath. "You can tell us how they are, assure us that they are safe."

Jak patted the table with his palms again, softly. "Then you can have your contract back, Your Honor, to do with as you please."

"And if we *never* meet up with the *Tamaroan* again after that, then no one will ever connect the delivery to you, or you to the children, is that it?"

The hard look that showed for a flash in Jak's eyes hinted of the vengeance that would follow should the wrong people be allowed to make such connections, but he said only, "Could I have another mug of this cocoa before I return to the bridge, Your Honor? It may be a long time before I find any again." Meaning that the *Shadow* should leave quickly. Ray and Rokey were dismissed.

Rokey was almost humming to himself while he poured another round. "By the way, when you are carrying cocoa, be warned that some people react, how should I put it – oddly to the stuff. For example, have you ever encountered the flying peoples of Baturn?"

Jak tilted his head, and squinted thoughtfully as he searched his memory. "Little guys? They trade miniature dinosaurs and such, and make really good black wines that, alas, do not travel well?"

Rokey nodded. "Don't ever serve cocoa to one of them. Makes them completely silly. All you'll get is giggles and bad puns until they sober up."

Jak was amused by this. “I will remember. They are silly anyway – hanging upside down to talk to a person, and flapping away without a word if they don’t like your terms.”

“That’s the Baturn, alright.”

Lord Jak abruptly changed subjects, as though troubled by something deeper. “Briggs has never been to Wozur. She is from the colony on Askhat, which is about as far from Wozur as you can get. She has some very romanticized visions of the Home World.”

Rokey did not say anything, since he could see that Jak was working up to another difficult confession.

Jak sipped the cocoa again, letting his thoughts settle. “I think she is attracted more to my roots on Wozur than to me, more impressed by my family’s history than my own life.”

“She seemed quite genuine in her affection for you, Jak. You may be worrying for nothing.”

“I am five times her age, Your Honor. I do not fool myself. I do trust her loyalty, but I would prefer,” Jak paused, and the distress in his eyes was difficult for Rokey to comprehend.

“I would prefer,” Jak went on more strongly, “I would prefer that I am not in daily competition with the great Lord Rokhmyr of Wozur. I cannot compete with your titles, your property or your status.”

Rokey spoke carefully. “I have not seen my own wife in almost half a century, but I haven’t forgotten what she means to me, what we mean to each other. I can understand why you would worry. I would hope that no one ever tests my wife’s loyalty, either.”

Jak nodded, meeting Rokey’s eyes for a moment with a flash of pure gratitude.

While they savored the warm flavors of the second round of cocoa, Lord Jak talked haltingly about his children, little Wennofar, barely twenty yet and still awkward with childhood when last seen, and his twin sons, Sedge and Sejan. Although in their thirties, they had not yet furred when the *Tamaroan* left them in hiding, and Jak was sure he had missed out on the time of their change.

Rokey let him talk, asking questions to encourage him to talk. Rokey did not ask the obvious question: do you think you will ever see them again?

Captain Briggs came by for a quick farewell, giving Rokey a breathlessly whispered, "Thank you!" that was all the payment he needed, and left him breathless, as well.

"Do you forgive me for not telling you about the children?" Briggs asked. Her eyes looked sad. She clutched to her chest the box of cocoa Rokey had given her as a farewell gift.

"Forgive you?" Rokey said. "My dear, I applaud your discipline. I would have found it more difficult to forgive if you *had* revealed such a dangerous secret to a stranger!" He bowed formally, pressing his forehead against the back of her hand. They stepped away from each other too quickly, as though sparked somehow by the touch. Rokey brushed back his flared whiskers with trembling fingers. Briggs then shook Ray's hand solemnly in farewell, an antiquated gesture she had picked up from watching movies with Rokey. Rokey and Briggs had had time to watch a lot of movies together on the ride here.

The *Tamaroan* disappeared behind them, obscured by the glittering dust cloud of the rendezvous point. Ray fired up the main engines, humming happily, and spun the *Shadow* around to orient the main thrusters for the window jump. Rokey laid in the course for the resort world and the children of the *Tamaroan.* He did not really feel the same elation as his partner, and Ray seemed to sense that. He said nothing, but as he launched the starship, he let out a happy, if somewhat restrained whoop of joy.

Everyone Comes to Club Sargasso

Rokey sat slumped at his table at Club Sargasso, brooding over his drink. He could feel himself slip into deepest, weary boredom. The musicians raised their instruments to play yet another variation on the theme, and the dance floor filled up. Rokey hunched closer over his table so that the mechanical silence of the HushaBoom could wall out the music. He turned his palm up on the table with a long-suffering sigh and stared down at the curve of his fingers.

He had been amusing himself with a private intellectual game: speculation on why carbon-based life tended to evolve toward humanoid forms. This was a favorite question because there was no answer, or rather, any reason could be given as the answer. The facts were the facts: accidents of evolution that led to consciousness averaged out to the norm of statistical events in the skillions upon skillions of life-hours that ticked away in the altogether of reality. With the unthinkable numbers of the universe involved, even non-statistical events happened in statistical numbers. Rokey liked to muse upon the infinite variety of variations that proved the rule, and Club Sargasso's clientele provided a valid sampling. The pentacle was not universal simply because it was easy to draw. Non-aerobic life-forms, of course, drew very different patterns of their psyches, yet they all led ultimately to people learning ways to talk to each other: "Hello. This is me. Is that you?"

Rokey caught himself mumbling these last thoughts out loud. He frowned, flicking his ears around quickly to be sure that he was still within the artificial silence of the HushaBoom over his table. He sighed and closed his fist, raising his hand to rest his chin wearily upon his knuckles. Ray and Rokey had been waiting at Club Sargasso for more than a week. Boredom was leading to carelessness.

He watched with momentary interest as a tall, black-clad Earthman walked into the Club, backed by a swish of cool night air. Rokey noticed then that the tall man was following a short, dark Earthman who would be generally unnoticeable in the eccentric atmosphere of Club Sargasso were it not for the stone-carved being who followed him.

After studying the pair, Rokey concluded that the taller man was an android. Living flesh could not develop that kind of standing-still intensity. The short man whom the android followed must be wealthy. Only wealth of a peculiar degree could buy mechanical flesh with such vivid details of life, and only *innocent* wealth would walk into the Sargasso with such a fortune at his heels.

Rokey looked more closely. The thing was easily two meters tall, a chunk of carved granite shaped like a man. The work was boldly cut and stark, yet the eyes were curiously lifelike, large eyes edged with curling black lashes as beautiful as a woman's, fierce amber eyes like a wild bird.

An expensive-enough android might have the intelligence of a bird, Rokey thought to himself. Such a bodyguard could keep a rich man alive, even at the Sargasso.

The rich man and his android disappeared through a back wall into the Sargasso's inner sanctum and the offices of Club Sargasso's owner, a Wozurn named Ricmorran.

Rokey lost interest and went back to his own problems. Ricmorran was an old friend. He would tell Rokey their story soon enough. A rich man with an android bodyguard was not part of Rokey's problems.

Waiting for Lord Jak's agent to appear with their contracts was Rokey's problem.

Rokey had always been a rich man himself, but, in this place, he was trying to remain unnoticed, just another Wozurn in a roomful of furred faces. He cherished the security of that anonymity. The Sargasso was crowded with freemerchants, smugglers, thieves, pirates, and worse. Rokey was not new to obscurity. He had not been born into it, either. He knew its values and uses. He was finding out that obscurity was boring, even in a place as vibrantly dangerous with excitement as Club Sargasso.

In the academic circles of his younger years Rokey had been raised on the romance of candlelit reunions in exotic nightclubs, but a steady diet of such romance had left him hungry for a comic interlude or even a nature documentary. At the very least, he might have been comfortable in his own quarters aboard his starship, watching a hand-picked selection of well-loved movie classics or just some good cartoons.

Rokey sighed, feeling the lure of his trideo viewer. He and his captain had few rules, but foremost among them was "No splitting up." Rokey could not go home to the *Yankee Shadow* until Ray was ready to go. Rokey could see by the size of the gathered crowd in the games-room that Ray was still online, which meant they were not going home for a while yet. Computer circuits were raking in fortunes for some while ruining others, guided by Ray's nimble fingers. Such recklessness was not a survival trait.

Never mind that Ray was good. Never mind how much he was winning. That just spiked up the inevitable punch line. These people really *were* pirates. Rokey mourned to himself, watching Ray at the gamefield across the room. His ear tips flicked in a rueful gesture at the cheers of the crowd, and he sighed.

Rokey's morose contemplation of his lack of options was interrupted by the touch of a white, sylphlike hand stroking the fur on his forearm. He looked up, momentarily startled, to see a lovely Vangellan waitress smiling at him. Rokey's eye was caught by the fine down on her bare white shoulders sparkling in the purple light of the HushaBoom over his table. He did not hear her words at first, distracted as he was by a memory of white fur sparkling on another pair of smoothly rounded shoulders, long ago.

"Ricmorran asks if you would care to join him in his office for a drink, Your Honor?" the woman repeated what she had just said to him.

Rokey smiled at the young girl as he rose, steadying himself on the back of the bench for a moment before following her out. He had been expecting this. He was pleased to know that he could still count on Ricmorran.

Ricmorran was the owner of this phenomenally successful oasis, Club Sargasso, yet he would not own even the fur upon his face were it not for Rokey. He also knew why Lord Rokhmyr was only "Rokey" now. He could be trusted not to tell. Rokey followed the lovely white shape of the waitress through the dissolving wall into Ricmorran's inner sanctum.

"He goes by the name of Rufus T. Firefly," Ricmorran said quietly, referring to the strange little man with the android following him. Ricmorran said the name with a completely straight face.

Rokey looked at him sharply, waiting for the punch line.

Ricmorran paused at Rokey's sharp look. "You've heard of him?"

"I've heard the name," Rokey said carefully, trying to remember what movies he had watched while traveling with Ricmorran. The man might honestly not know what an obvious alias it was.

"It's not his real name anyway," Ricmorran went on, toying with the tiny bone sculpture on his desk. "That's all I can tell you, and I do mean strictly all, Your Honor. I only tell you that because I owe you."

Rokey knew that when Ricmorran began playing with the toys on his desk he was either embarrassed or covering something. Rokey studied the twitch of his fellow Wozurn's scarred cheek. "He paid you that much."

"Your Honor, I swore a genetic oath! *That's* how important he is!"

Rokey chuckled, leaning back in the overly comfortable chair beside Ricmorran's desk. He watched without speaking while Ricmorran pushed a small silver box with his fingertip, first to one side of his desk screen then to the other. He studied the box lid as though it held a secret cue card.

"Your Honor," Ricmorran said finally as he tilted his head to grin at Rokey. "He paid me a *staggering* sum not to ask, inquire, ponder, wonder, muse, or allow speculation on his identity – and I quote!!"

Rokey chuckled, also tilting his head, matching the scarred grin. "A *staggering* sum, you say?" he echoed pleasantly.

"An *outstandingly* staggering sum, Your Honor!"

"No wonder you've been in such a good mood."

Ricmorran's face lit with a grin. He winked at Rokey. "You better know it!"

They toasted each other and drank to "Rufus T. Firefly."

The fact of that mysterious stranger having bought Ricmorran's loyalty did not disturb Rokey. If the man's real identity *were* any threat, Ricmorran would not hesitate to tell. Ricmorran kept the secret even from Rokey for the simple reason that he had promised he would. He succeeded in running the biggest pirate watering-hole in the quadrant because he maintained iron-clad codes of honesty. Even the boss obeyed the rules.

"Rufus T. Firefly," Rokey repeated thoughtfully. "What's he after?"

"A navigator. He wants the best navigator money can buy."

"I've certainly got that," Rokey said, thinking of young Raymond at his games.

Ricmorran nodded, with a rueful grin drawing his lopsided whiskers back. "That captain of yours has made and broken some major betting fortunes since he started playing my machines. He flies those scubbing cartoon fleets like he was some kind of demon!!"

Rokey winced at the aptness of the metaphor. Raymond Harris flew real starships the same way. "You made the money back on Firefly," he suggested.

Ricmorran's grin sparkled in his copper-shiny eyes. "Indeed. And more to come on my commission."

Rokey laughed out loud. Ricmorran's audacity had always entertained him.

"This isn't a Humphrees Agency gig, is it? Ray will skin my face if I take another job sent by George. He hasn't forgiven him for the last one yet." Rokey paused, giving Ricmorran a meaningful look. "I'm not sure I have, either."

Ricmorran had to hear about that one. Another round of drinks went into the telling. Rokey always enjoyed bragging to Ricmorran. The man always got so caught up in the story. Rokey was ready to launch into further tirades against his former partner, George Humphrees, but Ricmorran reluctantly interrupted him. "Time is actually important in this,

Your Honor. I hate to interrupt, but this Firefly person is in some kind of hurry."

"What's the gig? A race? A treasure hunt? Lost love?"

"A Quest."

"Ouch." Rokey winced. "I might have known."

"A capital-Q Quest, no less," Ricmorran added, shrugging with an easy gesture of big shoulders. "I doubt the travel will hurt your reputation much, Your Honor." He twisted his scarred cheek up to wink meaningfully at Rokey.

Rokey nodded at Ricmorran over his glass before draining the last of his drink. The sweet scald filled his nostrils, momentarily burning away all concern with "Rufus T. Firefly," "Lord Jak," and the host of pirates and pseudo-pirates' squabbles. Ricmorran was known to serve a wickedly potent witches' brew to his special friends.

Once he had swallowed down the dizzy swirl of the fumes and brushed back his suddenly flaring whiskers, Rokey folded his big arms across his chest and tried to look serious. "What's the punch line to this, my friend? You're saving the worst for last."

"Colonel Johann Mohammed van Zandt."

Rokey's whiskers flared out straight again.

Ricmorran did not need to say more, but he added, "His fleet has been sighted coming through the window. They'll be landing in a matter of hours."

Rokey swore softly to himself, shaking his head. That was very bad news, bad news of the worst sort. It was also something of an explanation for the *Tamaroan's* delay. He closed his burning eyes wearily and leaned back into the cushions of the overly comfortable chair. "Pirates with names that sound like stupid sitcom musicals, and I have to be in the one place in civilization where those names are disgustingly real."

"And looking for you."

"And Raymond Harris."

"Especially for Raymond Harris."

The arrival of van Zandt was the leverage that would pry Ray Harris from his games machines. Rokey was sure of that. The stink lingered from their last brush with him. Apparently, even the powerful arm of Lord Jak and all the *Tama-*

roan's troops had failed to wipe away that smell.

A Glass of Ice Water and a Navigator, Please?

Rokey sighed quietly to himself and leaned forward over the table so that he could hear the little Earthman's voice more clearly. Music from the live band on the distant stage pulsed around them, shielding their conversation.

Seen more closely, "Rufus T. Firefly" was as strange as the handmade man-shape seated beside him. Both were dressed in black, both pale as cave-newts, both of them out of place at Club Sargasso. Firefly was fluid and eloquent in his motions, middle-aged, with a lifetime of money and privilege showing in his every gesture. He had a fancy walking stick that had a silver Anubis head-stock with ruby eyes. He kept one hand gripping this as though it were holding him upright as he sat there. He reminded Rokey of someone in some distant time or place, but the trace was elusive in this atmosphere. Rokey told himself they had merely grown up watching the same movies.

"He had remarkable style," Firefly went on with the anecdote he had been telling. "You couldn't have gotten a postage stamp between them – Oh! Is that the waitress there?" He interrupted his story to hail the black-clad woman passing by their table.

The woman was not a waitress, but she did not mind his attention. "I'd love a drink," she purred as she slid onto the booth seat beside the pale little man. "A double of whatever you're having, dah-link."

Firefly was momentarily delighted by the woman's presence. "My dear, you are a surprise in the night!" he exclaimed gently, shifting away from Rokey to smile at her with his whitely luminescent teeth.

"It's always night at Club Sargasso, dah-link," she purred, pressing herself closer to him. She had a geisha face as perfect as a computer composite. "And I have lots of surprises."

Rokey's nostrils were spiked by her powerful perfumes. "How much cash are you carrying?" he said to Firefly.

Disappointment showed briefly in the little man's black-olive eyes, and his wolf-white smile swallowed itself politely. "Perhaps later, my dear. I am here on business."

"So am I, dah-link." She swept Rokey with a scathing glance, then purred to Firefly, "I do take cards." Her rich, velvet voice was sweet in the mechanical silence under the HushaBoom. "Any kind."

"Later, my dear," Firefly repeated, less firmly.

Rokey was not surprised by the wistful note in the man's voice. The woman shrugged with a gesture of smooth, round shoulders under her loose dress, a gesture as childlike and pure as candlelight shining in the murk of the Sargasso. Rokey and Firefly watched appreciatively as she drifted away.

Firefly's sigh was deep with regret. "I must be getting old." He shook himself and drew a lit cigar from his overcoat pocket, grinning up at Rokey as he puffed on it. "Now, this navigator of yours – Ah!" He interrupted himself as yet another candlelight-beauty drifted by their table. "This must be the waitress!!"

"No, she isn't," Rokey said gently. He put his hand out on Firefly's sleeve as the man reached up to signal her.

Firefly patted the back of Rokey's hand, smiling weakly, then sank back into his seat. "I'm sorry," he said, rallying his smile. "I really would like a glass of ice water, but you can only order that in person here. The table doesn't seem to have it on the menu."

Rokey raised his hand to signal for the Vangellan waitress. "This is a very dry world," he explained. "Drinking water is a special order here." He looked more intently at Firefly as he spoke. The man's fingers had felt hot, even through Rokey's fur. Rokey had to wonder if it were fever or excitement.

Firefly looked deeply puzzled for a moment. He leaned forward to ask, in most studious fashion, "But – how can there be air without water? I mean – I mean." He licked dry lips with a sharp tongue point. "How can this planet have a breathable atmosphere without any water? There's not a bit of it on the surface. You can see that from orbit!"

Rokey was as impressed by the question as by the man's sudden intensity. He decided against giving a flippant answer, even though one occurred to him. The man seemed genuinely hungry for some piece of information, some clue locked up in his question.

"This planet recently lost the race to keep its native life-forms alive," Rokey explained, letting his voice slip into professorial and reassuring tone. "When Club Sargasso is a thousand years older, you won't be able to breathe so easily anymore. That's why Ricmorran built most of it underground."

Firefly grinned whitely, as though this were precisely the answer he had hoped to hear. He nodded, his gaze turned inward, and licked dry lips again.

The waitress appeared and stopped beside the Wozurn. "Yes, sir, Your Honor?"

Rokey leaned out of the HushaBoom's field so that she could hear him. "A pitcher of ice water and three glasses."

She was visibly startled. "A whole *pitcher*, sir?"

"Yo." Rokey smiled sharply at her. "A big one, full. With ice."

Her eyes got big, but she shrugged and melted away.

"Thank you," Firefly said. "You seem to have an enviable status in this place." He raised his vodka glass. "In a river of whiskey may you swim like a duck," he recited the old toast.

Rokey gave the second half. "May you never be thirsty nor run out of luck."

Firefly tapped the square glass side of his half-finished drink, glancing up to Rokey with a peculiar look. "Did you know that the single most universal form of nourishment is alcohol?" he said brightly. "Distilled, of course, to pure and identifiable form. It can be mixed with water – preferably in frozen form to maintain its essential purity. From planet to planet, these are guaranteed to be safe for everyone. If you can breathe the air, alcohol is consumable, digestible and even nutritious, although, alas, not everyone gets drunk. A human being of any kind, so long as he can pour it into the glass, can trust the vodka at any local tavern among the stars – even if the pretzels would kill him!"

He laughed with a surprisingly hearty chuckle. "I travel so much, don't you know," he said as conclusion. "I always find great comfort in that thought."

"Only too true," Rokey acknowledged agreeably. "I've tested the truth of it in taverns on both sides of the sky."

The two men grinned at each other. Firefly raised his glass in salute to the Wozurn and drained it slowly.

Rokey knew the facts of Firefly's curious little dissertation quite well. He had, in fact, said the same thing, in almost those exact words, in a favorite lecture to every graduating class of "This is *Your* Milky Way" for decades. The very same lecture, in fact, he had been reminiscing on when these two strange strangers had wandered into the Sargasso. No doubt, a holusion of Lord Rokhmyr gave that same lecture year after year. Rokey pushed away that uneasy sense of recognition. He had taught a lot of students.

"It is reassuring, isn't it?" Firefly said pleasantly.

Rokey shrugged, glancing over his shoulder at the games machines and Ray's audience of onlookers. The game was still on.

"Your friend, the navigator – could he – would he?" Firefly interrupted himself with a wry smile and a shake of his head, wreathed in the sweet smoke of his cigar. "I suppose it's best to ask him, isn't it?"

Rokey nodded. "I suppose."

Firefly's smile relaxed and the look in his eyes was less strained. "He is the type who likes a challenge?"

"To a fault."

The Vangellan waitress reappeared, carrying a tray with a tall, shining pitcher of ice water and three tumblers. Water drops glistened on the sides of the pitcher as she set the tray down. She brushed her fingertips through the wet beads, touching the coolness to her face.

"Please, my dear," Firefly offered cheerfully, "Have an ice cube."

She glanced back and forth between them with a delightful, uncertain giggle, flashing the look that gave Vangellan women their Helen O'Troy reputations, and dipped quickly into the pitcher. Her purple nail polish sparkled in the HushaBoom's light as she fished out a diamond-bright cube. Her purple lipstick sparkled as she blew a kiss to Firefly and held the precious ice cube to her temple so that water drops pearled down her cheek and her smooth, white throat. She was a cream and ivory shape with long arms and slender wrists, swaying gently as she walked away.

Even Firefly's android, introduced as "Mr. Burke," turned to watch her leave. Rokey had been deliberately ignoring "Mr. Burke," because mechanical bodyguards tended to get nervous if looked at too closely.

Burke's reaction to the woman, however, changed Rokey's opinion and made him start thinking of "Mr. Burke" as "he" rather than "it." An android would not have noticed her unless she were a threat. Rokey became even more curious about "Rufus T. Firefly." He had managed to find as bodyguard a most peculiar human being, or was he perhaps a *cyborg?* Rokey wondered how one asked. "Excuse me, are you entirely real?"

The third glass had been ordered for Ray once he arrived. Rokey slid it over in front of Burke and filled it after Firefly's glass and before his own. Burke did not move.

"Ah!" Firefly sighed noisily, setting the empty glass on the table with a clink of ice. "That's much better! I feel as dry as this whole dusty planet!"

Rokey refilled Firefly's glass again. He was beginning to wonder about Firefly. The man's eyes were fever-bright and his skin was so hot. Rokey sniffed, nostrils gently flared. The man's scent was human, irritatingly familiar yet unidentified and masked, for the most part, by an expensive cologne. Rokey smelled nothing of disease or infections. The man was burning up with excitement perhaps? Rokey could only wonder if insanity or fanaticism in Earthmen had any distinguishing scent. For his own people, the answer was yes. As much as he knew about Earth, Rokey did not know that.

Mr. Burke took his glass finally and sipped at it, watching Rokey over the rim with his amber, bird-of-prey eyes.

"Would you care to order something else?" Rokey said to Burke.

Burke stared at Rokey unblinkingly for nearly half a minute before slowly shaking his head. He drained his glass and set it back on the table.

Rokey refilled their glasses and turned to survey the room, noticing that the gaming festivities were breaking up amidst cheers and catcalls. "Ray should be here in a moment," he said to Firefly. "Ricmorran's messages are difficult to ignore."

Ray worked his way through the crowd to Rokey's table, pausing to accept congratulations and exchange cordial threats. He did not hurry and did not glance over to Rokey's table as he went. His well-tailored suit made him nearly invisible in the murky light despite his pale colors. Rokey could smell the mingled traces of weary triumph and uneasiness in Ray's familiar scent as he approached. Ray's reluctance to quit the games was out of desperate boredom and not the pleasure of the hunt. Ray was more than two hundred years younger than Rokey, thus more vulnerable to boredom. Rokey's whiskers twitched in an almost smile as he braced himself for Ray's display of pique.

Ray sat down at the table and leaned forward on his elbows. He folded his black-gloved hands one across the other and smiled over at Rokey. The smile did not touch his green-as-glass eyes.

Instead of hello, he said, "It was a very good game. My fleet was winning."

"Your fleet is always winning," Rokey said soothingly. His pride for his captain showed in his smile. Ray was lean, and strong, and taller than Rokey's own sons, but Rokey felt the same surge of paternal concern over the man's naked skin and childlike self-confidence. "You'll win next time, too," he added.

"I could be winning right now." Ray turned to look over to the now-abandoned games machines.

Rokey knew the look. Ray paid close attention to what he did. Sometimes effort was needed to redirect that intensity. "These gentleman have some business for us."

"You sure George didn't send these guys looking for us?"

Rokey nodded. "No business card this time, honest."

Ray finally looked at the two men across the table. Firefly was smiling. Burke was not. Ray stared longest at Burke and snapped sullenly, "We're waiting for the *Tamaroan.*"

"The *Tamaroan* is late."

Ray grinned, with a sharp, dangerous look in his eye. "Yeah. Ain't it been fun."

Rokey shrugged, turning back to Firefly. "What he means is that we have time on our hands."

"Excellent!" Firefly exclaimed heartily. "Time is what we need, because they are running out of time and we don't know where they are so that ought to take quite some time to find, don't you think!"

Rokey suppressed a grin as he watched the pupils of Ray's green eyes contract to pinpoints of attention. The scent of "rich kook" wafted around Firefly with the sweet smoke of his cigar, and Ray had just noticed.

"I see," Ray said carefully. "This is what 'Morran meant about a navigator."

"Well," Rokey kept his voice deliberately even. "He does have a map."

"That might help." Ray glanced quickly around the little table, taking in the solemn faces turned to him.

"Mr. Firefly is looking for a particular star system, Ray," Rokey said. "A very particular star system."

"It is probably unique, Captain Harris," Firefly added eagerly.

Ray had given a start at the name "Firefly." He studied Rokey's face with narrowed eyes as Firefly spoke. Ray *had* watched movies with Rokey, lots of movies.

"What kind of map?" Ray demanded, in a tone that suggested he thought it would be scribbled in sauce on a tablecloth.

"It's a place to start," Rokey answered lightly.

Firefly grinned at Ray, resting both hands across the top of his curiously carved walking-stick. "I have a starting place, Captain Harris, but only a truly gifted navigator can discover which window to jump through!" Delight showed clearly in his oversized eyes.

"I'm flattered," Ray said finally. "I didn't realize my reputation had gotten ahead of me."

"You *are* a good navigator," Rokey said with a flick of his whiskers.

"I'm a pilot," Ray countered with sudden stubbornness. "I just know my way around real good."

"Excellent!" Firefly said. "I have a ship that deserves a good pilot, especially one who knows his way around!"

"What ship is that?" Ray asked.

Firefly's eyes twinkled. He grinned at them, pausing to puff sweet clouds of blue smoke around his head. "I'd love to show her to you."

"Rufus T. Firefly" had a lot of identity to conceal if the mere mention of his ship's name might give him away. The nagging suspicion that he recognized the little man touched the pit of Rokey's stomach once more. Earthmen sometimes looked uniformly like Earthmen to Rokey, but he never forgot a smell. Evidently Ray recognized this as well because he did not inquire further into the ship's name. Rokey could see the curiosity burning in his look, even though Ray said only, "Wouldn't that be nice?"

"At your convenience, Captain Harris."

Ray hooked a thumb in Rokey's direction. "His Honor here is in charge of the menu. I just take orders."

"Like hell you do," Rokey broke in cheerfully. "Although I will admit you do read the directions on a package before opening it."

"I like packaging," Ray said, with a brief smile in the midst of his sullen scowl. "I just don't unwrap anything I can't afford."

"Can you afford to leave Club Sargasso for a time?" Firefly asked.

Ray shrugged and glanced over to the games room.

"We can't afford *not* to," Rokey answered. Rokey cut off Ray's protest by repeating the name Ricmorran had dropped earlier. Ray's pale face hardened into tight, angry lines, and he stood without speaking.

"I think we're ready to go, Mr. Firefly," Rokey said pleasantly.

The men rose, Firefly grinning with his white, white teeth. "Wonderful!" he exclaimed breathlessly. "Wonderful!"

Ray led the way out. He seemed now to be in a great hurry

to quit the Sargasso. Sand scraped under their heels at the door, and the crackling buzz of the neon signs singed the smoky air.

A Gentleman's Grasp

The night outside was cold, with a thin, chill wind whining around the door and chasing them across the entry portico in a flail of sand. There were many ships, each parked at its own mooring post in the dark. The multicolored lights of the crowded landing field stretched off into the dusty distance, covering the dark ground with pools of glowing mist. The stars were bright and close overhead.

Once they were out on the pavement and under the cover of night, Ray said, "Where are you parked, Mr. Firefly?"

Mr. Firefly seemed lost in contemplation of the starry heavens, gazing upward with a rapt look. Mr. Burke answered for him. "Lot thirty-four, berth thirty-seven-c."

Ray squinted into the dark, sighting landmarks and reminding himself of how the field was laid out. "Blast. Halfway around the field from the *Shadow.*"

"They're all in shadow here," Firefly said mysteriously. His white face seemed to glow in the reflected mooring lights. "It's all shadows out here."

"*Yankee Shadow* is the name of our ship, Mr. Firefly," Rokey said. "We aren't parked in the same part of the field as you."

"Oh dear, I don't think we're allowed in the park after sunset, but I'd be happy to walk you home!"

Even Burke looked over to him, puzzlement showing on his hard, craggy face.

Before anyone could react to this, Firefly whisked away into the night, vanishing except for the tap-tap-tap of his walking stick on the pavement. The three men quickly recovered from their surprise and hurried after him.

Burke caught up with him first. Rokey heard the his massive, gravelly voice calling ahead. "Boss?" he rumbled softly, "Boss?"

"Ah, Burke, my good man!"

Firefly emerged out the night, standing with his walking-stick in hand. The ruby eyes in the silver Anubis head were glowing. Rokey was startled by the flare of light. Firefly smiled around at them, leaning up close to the giant man-machine beside him. "Burke, my good man – do you happen to know whether we're coming or going? I can't seem to tell. It's a marvelously entertaining sensation, but I do think it's getting late."

"Home, boss," Burke rumbled at him gently.

"Very good. Excellent. And your friends, here? Which way are they going?"

Rokey broke in. "Ah, Firefly, you feeling okay?"

A sudden flare of lurid red light and a BOOM! rocketed through the night and shook the ground. Ray and Rokey ducked and spun around toward the explosion. Firefly grinned appreciatively, leaning against his stick with one hand. "Bravo!" he called cheerfully. "Good show! Will we have a parade now?"

Mr. Burke stood studying the dark of the distant horizon where the after-flash of the explosion burned dimly. The reflected lights of the ships were shiny on his face.

Ray and Rokey rose from their defensive crouches. "What the hell?" Ray demanded.

Firefly grinned, shaking his head, evidently impressed. "Well, we won't find a taxi out here, you can bet a buck on that!" He took a lit cigar from an inner coat pocket and began puffing away at its sweet smoke. "Not for where we want to go."

"That wasn't anywhere near where the *Shadow* is parked, was it, Ray?" Rokey said to his partner in a low voice, feeling suddenly anxious.

"No, not at all. But it's damnably close to lot thirty-four."

"Berth thirty-seven," Rokey finished in dull tones.

"Yeah. Right around there."

"Oh, yes, indeed, gentleman!" Firefly said brightly. "I doubt anything as expensive as that has exploded in this place in the last hundred years. There are only seven destruct-secure security systems like that in this quadrant, and I own them all."

"Six now, boss," Mr. Burke said.

"Right you are, my good man! Right you are!" Firefly puffed grandly on his cigar. "Now there are only six."

"What?" Ray demanded, packing a lot of question into that sharp, clipped syllable.

"I have a security system like no other, Captain Harris, like no other. Whoever tried to break into my shuttlecraft just got the surprise of his life." He finished somewhat sadly. "I'm afraid, though, that it taught him a lesson he'll never remember."

Somewhere behind them, in the direction of the Club, a distant siren began to wail.

"Here comes the parade!" Firefly said around his cigar.

"That was your ship that just blew up?" Ray dropped his voice to a fierce whisper, suddenly alert to the night around them. Firefly's point had just made its wavering way into his attention.

"Why would it do that?" Rokey asked, feeling a daze of apprehension.

"Somebody tried to get in and it wasn't me." Mr. Firefly cocked his head, listening to the sirens approaching on the crowded field. "It's a funny thing, you know. I very rarely bother to set that security system when I travel, but every time I do, I have to use it." He grinned at them with a mischievous gleam in his big, moist eyes. "I used to have thirteen of those shuttles, you know!"

"Six now, boss," Burke repeated.

"And worth the sacrifice every time, my good man. Every time. But it does remind me." He turned to Ray. "Do you think Mr. Burke and I could impose on you for a ride home? I think I shall need a ride now."

"Yeah, Firefly, and the sooner the better. The night is full of ears and eyes." Ray gestured curtly in the direction of the Yankee Shadow.

"And claws, Captain Harris," Firefly said dreamily as they followed Ray into the night. "Don't forget the claws."

Sirens wailed and fretted behind them. Field lights began

to spring up around the burning shuttlecraft, outlining the billows of black smoke against the night sky and crawling with the headlights of emergency vehicles.

The noise and excitement on the field behind got noisier and more excited as drunken patrons became concerned about their own ships in the fire alarm. People ran past in the dark, heading in all directions, shouting orders.

Their progress was limited because Mr. Firefly was persistently distracted by the chaos, which was, to him, an entertaining parade in the night. "Are the balloons next?" he said eagerly. "The really big ones? Will we see Moose and Bat, or Betty?"

"No parade, Boss," Mr. Burke rumbled.

"Then why are the lights so bright?" Mr. Firefly argued agreeably. "Is this a cave? It's so dark."

"Nighttime," Burke's massive voice explained softly.

"Ah. Of course. It's always night at the Sargasso. Let's have a drink. I'm very thirsty."

"Later," Burke apologized.

"Have we reached Emerald Towers yet, Mr. Burke? Or was that last time?"

"Wysteria, Boss," Burke corrected him gently. "For Wysteria."

"Ah, dear Wysteria. Stubborn as paint and cold as a fish. Have you ever tried to paint a goldfish silver? I lost every argument with her except for the one that counted. Of course, every fish at Emerald Towers is green, not gold. I think it's because of the filters. Green lights and red lights." He paused. "May we go now?"

"Keep moving, Mister," Ray snapped, "Or we'll end up as lost as you are!"

"Oh, dear me, no. I'm not lost. I'm right here with you."

"Yes, so it would seem," Rokey said, sounding more cheerful than he felt.

"I may not know where *you* are, of course," Firefly continued. "But I've got the key to my hotel room. In fact," he went on brightly, "I've got the key to the whole hotel." He then reeled off, in a sing-song chant, a series of orbital coordinates in the short-hand slang of seasoned sailors.

Ray and Rokey recognized the indicated orbit at once –

and knew that any other sailor handy would recognize it as well. They hustled as best they could. There were too many people out here shouting, and listening, with enough confusion to cover any kind of attack.

"There was a young man owned a rocket," Mr. Firefly broke into a limerick, chanting it out as they walked. "Who carried his keys in his pocket." Firefly finished the verse slowly, as though trying to recall a missing scan, "In hopes of the day, some young lady would say, when you get to my door, please unlock it."

He tapped Ray with the tip of his silver-headed walking cane and winked at him knowingly. "You'll be glad that you have your keys, Captain Harris, won't you?"

Ray tried to smile. "Never leave home without them," he mumbled.

"Pirates never use keys, do they, Captain?" Firefly went on. He nodded at Ray, and gestured toward Rokey. "I'm sure he's told you that before, hasn't he?"

Rokey wondered what this absurdly illogical little man could be hinting at. The scent of a bizarrely arranged trap was easy to imagine.

"I know he's out there, Rokey!" Ray fumed quietly. "I can just smell him!"

Rokey chuckled. "I can't smell him, mate. If I can't smell him, you sure can't. You can't smell your own sweat in a spacesuit!"

"I'm learning," Ray countered warmly. "And I can smell him out there looking for me!"

"You cannot smell him! Calm down!"

"I smell something. Don't you smell something out there, mate? You and your famous nose?"

"Me and my famous nose."– Rokey interrupted himself, raising his head and focusing on the cool night air. He did smell something new, something disturbingly familiar.

"Van Zandt, right?" Ray demanded in a low voice. "Now you smell him, too."

"You cannot smell van Zandt out there, so calm down!"

As they approached the berth where their own starship freighter was parked, the scent of burned plastics began to alarm him as well, but for different reasons.

The ramp leading up to the airlock entry was gone.

Rokey stopped short in the safety of deep shadows. He was puzzled. He had left the ramp down. He was sure of that. He had assumed his walk home would be a tired, drunken stagger, so he left the ramp down to save himself the trouble of finding the controls.

The ramp was not there.

Rokey peered up at the starship's gleaming white side and saw that across the control panel for the airlock was a blackened scorch mark. He moaned an appropriate curse to himself and pushed the others deeper into the shadows. Ray had seen it as well. His anger-sweat caught Rokey's nostrils like a shout in the darkness.

"Van Zandt?" he said in a tight, demanding whisper.

Rokey shrugged in the darkness. "Or maybe somebody just wants his money back."

"Alice? Is that you?" Mr. Firefly said brightly. "I thought I saw the sheep go through here."

"What's he on about?"

Ray gestured for Burke to follow, then went up to the edge of the *Yankee Shadow's* berth, where the starship's hull curved sharply above them.

"Give me a hoist up," Ray said, leaning close to Mr. Burke. "I have to reach the control panel."

The airlock controls looked scorched, but Ray knew they would still work. He had had the intention of being boosted up to stand on Burke's shoulders in order to reach the panel above their heads. To Ray's surprise, Burke instead stepped up behind him, put his big hands around Ray's waist and lifted him up in the air as if holding up a child. Ray stifled his startled response and swiftly punched in the emergency codes to open the cargo airlock at the rear of the ship. "OK. Down, mate," he whispered. He was gently lowered to his feet.

He patted Burke's arm. "Thanks."

Mr. Burke sighed and stepped back into the darkness beside his boss.

The cargo ramp was broad and longer than the passenger ramp to lessen the incline. The end settled into a pool of dark on the concrete with a loud thud. Firefly applauded.

Rokey did not relax until they were safely inside and the

airlock hatch had closed them into the dim light of the cargo hold corridors.

Mr. Firefly, however, had vanished.

"Didn't he come in with us?" Ray demanded.

"Yeah. He was standing right here."

"That way," Mr. Burke said slowly, pointing down the corridor. The cargo-hold door was open.

"How'd he do that!" Ray hurried after in pursuit.

The cargo hold was dark and half-filled with empty crates of satellite parts. They had successfully delivered the solar cells to the *Tamaroan's* children. The long, low hold was filled with remains of the crates and spools.

"I get him," Mr. Burke said, and lumbered into the hold. His head and shoulders were visible over the tops of the huge crates. The maze was to him quite clear. His gray, wild hair whisked against the low overhead as he walked, turning his head this way and that.

"What is wrong with Mr. Firefly?" Ray said to Rokey in low, urgent tones.

Rokey shook his head slowly, turning away from the open hold door. "Long as it ain't contagious, mate."

"Oh, look at this!" They heard Firefly exclaim from the depths of the hold. "You *never* know what you'll find in a place like this."

"Maybe you ought to take him up front," Ray suggested. "Put him through a rinse and dry cycle in hospital."

"I wouldn't mind one myself," Rokey mumbled. "But I shouldn't operate heavy machinery in my condition."

"Customers first," Ray said. "You go start up the biocomp. I'll go start up the engines."

"Look! Here's *another* one!" Firefly exclaimed from the depths of the hold.

Rokey did not linger to learn what had been found. Rokey was already weary of the Quest.

The Gentleman's Reach

"Trees That Eat Things!" Firefly gasped as he clutched the edge of the hospital cradle, struggling to pull himself up. His hot, dark eyes were fixed earnestly on Rokey's face. "Trees That Eat Things!"

Rokey made reassuring sounds as he gently pried the man's fingers loose and pressed him back into the anti-gravity field. The headpiece encircled the back of Firefly's head, and electronic sleep closed over him.

Rokey set more controls, checking readouts and making fine adjustments until he was certain his "guest" was safe. He went out wearily, slowly climbing the stairs to the bridge on the deck above.

"Is our resident kook tucked away in hospital?" Ray said as Rokey slid into his copilot seat.

"Spinning comfortably," Rokey replied. "He should be nicely rinsed and fluffed in a few hours. Computer says he was pretty sick, running a high fever."

"That explains the delirium. Where's the tall spook?"

Rokey chuckled. "Seated at his master's side in unblinking vigil. Nothing's gonna get by him. Do you know where we're going?"

"Yeah. I just don't know what to do once we get there."

Rokey shrugged. "Wake me if you figure something out."

Rokey then drifted off to a half-asleep doze while the *Yankee Shadow* carried them further and further away from Club Sargasso and pirates and their many pseudo-adventuring ways. Rokey did feel a twinge of dismay that the parents onboard the *Tamaroan* would be sorry that he was not waiting for there. He fell asleep completely before regret really took over.

He was awakened later by Ray's exasperated snarl. "Did your Mr. Firefly tell you anything about how to get onboard his ship?" Ray's voice was tight with frustration. "The damn thing won't let us in!"

Rokey sat up with a start, blinking around in momentary confusion. Then he just stared out in awe at the sight of Firefly's yacht floating before them, a gold and crystal-faceted starship sparkling against the black of space. She was ornate, as big as a city-ship, with an erratic pattern of portholes, towers and antennae glittering around a golden sphere. The *Yankee Shadow* skimmed along beside her like a gull across the moon.

Ray repeated his complaint more firmly. Rokey tried to turn his attention to the readouts on his dash, but his eyes kept drifting up to the dazzling view of the starship. "He – uh, he couldn't really say much, and he's out now."

"I can't get any response from that thing, and I can't find anyplace to dock. What are we supposed to do? Sit here and wait for someone to notice *that!*"

With that last word, Ray gestured toward the view of the starship yacht. "Do you recognize her, old man?" he said to Rokey.

"I'm not even sure I recognize you," Rokey replied.

"That's an antique monstrosity name of the *Reach,*" Ray said. "Last I heard, she had been bought by Wystan Whytock the Second." Ray looked pointedly at Rokey, pausing to let him search his memory. "You've heard the name, old man, believe me."

"Oh, I remember," Rokey said finally. "The richest man in the galaxy?"

"The Second. This one is the *son* of the richest man in the galaxy."

"Our friends down in sickbay?" Rokey said in surprise. "Firefly is really Wystan Whytock the Second?"

"He could have bought the entire Sargasso with pocket change."

Rokey chuckled, remembering Ricmorann's shining-eyed delight. "Maybe he did."

"If I recognized the *Reach,* then others will, too," Ray said then. "We have to get her away from here."

Rokey realized that such a prize would be irresistible to certain people at Club Sargasso. To protect her, the *Yankee Shadow* might have to fight as hard as Ray's cartoon fleets in the gaming rooms. The odds would be harder to call. He leaned back in his seat with a heavy sigh and tried to think.

"It's a wonder she's here at all," Ray snapped, echoing Rokey's thought. "She should be crawling with pirates."

"Maybe they all killed each other off before we got here."

"Let us get us out of here before they start."

"We have to take her and our rich kook along. We'll have to park somewhere and get onboard."

"How!" Ray exclaimed. "She's already shot at us twice!"

"And you let me sleep through all that fun."

Rokey scanned his own controls, catching up with Ray's earlier attempts to dock with the starship.

"Whytock must have known this would happen," Ray said. "Didn't he say anything coherent?"

"Not once since I met him," Rokey replied. "The last thing he said as I put him under was about trees that eat things."

"That's pretty incoherent." Ray looked down at his dash controls with a deep sigh. "I feel like a bug on a map out here."

"Trees that eat things," Rokey repeated thoughtfully. "No, that isn't incoherent. I think that's it."

"That's what?"

"How to get in."

"You're getting as buggy as Whytock."

"I try to teach you things, Ray. I try to improve your mind and give you a little culture, but all this time you're just humoring me."

"I'm good for a laugh now and then, old man. But what's a tree that eats things?"

"It's a movie. I've shown it to you a dozen times, at least."

"You mean that confusing *trashe noir* thing, with the spooky garden and the Drug Store, and. . . and. . . I always fall asleep before the end."

"So did the Tree That Eats Things. That's the point."

"What's that got to do with how we dock with that yacht?"

"That's the key that Whytock was trying to tell me."

"Sounds crazy to me."

"No, not crazy, just delirious. Don't I talk like that when I get delirious?"

Ray had to laugh at that. "Yeah, you do, as a matter of fact. But you recite dialogue, not just titles."

"I'm better informed," Rokey replied absently, lost in a mental replay of his favorite B-movie. "The tree is guarding a secret passage. It shoots poison stingers so that no one can get past into the passage."

"That's us, all right. It's stingers aren't too poisonous but only because so far I've seen them coming."

"So keep your eyes open while I figure this out."

"How do you get past the tree that eats things in the movie?"

"You sing to it. Rather, you find a four-year-old child to sing to it, since it can only hear a specific frequency."

Ray flipped on the ship's intercom, signaling sickbay. "Mr. Burke, could you come up to bridge, please? We need your assistance here. Use the stairwell just outside sickbay."

Rokey chuckled. "You weren't asleep at all, mate."

"I sleep with my eyes open, old man."

While they were waiting for Burke to join them, the beautiful starship shot at them. Ray saw the flashing alarm on the edge of a scope, and leaped to his controls, spinning his ship up and out of the way of the missile.

"Mr. Burke! Hurry!" Rokey bellowed into the intercom.

Burke strode onto the bridge and stood behind Rokey's seat without saying a word. They explained to him as coherently as they could while interrupting each other in their haste.

Rokey indicated to him that the radio circuit was open.

Burke closed his eyes. "Twinkle. Twinkle. Little. Star," he chanted with a leaden rhythm, grasping for the ancient tune. "Don't you. Wonder. Who we. Are?" His heavy, gravelly voice was big in the compact bridge space.

The radio beeped on. "Ah, it is Mr. Burke out there." The starship's computer spoke with a pleasantly polished contralto voice. "Why are you returning without the shuttlecraft, may I ask?"

"Blew up," Burke replied.

"I see. How unfortunate. Is Mr. Firefly with you?"

"Yes." Burke nodded as he spoke.

"Is he uninjured, Mr. Burke?"

Burke seemed bewildered for a moment, and looked around, meeting Rokey's eye with his amber eyes wide and uncertain.

"He's only unconscious," Rokey said quietly.

"Unconscious," Burke echoed heavily.

"Oh, dear!" The computer sounded, over the radio, almost maternal in its contralto, machine-made concern. "Is he in danger?"

"Yes!" Ray broke in impatiently.

The starship ignored him. "Mr. Burke, is Mr. Firefly in danger?"

Burke nodded, then said, "Yes."

"Tell it to let us in," Ray growled softly, with barely restrained heat.

Rokey chuckled. "There will be people shooting at us at any moment," Rokey said to Burke.

"Open. Doors," Burke ordered, after a moment's intense concentration, during which his overly white face went even whiter.

Ray turned back to his controls with a disgusted look.

"Of course, Mr. Burke," the radio purred. "Do you require an entire landing bay for your vessel or only a docking bay for disembarking?"

"All. Whole ship," Burke gulped for air.

"Of course, Mr. Burke. Coordinates for landing bay eighteen veeping to you now."

"Yo! All right!!" Ray exclaimed as he went to work.

Burke returned below deck to sickbay.

The astonishing ship swallowed them up through a gold-rimmed mouth that lit up abruptly before them as they dove toward the gleaming hull. The *Yankee Shadow* swished down gently onto the landing deck and they were at once surrounded by a blaze of light.

As they waited for the rush of air against hull speakers that meant the landing dock was ready, Rokey unbuckled and stood up to stretch. This long night was wearing thin on him.

"Well, at least this is a change from the Club."

"I liked Club Sargasso," Ray snapped. "I was really beginning to relax."

"This trip ought to be real relaxing – a ship like this one, and with a kook at the wheel! We ought to have ourselves a very relaxing time here."

"More movies," Ray grumbled softly.

Rokey shrugged.

Shadow Games

"Does this ship have a crew?" Rokey inquired of Mr. Burke.

Burke shook his head without looking up from his vigil beside Wystan Whytock in hospital in the *Yankee Shadow's* sickbay.

"We have to find the bridge-controls of this ship," Ray said. "She's been in orbit here too long already."

"Boss flies ship," Burke offered in his heavy voice.

"Can you take me to the bridge?" Ray said. "I can fly this ship. We have to get out of this system – and fast."

"Boss flies ship," Burke repeated.

"And I'm sure he does a fine job," Ray said. Rokey frowned at his partner's growing exasperation. "But since he's unconscious, I can fly the ship to get us out of here."

Burke considered this for a moment, staring down at the sleeping form in the hospital cradle, then stood up. "I take you."

Ray scowled at Rokey and shrugged, following the big man out.

Rokey went up to the galley to make cocoa. The sour taste of hours of drinking was building in his throat, and he would not get to wash it away in hospital until their passenger was recovered.

Ray returned a half an hour later, alone, with an even darker scowl across his finely cut features. "You'll have to wake Whytock," he said. He did not sound pleased.

Rokey was shocked. "A starship that Raymond Harris can't fly?"

"I never saw ship's controls like that before in my life!"

Ray was on the verge of shouting. "Not even in comic books. That's the damned most archaic instrument panel layout ever made. All I could make out of it was the command center for the garden. Did you know this ship has a garden?"

"I wouldn't put it past him," Rokey was genuinely surprised. His partner's familiarity with starship design and control was legendary in Rokey's mind, legendary even in some quarters of the galaxy. For Raymond Harris to be defeated for the first time in his career, not by the complexity of a starship's controls but by its archaic simplicity, was remarkable.

Ray tossed a book onto the galley table in front of Rokey. It was a lovely thing, with four-color art of the starship on the cover, blazing against a sky of stars. Rokey picked it up and thumbed through it.

"That's the manual for this ship," Ray said with a sneer.

It was printed on ultra-thin sheets of prismium between covers of metallicized isolucite. Rokey was impressed by the precision and beauty of its production. It was written in Chinese. "I see," he said finally. "I guess we better wake Mr. Wystan Whytock and fill him in."

"The *Reach* really was built by a monkey and a madman, you know," explained a now conscious and apparently coherent "Rufus T. Firefly," a.k.a. Wystan Whytock II.

"She was the very first luxury-styled, personal star-yacht built in the Solar System's space-docks in orbit around Mars," he went on proudly. "That was over a thousand years ago. After four hundred years of travel through the galaxy, the surviving member of the family turned her into a hotel, back in orbit over Marsport. She was quite a fixture there, but you know how things got to be on the old home turf!"

Whytock interrupted himself and turned to Ray with a startled look. "Of course, it's not your old home turf at all, is it? Not at all. Ancestral blood-lines and all that, but no wistful childhood memories of Earth."

"Not a wistful between us," Ray quipped.

"Heh, heh, heh! Not a wistful between you, indeed! Then you do understand why I didn't mind buying her out of orbit and taking her with me in my travels. She was made to travel the stars, taking someone in luxury and style to all the places in the sky. I thought Marsport had seen enough of her."

"And her enough of Marsport, too."

"I had to modify the *Reach* some. She used to have a crew."

"At least someone to do the jump calculations," Ray said. "She has the most primitive navicomp system I've ever seen."

"The first one ever built out of the Solar System, Captain. A thousand years ago, it was the finest product of Earth's technology."

"How do you do the jump calculations to get from here to there?"

"Usually I just ask directions before leaving, but there is an instruction manual."

"I've seen it. I don't read Chinese." Ray gave the fancy booklet to Whytock, who pocketed it automatically without comment.

"Never mind. I'll work it out on my fingers," Ray said. "Can the *Reach* cross link with my ship so that I can steer us through a convenient window?"

"Oh, yes, certainly. That she can do just on voice command. If you would be so kind as to hand me my walking stick?"

Ray turned to the main console of hospital controls and called up the bridge link and through it, the radio.

Even with Raymond Harris controlling her through the *Yankee Shadow's* bridge, however, the *Reach* was a slow ship. There were too many hours left for pirates to catch up with them. Pirates do not have slow ships. Ray aimed the gaudy starship toward the intraspace window for the system Whytock had selected from the many choices available from the Sargasso system. Having a place to go did not calm Ray's nerves as much as some answers would have. Nevertheless, once the *Reach* was safe within warp shields in the intraspace window, Ray went to sleep. Rokey went back to his cocoa, to await his turn at hospital. He would not really trust his judgment until then.

Parlor Games

When Rokey awoke from his "rinse and dry" cycle in hospital, the ship was quiet, with the silent throb of the drive engines a comforting and familiar sensation against his bare soles. He smelled cocoa and went up the galley. Ray was slouched back on the bench, his dark with a sullen scowl.

"Morning," he said as Rokey walked in.

Rokey was pleased to see that there was cocoa was already prepared and keeping warm in the range. "Thanks, mate." He curled his hands gratefully around the mug and slid onto the bench across from Ray. Rokey took a long drink of the foaming, wonderful brew, feeling a curious pleasure simply in being alive.

"Want to go for a walk?" Ray said abruptly. "This ship is like a museum. You should see it."

Rokey shrugged and drained his mug. "Why not?"

Disembarking the *Shadow* into the landing bay of the *Reach* was like entering the lobby of a five-star hotel, with hushed, gentle music and soft carpets. Gold gleamed amid marble and jade. The landing bay led them through a carpeted airlock tunnel to another oversized lobby, ornamented as richly as a planetary hotel, with marbleized wall covering. Art from a hundred different cultures hung in lighted niches at different heights. Snake-scaled brass railings rippled alongside stairwells and walkways in corridors of every size, style and color leading off in a dozen directions.

"Curiouser and curiouser," Rokey remarked, pausing before an ornate, wood-carved door only knee-high. "Why are some of them so small?"

Indeed, even Ray with his narrow bones would have had a squeeze. "Designed by a madman and a monkey," Ray quoted. "Remember?"

Rokey peered through the nearest tiny door into the tiny corridor beyond. "Beats me. A monkey's as good a reason as any other."

They walked on in silence for some time, randomly opening doors and choosing directions. They passed through huge ballrooms, now silent and dark, through elaborate bedrooms and theaters and halls, corridors, bathrooms, poolrooms, and closets. Each was different, each magnificently made.

"Everybody in the world was rich when they built this ship," Ray said. "People made things for the honor of it, for the honor of making the best."

"The rich can afford that kind of honor." Rokey's voice betrayed the cynicism of sure knowledge. Rokey had once been very rich, born rich, the rich master of a wealthy house that had been wealthy for a very long time. Now he dealt with pirates and weirdmen, and counted his change.

"I used to be rich," Ray said quietly, almost wistfully.

"You still are," Rokey snapped. "You're just short on cash at the moment."

"Short on luck, mostly."

"No, Cap'n, I have to disagree. You've been splashed by Curley's Oil Well, and you fair drip with the stuff."

Ray laughed softly, letting his fierce gaze sweep once across Rokey's face. "You and your theories," he said fondly.

Ray and Rokey argued often about theories of luck, but pleasantly. Ray's own theory was that luck bled away if counted on. He found it best to pretend he had none, but he liked to hear Rokey's "theories."

Rokey brushed his knuckles across his sweep of whiskers in a time-honored pre-lecture gesture.

Ray cut him off abruptly, stopping to point down the corridor ahead. "It's another dead end down there."

"Pick a door then. Have you made any sense out of this maze yet?"

Ray nodded absently, turning slowly on one boot heel to scan the corridor wall curving out of sight behind. On one side were three tall, narrow doors of differing textures and colors of stone, alternating with enigmatic miniature copies. On the opposite wall was a pair of plain, ivroid doors of normal size, with golden, recessed handles. One door had a green *Watch It Eye* in its center, the other a blue one.

"The green doors are always locked," Ray said finally. "They weren't locked before, when I went through here to the bridge."

Rokey tested this out on the nearest greenstone door. It was locked.

Finely beaded threads and wisps of gold traced gleaming webs across the door's polished sheen, winking and flashing as he moved. He touched the cold surface with his fingertips and the golden tracings flared brightly, fading back slowly from warm honey to a sullen red. "Hmmph! Greenstone of the South," he quoted. "That's supposed to be for good luck."

"They're locked," Ray repeated.

"Maybe they're Soul Doors," Rokey suggested. "That was new in the days this thing was built, and much in vogue at the time."

Ray shrugged. "You're the historian."

"It's history now."

"A lot of souls, though, don't you think? One in six doors so far has been green."

"And all locked," Rokey muttered. He had a momentary qualm, a surge of starship claustrophobia he had not felt in a hundred years. His ears fluttered back and his hackles ruffled up and then flattened in an abrupt gesture, responding to his feelings.

Ray said nothing. He strode over to a door of zebra-striped stone, far down the hall from the locked "Greenstone of the South" door. The zebra-stripe effect was created by a design carved into multi-layered stone, black obsidian stripes on an ice-white layer beneath. The design cracked and slashed around the centrally placed handle, a recessed knob of greenstone. When Ray turned the knob, the door divided in a ragged diagonal slash, corner to corner, and the divided halves slid silently aside.

The room beyond was lit blue and green in a watery, pseudo-underwater light. Dry-ice fog rolled across the plush floor. Blue and purple shadows pooled along the corridors and surged in the mist.

"I smell flowers," Rokey said. "Expensive flowers."

"I don't know about that, but it's bleedin' damp!" Ray quipped.

"Do you hear that?" Rokey stepped up to the door.

"No! I do *not* hear flowers and neither do you!"

Rokey chuckled. "You're cute, son, but it's been done. I smell flowers and I can hear bells. Little, tiny, tinkling bells."

"If I smell the flowers, will I hear bells, too?"

Rokey shook his head and brushed past him to go in. Ray followed after. The corridor was wider, with mist that chilled where it touched skin. Ray took his gloves from a jacket pocket and pulled them on. After a few paces the mist closed around them. Ray, too, began to hear bells: tiny, tinkling silver bells, shivering in the distance. The shivering bell chimes faded away, as though rounding a corner somewhere in the blue-purple shadows ahead.

Rokey continued on, his big ears arched forward, fixed on the invisible source.

"Wait a tic, pal," Ray called sharply. "We're on some kind of leash."

Rokey paused, looking back over his shoulder at Ray. "I smell flowers," he repeated stubbornly.

Laughter, as silvery and silken as the distant chimes, sounded ahead in the mist.

Rokey turned back to stand beside Ray, scanning the corridor, his ears swiveling delicately, whiskers taut.

The fog was rolling in more thickly and the blue glow began to dim to a purple twilight. Rokey crossed the corridor, swirling through the fog in angry strides. He put his hand out to the wall and followed it along until he found a door. He tried the handle.

Even in this colored light, Ray could tell the door was green. Rokey angrily rattled the unresponsive doorknob, then strode back the way they had come, trying the next door.

"It can't be!" he said. "It's locked!"

Ray had not followed Rokey, merely turned on his heel to watch.

"This can't be the door we came through!"

Ray was quite sure it was. He liked to keep track of exits

and escape routes.

Rokey stood at the door, one hand on the locked knob, looking back helplessly at Ray. "It can't be," he repeated, his rumbly voice sharpening in protest. "There's no trace of me – there's no – no scent! I can't smell."

Rokey spun on his heel and sniffed the wet air with exaggerated care, then knelt and bowed his head to sniff the floor.

"Rokey!" Ray was startled. "That's undignified! And unnecessary!"

Rokey did not need to sniff tracks like a bloodhound to identify traces of scent. His brain was even keener and more finely trained than his nose. If there were scent, he would have known. The chemical blankness around him was as puzzling and alarming as an unexplained visual blackout would have been for Ray. He sniffed his own hands, then hurried up to Ray and sniffed at his jacket and his hair.

"Nothing wrong with my nose," he muttered with relief, brushing down, once again, the ruff of mane that had risen around his face in alarm. "Something has wiped away more than our fingerprints, Ray – we've been erased! We're being led somewhere, and the traces of our going there are being erased behind us!"

The shivering tinkle of bells sounded ahead as if to answer him. "What the hell's going on?" he muttered quietly, trying to see through the mists ahead.

"But why?" Ray said. "What's the point?"

Rokey put his hand to his face again, for the momentary reassurance of his own scent. The blank, invisible smell-dimension around him was cleaner than clean, with no chemical sting of cleansers and antiseptics, just the scentless, frustrating sterility of ionic scrubbers. Against the stark, clean air, Ray's scent identity loomed in the fog like a shadow cast oversized against a wall. Rokey shook his head abruptly in protest at the disorienting effect.

"We need to get back to the *Shadow,*" he said to Ray. "I don't like this place."

"I couldn't agree with you more, mate – but how?" Ray asked.

The blank end of the corridor behind them and locked

doors left them nowhere to go but toward the lure of the bells in the mist ahead.

"Why would anyone try to keep us from finding our way back to the *Shadow*?" Rokey asked.

"I don't need my nose to find my way."

"Because your nose is ignorant and can't tell stink from instinct!"

"There's nothing wrong with my nose, Rokey. I just don't need it to find my way home."

"I do," Rokey said mournfully, peering into the damp gloom around. "We're locked in here, wherever here is inside this big bauble!"

"Here is three decks, eight corridors, fourteen doors, and about half a kilometer from the dock where the *Shadow* is parked," Ray said.

"You sure?"

"Three decks, eight corridors, fourteen doors, half a kilometer. You want the sequence of port and starboard turns?"

Rokey drew back, and the tight curve of his whiskers showed that he was not reassured.

"I want to know why this ship is erasing our tracks," Ray said. "What would be the point? We're in intraspace. Do they expect us to run away?"

"They who?"

"Could the strange Mr. Burke be behind this?"

"He didn't seem to know much about this ship when we got here," Ray protested. "He didn't seem to know to much about anything."

"Charlie Chan say ignorance easy to fake."

"I wouldn't know about that," Ray countered.

A single horn note, pure and thin, sounded ahead, a simple challenge. Ray shrugged loosely and set off after it. Rokey kept pace just behind him. The tinkling bells shivered with an angry sound that dissolved then into whispery laughter.

They rounded the corner. The corridor here was the same, although the fog swirled more thickly, the lights dimmer, even more purple.

"Nothing. If the speakers for that noise are in here, they're damn well concealed."

"The sound is being projected off inset reflectors in the

walls," Rokey said. "The source is up ahead."

In the mists and gloom far ahead, a sliver of light appeared, widening slowly to a wedge of watery twilight falling through an opened doorway.

"Now I *really* smell flowers!" Rokey said.

The artificial mist rolled through the door ahead of them, pale white in the wedge of light. Ray and Rokey stayed just outside the doorway and peered in. Even Ray could smell the flowers.

There was a garden inside. They entered through a rough stone gate, a trilithon of hewn obsidian, into a single, domed chamber as large as a stadium, filled with night sky and a garden that, with water and stone and plants, cleverly created the impression of a towering woodland park beneath the stars. Mist swirled around, lending the illusion of distance to the garden. They stood at the bottom of a gentle slope, on a narrow white-pebbled pathway that curved up and away through autumn-colored trees into darkness and mist. Twilight hung on the crest of the tiny hill beyond, pinned with the sparkle of artificial stars. There was green moss beneath the trees, spread with golden leaves like dropped coins.

Rokey was enchanted enough to forget his irritation at the mystery that had led them here. The air was moist and rich with smells, small, subtle smells from a carefully limited palette, soothing and remote. Water against stone made a noise like low voices. Not even the crushed white stone gleaming on the pathway could muffle from his nerves the particular vibrations of a ship in flight.

Ray looked around carefully at this sky, studying the ornate stars. He went across the green moss and buried stones to the curve of twilight-blue that was the domed ceiling of this chamber. It was surprisingly close, the baseline disguised by moss-covered boulders and the tall spikes and blossoms of some dark, purple flower. Rokey followed him.

The substance of the sky was deep blue glass, shaded at the horizon, translucent, lit by an internal glow. The stars were five-pointed outlines of gold, shining in the glow of the sky. Each star was a frame for a portrait, faces of every race, people, and time. Some were holos, some flat. Most had been taken with the eyes focused at the lens so that every portrait seemed to stare back.

Ray pointed. "That's you." He was frowning. "What's he doing with a picture of you, old man?"

Rokey had trouble for a moment finding the particular star-framed portrait that Ray was indicating. He was startled when he realized it was, indeed, himself, an old publicity holo from his first days as president at Rokherton. He chuckled. "Haven't changed much, have I?"

"What's he doing with a picture of you?" Ray demanded.

Rokey put his hand across his heart in a gesture of false modesty. "Well, it was in all the news at the time."

Ray grimaced. "You recognize anyone else up there?"

Rokey scanned faces he could see for a moment, then pointed to a spot close to his portrait. "Yes. That's Hohlar Ayannar, head of the Genetic Survey Board." He studied them in silence for a moment, then pointed to another, and a third and fourth. "Those are members of the teaching staff at Rokherton. And that," he pointed further up, "That's the head of transportation on Wozur. Nice lady, knows every inch of the planet and how to get there."

He clasped his hands behind his back, surveying the once-familiar faces carefully, long-lost memories surfacing unbidden. "It's been a long time," he said finally, speaking in Wozurn.

Ray made a sweeping gesture with his arm that took in the whole range of the starry ceiling. "This is crazy!"

"Pretty, though."

Ray turned and went back to the path. He was shaking his head.

There was the chuckle of water from the other side of the dark crest of the small hill. They climbed the sloping pathway, ducking their heads under the boughs of the miniature trees that bent gracefully over the path.

Water sparkled below them on one side, with the glowing stars reflected off tiny pools and waterfalls scattered among reeds and night blooming lotus plants. Great white blossoms rose from the dark water like spiked ghosts around a high, long, sinuous curve of black stone.

"This is a beautiful place," Rokey said in a hushed voice. "Reminds me of home."

"I'm glad you like it," Ray replied tensely.

They walked down together to look at the dully gleaming stone. The bone shapes in stone of some giant, petrified beast were sprawled along the hill down to the dark water on the other side. At the far end of the curve of stone was a dinosaur-like skull, with huge, empty eye-sockets, resting its chin among the spiked lotus-ghosts.

Rokey sat down on the spine of stone. "My feet hurt and this place is very restful." He had not thought about his own garden in decades. The faces in the sky and the groomed perfection of this place brought a wash of memory. Each leaf was an understatement of an ideal, grown and arranged with nothing accidental or casual, yet utterly natural. Timelessness hung over the scene as densely as the fog.

The gardeners of this ship were the best Rokey had ever encountered, but of course, why not? Who was in charge, Rokey wondered. Did Wystan Whytock and Mr. Burke come down here in person to trim and prune, water and fertilize? Ray's casual comment finally got Rokey's attention. A Tree That Eats Things? Where was the gardener?

"Computer?" Rokey called aloud, clearly. "Computer, where is the gardener?" Ray looked at Rokey in surprise, but said nothing.

"The garden self-monitors itself at all times, sir, from a variety of locations." The computer's voice was warm and filled the air around them. "What specific gardening service did you require?"

Ray broke in. "The gardener locked the door on his way out. Can you tell him to unlock it?"

"The garden monitor units are not involved with the primary substructure of the ship, Captain Harris," was the infuriatingly polite reply.

"All right then, computer," Rokey had a try. "Unlock the door nearest our location."

"Are you not comfortable here, sir?"

"This is the finest starship garden in existence, Computer. Now let us out. We wish to return to the *Yankee Shadow.*"

"I'm afraid I cannot permit access to that area, sir." The contralto voice sounded genuinely regretful.

"Why not?" Ray demanded.

"I cannot permit access to weapons."

Ray looked startled. "What?"

"There are weapons stored onboard the *Yankee Shadow,* sir. I cannot allow further access."

"That's nonsense!" Ray exclaimed. "I'm not going to use weapons in here!"

"It's not you we are concerned about, sir," was the baffling and infuriating answer.

"Me?" Rokey asked in surprise.

"I cannot permit you access to weapons, sir. I'm sorry."

"And why is that?"

"Wozurns present a danger to my boss, sir. I cannot permit that."

"But I'm no danger," Ray said. "Is that right?"

"You're an Earthman, sir."

"Scubb," Ray swore softly under his breath. "This is stupid."

Rokey shook his head with a sigh, looking around the garden in search of another clue. "She has to let us out of here," he protested. "She's only a machine."

"Damned smart machine," Ray growled.

"No such thing. Just a very well-informed machine."

"Then who erased your scent tracks?"

Rokey crossed his arms over his big chest, looking away from Ray's eyes. "Why don't you ask her why she did that?"

Rokey spoke only half seriously, but Ray brightened. "Computer, why are scent traces erased in the corridors?"

"Wozurns hunt by scent, sir."

"I am not hunting. I merely want to go home."

"Yes, sir. I'm sure, sir."

"You'll let *me* go back to my ship?" Ray asked.

"Of course, sir."

"Wait here," Ray said to Rokey with a sigh. "I'll go find someone to let you out of here."

"Take your time," Rokey said. He settled himself more comfortably into the curves of black stone. "I like it here."

Ray strode away with hard crunching sounds of his boots on the white gravel path.

He located Mr. Burke first, who walked back to the garden with Ray. When they arrived, Rokey was almost sorry to see them. The garden was an island of serenity, a place of timelessness in the heart of the stars. He regretted leaving. Ray, however, was so outraged by the computer that his distress forced Rokey to agree to leave.

"I'll speak to Whytock," he said to Ray, trying to sound soothing. "Don't take it so hard."

They followed Mr. Burke out of the garden and he led them along without comment. The computer made no effort to stop them, as though Burke's mere presence were enough to nullify whatever danger Rokey represented.

Burke strode off slowly but deliberately. He did not look behind.

They followed silently, a task made easy by the rich carpeting on the decks and the noiseless doors. Burke led them to the upper reaches of the vast ship through a complex pathway of corridors, doors, and stairs. He doubled back on his path occasionally, and changed levels in an apparently random way. After a half an hour or more of this purposeful meandering, Rokey began to suspect that Mr. Burke was either taking a deliberately roundabout course, or else did not really know his way around the ship.

Burke halted at last outside a tall, wide set of double doors of some dark wood, elaborately carved in deep relief. He stood for several minutes in front of these doors. Rokey could see by the slow tilting of his head that he was studying the energetic figure carved in the panels.

Then he put his big hands out, pushed the massive panels apart, and entered. Ray and Rokey stepped up silently and peered in. Burke stood in the center of the room, facing a tall, silvery woman swaying in a square of pearly light. Something strange about her held them hovering at the edge of the panel, looking in. Burke said nothing. He just stood, looking at her the same way he had studied the carving in the door.

The woman was pale as rain in the light. Rokey realized that she was a holusion, a phantom of light, another ornament of the cluttered quarters. She had wide gray eyes and silver hair, and wore wispy, clinging folds of silvered glass-bead patterns. She shimmered like rainfall. She was tall and smoothly curved, and the light of the holusion made her a pale figure in moonlight.

The rest of the space inside was large, crammed with odd, handmade furnishings and glass lamps, shelves, cabinets, tables, and consoles. Nested against the back wall was an enclosed sleeping chamber, like a giant satin egg cracked neatly open.

Burke turned around, and seemed startled to see Ray and Rokey standing behind him, as if he had forgotten they were with him.

"Is this the dining room?" Rokey said smoothly.

"Follow me," Burke replied. He pulled the massive door panels closed behind them, leaving the strange, pale woman dancing by herself in the light.

"Nice place here," Rokey said.

Burke nodded.

"You like it here?" Ray asked.

"Yes," Burke answered solemnly, with remarkable feeling in his big voice. "Big place. Good food."

The dining room he chose was a pull-out galley off a side corridor, complete with surprisingly comfortable fold-down seats. They let Burke order from the screen menu. The resulting feast was wonderful, diverse, and satisfying. Burke ordered a considerable array of small but potently flavored dishes, each essentially one mouthful of wild, spicy aroma and outrageous texture, each one totally different from the last. When the emptied bowls had piled to a precarious height, Burke carefully put them into a slide-covered receptacle in the galley wall, wiped the table, and started over with a new set of equally exotic dishes.

"Is anyone else involved in this Quest you and Whytock are on?" Ray said after a time.

Burke looked over at Ray with a flash of alarm in his yellow eyes. "Wysteria," he said slowly, after a long moment.

"Is she the lady dancing by herself in that crazy room?"

Burke nodded his head, lowering his fork and spoon slowly to his plate. His dark-rimmed, yellow eyes showed a spark of alarm, as though he thought Ray might steal her from him.

"She suits you," Ray added that last because he recognized Burke's alarm.

Burke nodded again, almost smiling. Another pile of

dishes went into the bin.

Dinosaur Meat

Answers were given at dinner, in a larger, more elegant, wood-paneled dining room close by the *Yankee Shadow's* berth.

"I am sure that you gentlemen would like to hear some explanations," Whytock began suddenly during dessert. "I've left a lot to your imaginations."

Ray had a lot of questions and a lot of imagination.

Rokey spoke up first. "Our hospital couldn't pinpoint the cause of your, how shall I say it, peculiar symptoms at the Sargasso?"

"Ah, yes. There was a rather tantalizing edge to that place, as I recall," Whytock said. "Or I think I recall. I'm sorry, but I've never been in a room with so many Wozurn before, never in my life. I seem to have lingered in the Club far too long. I assume the antihistamines just couldn't cope with all of you!"

Ray and Rokey both blinked in surprise at this.

Rokey wondered if Whytock were having a relapse. "Are you feeling okay just now?" He tried to keep his voice soothing.

"Oh, yes. The antihistamines – Oh! I see, heh, heh, heh!" Whytock broke into his bright, cheerful laugh. "This is difficult to put into – I mean, when an allergy gets that much – well, it isn't," – he actually paused long enough to draw a breath – "You know, I've never tried to explain this before. Well, not since school, of course. Not since – Well, Wysteria knows, of course, because it's her allergy, too. And it is, after all, the real reason for the feud with father, isn't it? All this started when Wysteria found out what he had . . . Well! I can't blame her. Would you? But I do think her solution is just as extreme as his, don't you?"

He looked around to the three men at the table, as though expecting them to confirm his statement. Their stunned silence seemed adequate answer for him. "Indeed! Being allergic isn't just embarrassing, it's – it's archaic. Can you imagine, in this day and age, to have so serious an allergy; It seems so – so careless!"

"Allergy?" Rokey asked. "What allergy?"

"Yes! An allergy to you, to your very self, sir. Or rather, to your most noble and well-groomed fur."

Rokey harrumphed gently. "Even *my* hospital unit is sophisticated enough to reverse an allergy! I won't even charge you for it."

"My father, alas, is smarter than any med unit – and I've tried the best there are, you can be sure! I rather hate the things now. No." He gave a tremendous sigh, and began fumbling in his jacket for a cigar. When he had gotten it puffing, he went on. "My father made his children – us, that is – Oh, dear! I do so hate the sound of this." He puffed quickly on the cigar.

"He had the two of us genetically engineered." Whytock declared this last with such dramatic despair that Rokey almost laughed.

"The allergy is so deeply seated – a kind of 'asthma of the brain,' that in order to re-engineer the genetics, *we* would be re-engineered. It would remake what we are, our very identity. Father knew his children's pride, of course. Wasn't it the same as his own? He knew we would never give up being ourselves. We're too much like that."

Whytock shrugged loosely, setting off the dazzle of his smile. "Besides, if we change the allergy, he'll disinherit us. It's the single provision in his will – and he threatens to live for a long, long time. Will I want to change *me* once he's dead?"

"What did we Wozurn do to earn such passionate regard?"

Whytock sighed. His manner fell a little as he twirled the cigar slowly in his fingers, staring down at its glowing tip. He drew breath to speak and instead shook his head with a little laugh, and sighed. "Wysteria and I often debate his motives, but we may never learn the for-real truth. I think it is as simple as his jealousy and vanity. Wysteria has a theory about the natural antagonism of parents for their offspring. Wysteria herself has no maternal instinct, and I do believe she got that from father, so she may well be right. But racial chauvinism is an ugly thing in any form, and father has it to a wealthy degree. He's always been green with jealousy that you Wozurn were the first in the galaxy to discover warp drive, and the first to organize an interstellar union. He wants Earth to be first. First in everything, last to lose. He thinks his revenge on you is to become the richest, which he is. He could buy and sell Wozur in an afternoon. It's the only kind of insult he can comprehend."

"I'm afraid his logic escapes me," Rokey said. "Not the insult, just the logic."

Whytock shrugged. "You have to know the man, although I'd rather you didn't. Let's just be grateful Wozur isn't for sale."

Memories suddenly, painfully crowded Rokey's mind and clouded his eyes for a moment. He swallowed down the taste of anger, remembering Lord Jak's statement about the rule of Wozur. "At least, it wasn't the last time I looked."

"Rest assured, sir. I keep a careful check, and they may have sold out their Council vote to our galactic leader, but the heart and land of Wozur are secure." Whytock almost said more, then abruptly changed his mind, and puffed on his cigar. "Mr. Burke and I were there a few years ago, you know."

Rokey's narrow-eyed response was less than encouraging, but Whytock continued on quite unaffected. "We visited Dr. Hohlar at the Index itself. I think Mr. Burke and I gave him a bit to think about, as well."

Rokey felt that some kind of net were closing around him, an elusive bond he was not sure he wanted to acknowledge. "You were a student at Rokherton?" he asked, with a grim tone growling in his voice.

"Indeed, where else? Of course, you can imagine how much my, uh, my peculiar affliction limited my classroom attendance, but that never stops a determined student, does it?"

Ray leaned forward then, elbows on the finely polished

wood of the table. He looked back and forth between the two men. Rokey's copper-plate eyes were getting red. "How did you know to come looking for us at the Sargasso?" Ray spoke sharply, watching Whytock's eyes. "Are you quite sure you weren't sent by George Humphrees?"

"Sheer good luck, sir. Sheer good luck. I had no idea nor any reason to suspect you might be – but once I knew you were there, I certainly wasn't going to miss an opportunity to be introduced. I said I needed a navigator, and Ricmorann suggested I hire Captain Harris. How could I pass up the chance?"

Whytock leaned forward, grinning. "You know, I did rather suspect he was eager to get you safely away from the Sargasso."

"Him and me, both," Rokey grumbled.

"You can find anything at Club Sargasso," Whytock went on. "I've heard that all my life, so when I needed to find a navigator, I went straight to the Sargasso."

"And just happened to find a navigator who needed to find a way out of the Sargasso?" Ray said.

"These things have a way of working themselves out," Whytock answered dreamily.

Rokey found himself thinking of the children of the *Tamaroan.* He had to wonder if this meeting was truly coincidental. What would a rich man want of pirate children?

"You seem to have a lot of ways of finding things out," he said.

"Indeed I do. Finding out things is my business. Well, my favorite business. Fortune has led me into a lot of enterprises, but finding out facts is my favorite."

"You've made a business of it?"

"Talk To Me Enterprises, in fact. You can find a branch of my offices in the Yellow Pages. Any Yellow Pages."

Both Ray and Rokey smiled politely at the wordplay in the company title.

"And what do your Talk To Me Enterprises enterprise?" Ray asked curtly.

"Information. I collect information," Whytock replied promptly. "From anyone about anything. Information is always useful to someone somewhere. Mostly, I collect information for myself, but I'll collect it for anyone, and I share."

"You can certainly afford it."

"Indeed, I can! Father buys money. I buy information. People who know things are much more interesting than people who just own things, don't you think?"

"I've staked my life on it enough times," Ray said, grinning at his overeducated partner.

"Information can be expensive," Rokey said.

"Especially at my prices," Whytock replied solemnly. "But I have plenty of ulterior motive. My revenge is as private as Father's and even Wysteria's – I have come to think of all those people out there among the stars of civilization, spending my money, as part of my secret family. Most of them are people of whom Father would never approve."

"Somehow, that kind of revenge kind of takes the sting out of being occupied," Rokey said.

"Yes. I do believe I'm having more fun than Father." Whytock's tone changed slightly. His expression was open, less comical. "Keeping money safely piled up is far more taxing that spending it."

"What does your boss think of this?" Ray said sharply.

"My boss?" Whytock was startled by the question. "Boss?"

Burke leaned closer to the conversation, his yellow eyes narrowed.

"Yeah. The lady in charge of this operation. The one behind the pretty holusion in your quarters."

Whytock was genuinely taken aback.

"Whytock is boss," Mr. Burke broke in with his heavy voice.

"Well, I always thought I was," Whytock said thoughtfully. He met Ray's hard-eyed look calmly. "The holusion in my room is of my sister, Wysteria."

"Isn't she boss of all this?" Ray gestured curtly around to indicate the huge starship-hotel. "Why is she hiding from us?"

Whytock puffed at his cigar in silence for a moment. "I'd never thought of it that way, but perhaps you are right, Captain Harris. Perhaps she is more in charge of my life than I'd really noticed. Isn't it curious how one's blind spot is always at the center of one's focus?"

"What are you talking about?" Rokey said.

"Someone has been directing this ship's computer to keep

Rokey under control," Ray said, speaking to Rokey but looking hard at Whytock. "I don't like it, and I don't believe this ship has computers with enough savvy to work that all out alone – or to be able to run the ship with just one person."

Whytock sighed dreamily, his eyes glazing over, lost in thought. "Even in her distant, frozen crypt, half way across the galactic arm from here, yes – she does run my life, Captain. Now that you point it out, it seems obvious, even blinding. With all my good luck and fortune, I can't spark any happiness in her, and I do seem to have made her happiness the Quest which keeps me going."

"Hold on!" Rokey complained. "Can we rewind here a few lines and let an old man catch up?"

"Wysteria is not here," Mr. Burke declared darkly. "Only holusion."

Whytock leaned forward onto his elbows, staring down at the cigar tip. His white cuffs gleamed around his pale wrists, and the candlelight gleamed in his black eyes. "She's a bit older than I am, just thirty-five years older. But I am catching up, because one doesn't age in cryo. She's a rare fine lady, my sister, but a little wacky. In a nice way, I mean, but a woman with a mind of her own. At least, I hope it's her own. Most of it's her own. She is much like our Mr. Burke, here. The strong, wordless type. Of course, I usually go to see her in her cryogenics crypt back in Galactic Medical Central, before she's fully thawed out, so I do a lot of the talking. She only thaws out when I come to see her. It's really quite an honor. Did I tell you about her feud with Father? It's over this damned allergy. Why should I mention it? But my sister refuses to thaw out for good and get back to her life until Father dies. And Father refuses to die until she thaws out and apologizes. There are sizable bets going around certain parlors in the galaxy about which one of them will thaw out the other. I know how stubborn they both are. I wouldn't put my money on either of them. But I do enjoy traveling around for Wysteria. Did I tell you that? I visit places and look around and take snapshots to show her. I go to thaw her out every few years, and tell her about my travels."

He sighed. "Ah, Wysteria. She's as lovely as her name. I know you'd like her."

Candlelight glowed warmly in the silence when he had finished.

Rokey leaned across the wide, polished stone of the table, to take the crystal decanter and refill his glass. Then he refilled all the glasses and held up his own in a toast. "A salute to Wysteria and the heat of her passion."

All four men drank to the salute

Whytock set his glass down gently and smiled, but there was a sad, wistful look in his eye behind the smile. "I do so wish you were right, Captain Harris. I would be so glad to have dear Wysteria in charge of my life entirely, if only it meant she were actively a part of it. Have you any sisters of your own, Captain?"

Ray shook his head.

"Ray is an only child, Whytock," Rokey said. "He misses all the brothers and sisters he never had."

Ray shot Rokey a heated look, but said nothing because it was true.

"You have a sister, Lord Rokhmyr," Whytock said to Rokey. "I'm sure you do understand."

"Yes. Yes, I do," he answered gruffly. "But she and I always got along best from a distance."

Ray sat silent.

"Perhaps that's true about Wysteria and myself," Whytock said thoughtfully. "But I hope not. Perhaps it won't be so bad if I do get to be older than she is. Maybe then I'll get to be boss, after all."

"You are boss," Mr. Burke rumbled.

"That still doesn't explain why the computer here was able to play nose games with Rokey," Ray growled. "Or why Rokey's face is in your little collection of stars."

"I find it wiser, Captain Harris, always to *appear* to be stupider than I really am," Whytock said earnestly. "The same is true for my starship. She is fully as capable as she is glamorous, despite the illusion of simplicity in her controls."

"More magic tricks?" Ray's voice was tense.

Whytock smiled with his white teeth. "I had the ship's central processors redesigned by someone who might as well have been a magician. She gave me the freedom to run this entire complex myself. It's always seemed like magic to me, but it's all done with mirrors, lights, and shadows."

"Luxonics systems, you mean?" Rokey said.

"State of the art."

"Luxonics are a little too luxurious for me," Ray said uncomfortably. "I've met my match."

"The lady would be honored, I think, Captain Harris. She was proud of her work on my ship."

"I'd like to meet her."

"Stranger things have happened, I'm sure, Captain."

"I have an interstellar bounty on my head, Whytock, a big one," Rokey said abruptly. Ray's sideways questions were beginning to embarrass him, in some strange, old-fashioned way he had forgotten he knew. "Ray is understandably concerned about my future, and my publicity holo in your garden has alarmed him. Startled me a bit, too, I must admit. I never thought I looked that arrogant."

"Nasty business, bounty hunting," Whytock said with a sigh. His voice was dark with real emotion. "I've done what I can to legislate against it, but our beloved Galactic Leader will have his way, especially when he knows so well how to stroke the baser instincts beneath the skin."

Rokey grunted in terse agreement.

Whytock sat in silence a moment. "I do know what your bounties are, gentlemen – and how you got them," he said quietly as he took the convoluted wine bottle from the cooling stand and refilled their glasses. "I know, for instance, that Lord Rokhmyr took a singularly admirable but unfortunate political stance against a pet project of our leader. You were the only spokesman for the truth."

Whytock smiled up at Ray's dark look. "Captain Harris has a price on his head, with a deadoralive clause, because he is the lone survivor of an disastrous military exercise that our interstellar government has told important lies about. You were the only witness to the truth."

The two men met this with dark silence. Burke sat unmoving, holding his glass.

"Alas, I am too expensive to have had a price placed on my head for such noble pursuits," Whytock concluded.

"I used to think that," Rokey said.

"We are both expensive men, Lord Rokhmyr, from expensive families. It is only that you were not forced to acquire anonymity until late in life. I have been trained to it since birth."

"It is an acquired taste, yes."

Ray drew back uncomfortably in the oversized chair. "I'm sorry, Mr. Whytock. We have reasons to be careful."

Before Ray could finish the sentence he was trying to find, Whytock spoke up, flashing his candlelight smile. "Trust cannot be bought, signed for, or counterfeited, Captain Harris, I know. Believe me, I'm rich enough to know what can't be bought."

"And I know that you make some things worthless by putting a price on them," Ray countered.

"I do pay for services rendered."

"Getting out of the Sargasso was reward enough for me," Rokey cut in.

Ray shrugged in tacit agreement.

"Behave yourself, Ray," Rokey said then, lightly. "You're a guest here. Until you find this nice man the place he's looking for, he's taking us on faith, too."

"I'm a good navigator, remember," Ray snapped.

"You've already given me a better sense of direction about myself, Captain. Your insight about Wysteria guiding my life is invaluable." Whytock leaned forward with his cigar clenched in his smile.

"Is that what you hired me for?" Ray asked.

"Oh!" Whytock looked genuinely surprised. "Did I forget to tell you about that?"

Rokey hid a smirk behind his wine glass.

Ray laughed outright. "I think you have, yes."

"I didn't tell you about the dinosaurs?"

"Not a word."

"There is an enormous market for dinosaurs and dinosaur meat and dinosaur products out there, you know," Whytock announced this as though they had walked in at the middle of a lecture. "Worlds like Earth that lost their native populations of dinosaur-species pay outrageous prices. The black market on fresh dinosaur-meat alone provides income for tens of millions of people across the sky."

"Isn't there a government agency to protect them?" Rokey

said.

Whytock scowled. "They're the biggest part of the black market, as well," he replied. "Our Galactic Leader gets a considerable bit of personal income himself from illegal xeno-animal sales."

Neither Ray nor Rokey responded to that. The current government of their interstellar civilization was not a popular topic of conversation.

"I like dinosaurs," Whytock went on quietly, studying the glowing tip of his cigar as he spoke. "I pay a lot for information about them, information about people buying them – and especially information about people selling them, where they come from."

"Admirable work," Rokey said.

"Yes," Whytock said with a sigh. "But protecting exotic life-forms from extinction is no easier in the galaxy than it was at home on Earth – and you know how extreme my Father's solution for *that* has become."

"It's such a big galaxy," Rokey said, "so full of souls."

"But to the point," Whytock went on as he tucked the cigar back into his pocket. "I have discovered that a brand new species of creature is being sold on the dinosaur market, creatures of a most exotic DNA type. They aren't truly dinosaurs and not even truly *animals* as near as my experts have explained. The trouble is that the their native planet is unregistered – and so far, untraceable. Whoever is making money from this new planet is determined to keep it a secret."

Ray groaned. "I am a starpilot, Whytock. I cannot find a star system by reading DNA patterns!!"

Whytock chuckled at this, and poured more wine all around. The strangely shaped wine bottle seemed to refill itself every time he set it back onto the stand.

"Ah, that is rich, Captain! Rich, indeed!" He grinned at Ray, "But in point of fact, I happen to know an xeno-biologist who has mapped the galaxy by DNA patterns – and she has some very interesting theories about navigation and DNA!!"

"Which leads us back to dinosaurs," Ray said.

"Ah, but these aren't really dinosaurs!" Whytock said, with some heat. "That's why I have to find the world where they come from. We are going to chase pirates around until they lead us to their source, Captain. You will have to walk backwards through the windows pirates have used. I can take you to the zip-point where they transfer their cargo to legitimate merchant ships, but my sources have been baffled in attempts to trace them further. I need you to trace them for me."

Ray's dark look was replaced by a slow, pleasant smile. He picked up his wine glass and raised it in salute. "*That* I can do, Mr. Whytock," he said softly. "That I can do."

He folded the while linen napkin on the table and stood up. "I would like to check your data against my navicomp, Whytock. Can you have your computer send what you've got to the bridge of the *Shadow?*"

"In an instant, Captain!" Whytock replied merrily. "In an instant!"

His walking stick had been placed on the edge of the table beside him, as though the silver animal head were resting on the cloth awaiting a morsel of his meal. Whytock picked it up and twisted one ear gently until it clicked. The ruby eyes lit up. Whytock spoke a few commands, twisted the ear back into place, and the eyes faded. "Your computer now knows everything I do about this project," he said to Ray. "Let us hope you have better luck with it."

"That's why you hired me," Ray said. He nodded to Rokey and went out.

A few hours later Ray returned. Rokey and Whytock were deep in their after-dinner conversation about Whytock's student days at Rokherton University on Wozur.

"Ah, welcome back, Captain," Whytock said with a smile. He picked up a glass from the table and held it out. "Join us in a cordial?"

Ray accepted the glass and Whytock poured from the same mysterious bottle. The liquid it served had changed to a deep orange-colored liqueur redolent of peaches and some alien flavor.

"I've got a start on it," Ray announced. He paused a moment to sip at the drink, smiling in appreciation at the flavors.

Whytock took this news with great seriousness. He even put out his cigar as he leaned forward across the table to listen.

Ray had brought with him a small, portable holoplayer.

He set this carefully in the middle of the table, and switched it on. A star field opened up over the table in a globe of dark light. He touched more controls, and a series of red lines appeared, linking stars in a web. "These are the intraspace links between the systems where you have been picking up the ships with the dinosaur meat," he began.

Whytock made a soft noise in his throat, and Ray corrected himself. "With the *not*-dinosaur meat." He pointed to a single star where most of the lines met, gesturing with his wine glass. The globe of golden liquid moved among the star patterns like a caricature of Whytock's starship. "You've been assuming that *this* must be the zip link system where the main ships are emerging from the hidden system, and then shifting the cargo into smaller ships, for transport here, here and here." Ray indicated systems along the lines radiating out from the zip link system. "But there is data missing from your picture."

Ray clicked another control so that a second set of lines in blue appeared. "Very few people know about this place, a zip-link system known as Snugglers Notch."

He pointed to the star where the blue lines converged, this time using his finger to trace the specific lines of the intraspace travel links. "As you can see, the Notch links to points in line with your cargo destinations directly, *as well as* the central zip link system you started with. The Notch is known only to smugglers and independents. Its location is a well kept secret. Evidently even Talk To Me Enterprises doesn't know about it."

Whytock was fascinated, studying the holo display with an intense look. "Indeed!"

"I haven't been there since childhood," Ray went on. "And I didn't remember it right off, either, but I think it could well be the link to your missing star system. Their main ship comes out at the Notch, transfers the cargo, and the smaller ships move on to market. That explains the distribution of appearances, and I think that's where we should go to look for them."

"And so we shall, gentlemen," Whytock said happily, relighting his cigar. "So we shall."

Rokey gave up on sleeping after a few hours of staring at the back of his eyelids. When he smelled cocoa heating in the galley, he got up and padded out. He found Ray slouched back on the bench, studying the holo display of stars with a sullen face.

"Morning," Ray said as Rokey walked in.

"Find anything?"

Ray made a noncommittal noise in his throat and continued staring at the display.

Rokey curled his hands gratefully around the warmth of the mug and slid onto the bench beside Ray so that he could see the display from his point of view. Spider-web shapes of varicolored lines laced the stars, the trade routes of civilization, the legitimate and the secret, cracks in the dimensions of space that linked the stars. "Such a big galaxy," Rokey said in appreciation. "So many souls."

"Do you buy his story?" Ray said abruptly.

Rokey chuckled, and sipped at his cocoa. "Oddly enough, yes, I do. The man is so far into peculiar that he can't be anything but genuine. Whether or not he can do anything about the raids on this mystery planet, wherever it is, that is another question, but I applaud his efforts."

"Besides," he added, smiling. "I like him. And this is a lot more interesting than being stuck at Club Sargasso. With any luck, too," – he gestured to Ray with his mug to emphasize his words. "We may have seen the last of Lord Jak and the *Tamaroan* – long may she wave, but I did not like being a pirate."

Ray grinned. "However pleasant the pirates may have been – and don't call them pirates."

Rokey nodded. "Yes, sir." He gestured toward the holo display, and changed the subject. "It seems to me that if Whytock is right about where this stuff is turning up as cargo, then we are dealing with a *major* black market operation. This could be a much bigger kettle of worms than he knows."

"That is just what I was thinking about when you came in, as a matter of fact," Ray said. "I was thinking that what we see here probably represents just the dinosaur products end of their operation. I am getting a most unpleasant feeling about the size of what we are going up against." Ray reached up and swept his fingers through his hair. "I am not liking what I am thinking about how big."

Rokey studied the display, feeling a sense of Ray's alarm touching him.

He sighed. "We may find ourselves missing the *Tamaroan* after all."

Artlessly Remembered

Completely unknown to Whytock, Talk To Me Enterprises or anyone else in the galaxy, for that matter, someone else was out hunting for those strange not-dinosaurs.

The morning was foggy, the light too thin and pale to intrude on dreaming. When Nate awoke, he knew at once that he had overslept. "Seff will go without me!" he said aloud, propelling himself out of the gentle grasp of his sleeping twigs. They curled up slowly behind him as he drifted away.

Nate grabbed the edge of his treehome opening with his tail tip and drew himself over. He hovered there, peering out anxiously for sight of his friend, unable to deny his fear of the thick, wet sky. The village of treehomes was hushed with the drape of fog, and no one was out drifting about.

"He will get into trouble," Nate said with a sigh. "I *know* he will get into trouble!"

The night before, while they were out together floating among the topmost branches of Seff's treehome and watching mists slowly obscure the stars, Seff had talked about looking for new subjects he could paint. Nate, almost as a joke, had suggested that Seff paint the fog. "That would be a challenge, wouldn't it?" Nate had said. "To paint something that hides everything?"

Seff, however, did not take the suggestion as a joke. He saw in it far more than Nate had ever intended. Seff was consumed on the spot with the ambition that he would solve the Mystery Of The Fog, and paint *that.*

Nate was accustomed to his friend's instantly passionate

obsessions, but the Mystery Of The Fog was something far more serious than painting. People vanished when the fog rose up from the sea. There would be a shriek or a cry heard in the distance, but never a trace of the victim. The few who escaped reported glimpses of giant things swarming past, huge gray shapes looming in the gray fog. These mysterious creatures moved in some strange, indescribable way. Those who had seen them would not speak of it. The Mystery Of The Fog was the essence of fear. Children were frightened with the stories so that they would know to stay securely tucked inside their treehomes when heavy clouds sank across the land, making every surface drip water.

Nate peered out into just such a morning, just such a fog. He felt cold despite the humidity and drew back inside. Mystery stalked the land on days like this.

His treehome thrummed, the low notes of her voice purring through the dense wood, telling him that Seff had come by but had not waked him. Nate peered out again, realizing that this meant Seff was out there alone, stalking the Mystery Of The Fog by himself.

Seff was not looking for danger, and he did not know yet that he would be looking for not-dinosaurs. Seff was looking for Art. The idea had seemed so exciting the night before, when they were anchored safely in the treehome branches. To catch a glimpse of something so unknown and mysterious seemed the right kind of adventure. Nate knew that his friend Seff needed an adventure. Seff needed something to raise his flagging spirits, for he had a talent so unique that no one in his world could make sense of it except his friend Nate. Seff's frustration was keen.

It was not just that Seff could paint. Seff was the first one ever in the entire world of Hupp who could paint. Seff had *invented* painting. Alas, because Hupp were born with eidetic memory for every sense, and no one could ever forget anything, no one else in their village grove really understood painting, or its purpose. The tools of remembering seemed unnecessary because Hupp memories were perfect and indelible. What need of painted images when "art" lived behind the closed eyes, and only death could end remembering?

"Beauty," fellow villagers told Seff, "is in all the world

around us. What has that to do with your daubs of color?"

Nate, however, had a life-size portrait of himself hanging on his treehome wall. Seff had painted him in profile in that portrait. Nate had seen his own face reflected in tide pools on the beach, but not his profile, no matter how he stretched his rubbery self around to look sideways at his face in the water. Nate could feel the side of his face with his fingers, remember its line, but the painting *showed* what he could not see with his own eyes directly. Every time he saw this profile, he thrilled again at the wonder of it. He was proud to be the one who kept Seff's faith in his curious talent alive. The look in those painted eyes was startlingly real. Nate held the irrational belief that as long as this portrait hung here in his treehome, he himself would be safe.

Nate did not tell his treehome exactly where he was going, saying only that he would be with Seff. The tree rumbled sleepily, shivering warm scatters of dripping fog over Nate in gentle reply as he floated outside.

The rest of the villagers were safely tucked away inside their treehomes. The grove was quiet and seemed lost, fading away as though already vanishing in the fog. There were no shadows and the sky was too close. The sun was only a brightness in the pearly white layers overhead.

"Nate!" a familiar voice hailed him sharply. Nate paused. "What are you doing out there in this weather?"

Nate finally located the face peering out at him from a treehome mouth, a face the same color as the tree's luxuriant foliage and difficult to see in the expanse of green. It was Massay, the village eldest and leader. Massay's sharp ears missed little in his community.

"I'm going to spend the day with Seff," Nate said, speaking carefully. Massay expected respect and always got it.

"Go quickly then. Get back inside with your friend!" Massay made a complaining noise and turned back into his treehome.

Nate hurried, catching twigs with his tail tip and pulling himself along, in between bursts of speed from the wide-open vents down the back of his little body that puffed him forward through the air. His progress, even so, was labored and sluggish. There were no friendly breezes to fill his ears and lead him over to Seff's tree. The air was thick.

When he finally arrived at Seff's spacious treehome, he peered in through the opening. He saw the lichen shelves on the walls of the interior, jammed with seed-cups and paint ingredients, the usual litter of paintings and bleached-bark sheets piled everywhere. Seff was gone. Nate felt a momentary flash of alarm, then he was distracted by a row of brand-new paintings, just sketches really, hung opposite the entrance, hastily placed in a line. Nate saw himself in the paintings. He floated up closer. He had to study them for a few moments.

Understanding struck him all at once as the quickly drawn scenes resolved into a story.

The first sketch was of the pale half-light of dawn, showing Seff peering into the entry of Nate's treehome. Nate was curled up asleep in the green twigs of his sleeping rack like a leaf-colored ball held in a pair of cupped hands. Nate had not realized that this was how he looked when asleep. Seff had managed to show just how cozy and secure he felt while enfolded by the inner twigs of his treehome. The next was a sketch of Seff puffing across the gardens, returning to his own tree. The third was of Seff painting, with brushes and paints swirling around him. Tiny versions of the first drawings were shown beside him. The fourth painting was of Seff disappearing into the mists of the swamps below the ridge on which the village grove stood.

These were images of Seff's own morning experiences. The final series were a wonder to Nate, another dazzling new possibility of this strange new thing, painting. The last sketches were of Nate emerging from his treehome and drifting over the treetops to Seff's tree. Nate noted the absence of the momentary diversion of speaking to Massay, showing that Seff had painted from imagination, rather than observation. Nate saw himself peering around Seff's cluttered space, finding the row of new paintings. Seff had not witnessed these things, yet he had anticipated them so well that Nate recognized the moments at once.

The next-to-last showed Nate vanishing into the mist over the swamp, just as Seff had. The very last was of the two of them floating hand-in-hand through thick, white fog.

Nate was delighted. This was thrilling. The message was clear: "Follow me."

No one had ever left a note before, not in all the history of Hupp.

"Follow me."

The very first note left on a wall in all the world – and it was to him!

Nate puffed out after Seff without another thought.

Follow Me

The village grove of Stand Alone grew on a ridge of mossy rock atop a narrow ribbon of land between oceans. This ribbon of land stretched along, it seemed, forever, from horizon to horizon. Beach and marshlands led up to the top ridge from both shores. The marshes were flat, with expanses of tall reeds crowded by the sand and the wide ocean on either side.

There was a simple stability in the chaos of the marsh life that usually pleased Nate. Bubbles abounded – leaf-bubbles tugging little plants upward and spreading their gossamer structures out into the air and light. Bubbly body-parts supported tiny insects on impossibly filmy wings. Egglets and grublets and spiderlets and seedlets wafted through the air on bubble-membranes, sparkling over moss and in the frothy twigs of berry scrubs. Clumps of massed balloon-plants, the deepest of twilight blues, rose everywhere on tall, wiry stems.

Nate clung to the reeds, trying to see through the fog that drenched everything and frustrated vision. He could make out only the blue balloons, bobbing in thick clumps, and black shapes of reeds with moss hanging from them. He drew himself down closer to the water's murky surface, one reed at a time, wrapping his tail around the stalks to keep himself anchored as he tried to see.

Nate cupped his hands to his mouth and hollered through the wet air, "Seff? Seff, where are you?"

Soft snickers of mud-feeders murmured back, but nothing that sounded like Seff. The liquid mumbling of open water echoed loudly in the fog-thickened air. Nate spread his ears wide, trying to listen yet not hear words in the wind's voice. Ominous things sounded in the wet distance. The sunlight was so thin here that there was no time. The shadows by which Nate measured the day were missing. Where was Seff?

Nate saw at last a flash of red-orange over a stretch of open water, a color that he knew as clearly as his own – Seff was in sight!

Nate puffed over to his friend, grabbing him eagerly in both arms and swirling him around. Seff was shivering and wide-eyed. He gasped as he clung to Nate, drawing them both closer to the water's surface with his uncontrolled and emotional movements.

"Be still!" Nate hushed him, breathless with relief yet flush with a wash of anger at Seff's rash and dangerous actions. "You were crazy to come here alone!"

"I became afraid that you would talk me out of it, Nate."

"And you were right!"

Seff drew back, all the way to arm's length. Nate had to snatch at his hand to keep him in reach. "I am doing something important, Nate!" Seff cried. "You of all people know that!"

Then he huddled in close, his fervor dissolving as quickly as it had appeared. "I've been so dreadfully terrified, Nate. But you can't know how much I want to see what the Mystery Of The Fog really is. You're right."

His excitement became something different, intense, thoughtful. "Perhaps I've been too quiet, and that's why I haven't seen anything yet." He pressed close to Nate as they drifted. "Now that I have the idea in my head, I just can't give up. If I could see one really tearing up the land like the legends say, then I could paint it. That would show everyone that there was a purpose to my painting, to show them what they can't see for themselves. Then no one could make fun of me."

Nate caught his breath on an outcry of despair, and answered coldly instead. "They could, and they would, and they will," he said. "You are going to get us both killed if we don't get out of here!"

Seff dangled limply at the end of Nate's fingers, staring out into the fog without seeing. "Yes. You do know, don't you.

But that makes it even more important that I see for real. I only need a glimpse. That's enough to show people!"

Nate wanted to argue but he could not. The notion of Seff's quest did work on him, despite his fear. Paintings that showed people things they could not see themselves was brand new. His envy of Seff's peculiar skill of hand made Nate even more envious of his daring idea. The fog thickened around them as the air grew wetter. Nate shivered, shaking off the lure of adventure. "You can't paint pictures of the Mystery Of The Fog if you've vanished into it!"

"Why did you come here?" Seff said, suddenly calm.

Nate was not particularly surprised by Seff's change of direction. Their friendship had covered many such conversations. Nate calmed himself. "How do I know? You left a message and I just had to follow."

Seff patted Nate's hand and drew closer, peering directly into Nate's golden eyes. "Exactly, my friend!" he said urgently. "You acted upon the most immediate of feeling, and here you are. Maybe inside you were thrilled by the idea of seeing the danger yourself?"

"Of course, I was!" Nate said with a groan. He tried to direct them away from this stretch of open water. The air was getting thick with the smell of the sea.

"Of course, you were!" Seff echoed. "Even a hint of the danger shown in my sketches was enough to bring you out here. Think how much I can move them all if I could paint it for them – not a hint, not a sketch, but a real picture!"

"Yes! Yes, you are right!" Nate hushed his own voice, peering around. He could almost hear the rush of waves. "Of course, but we can see them just as well from the safety of the reeds, Seff! I am frightened out over the water like this."

"There!" Seff cried suddenly. He was clinging to Nate so tightly that Nate could not turn to look.

"What?" Nate remembered the last of Seff's note-sketches, the two of them vanishing into the fog – and now it was really happening.

The air was darkening as though the fog were changing color. Salt in the wet air tingled against his skin. The fog hanging down to the surface of the water filled with dark, looming shapes that had not been there just a heartbeat before. The hulking fog-dark shapes came closer as Nate stared in horror.

"There!" Seff whispered with clear triumph. "Now we will see something, my friend!"

"No!" Nate puffed as hard as he could, scooping the fog into his ears to swoop away. He had never been more afraid in his life.

"I want to see!" Seff cried, tugging instead toward the disaster bearing down on them. *"I want to see!"*

Nate's fear raced ahead of him, raced through him, raced away. "Be silent!" he begged his friend.

Seff only struggled more.

Out of the cloud-touched water, dark shapes swept past. For a brief flash, an instant that lasted a lifetime, they could see clearly the gray shapes of the creatures and their peculiar, oversized, ground-hugging limbs. Their long heads were mostly mouth and dark, moist eyes. They moved swiftly for such enormous beings, despite their unusual limbs or perhaps because of them. Just as this registered in Nate's mind, one of these creatures loomed out of the fog, coming at them. A clawed limb was reaching toward them with a dangerous sweep.

The creature was upon them before their eyes had adjusted to the sight of it. It snatched at them, almost losing them in the swish of air of its own movement. Their whole world was wiped away by the wide black gape of its mouth closing over them. They were scrambled together by its many teeth.

It swallowed them.

Nate contracted himself into a tight bundle, squeezed down into a lump by the press and cramp of the creature's gizzard. He could not breathe. He could *not* breathe! He could not think. He could not tell even if he were intact. His hope went into shreds. Nate fled, not physically, for he had been swallowed and was churning with food inside the thing's belly. Nate went blank. He let himself disappear. He assumed he was dead.

His last thought was to wonder if Seff were dead.

"I Stink, Therefore I Am."

Death stank.

Finally, most of all, Nate had to admit that death *stank.* Death stank meaner and fiercer than anything Nate had ever smelled, real or imaginary. The stink was as big as the world, as big as the sky and night and day combined. Nate waited without thinking. He was getting used to it. Nate had to concentrate hard on not breathing. Breathing made the enormous stink a part of him inside and the stink was awesome.

Not breathing.

He had to think about not breathing. His tough, rubbery, stubborn little body still wanted to breathe outside air like a living being.

He was alive!

The world stank like filth because he was buried in filth, but he was *alive!* Nate struggled and writhed and flung himself free, spitting filth out of his mouth. *"Seff!"* he shrieked with his first gasp of real air. *"Seff, look what you've done!"*

The only answer was the surge and pound of ocean waves on the beach.

Nate rubbed his dirty fingers across his dirty eyes and peered around through the shimmer of stink surrounding him. He was alone.

The sun beat down brightly on the broad expanse of pale green sand and the black turds. Nate had survived undigested through the creature's gut. Seff must be there somewhere, too. Nevertheless, for long minutes Nate could not make himself dig through the sand-crusted pile for his friend.

A long curl of broken sea-snail shell, sparkling like pearl

in the sand, caught his eye.

Nate snatched it up with a cry of relief. It was nearly too big for his hands, but the broken end was scoop shaped. He wrapped his tail around the nearest rock as anchor, and used the shell to attack the rank stuff, stirring it about with short, jerky stabs. Insects and stench and steam rose up around him. Lumps of unknown, undigested things thumped against the scoop. None of it felt like Seff.

"Seff! Seff!" Nate called as he worked, gasping against the horrid smell each breath brought him as he drew air for words. The scoop got stuck and he could not drag it free. His strength was spent. Despair blurred his vision. He pulled back, choking down a fearful urge to fly away, and fly and fly.

The snail-shell wobbled of its own accord, fell over and, with a slurping *pop!* Seff burst out. He began screaming as soon as his face was free. He screamed and waved his hands and tail until he had spun himself furiously about in the air.

Nate sprang after him, relief overcoming the smell. Seff propelled himself on in mad, frenzied flight. Nate's own reserve broke and he fled as wildly after. Together they streamed over the clean, flat stretch of beach, dashing themselves against the sand and puffing themselves upward into the air. No matter how they raced, they could not out-fly the stink. The sunlit beach, the ocean breeze, the sparkling sunlight mocked them with cleanness. The stink was livid and a part of them. They could not escape it.

Seff collapsed into himself at last, gasping. He spiraled down into the shelter of a piece of ocean-bleached driftwood. Nate floated in the beside him, his feelings in wild disarray, quivering with weakness. They cowered in the fingers of driftwood. From there they could see, at last in plain sight, the Mystery Of The Fog revealed.

Far across the beach, the fog creatures played and frisked about in the surf. In the broad daylight they were almost beautiful. They were huge, and bizarre and unlike anything known, but they were no longer Mysteries.

"Why didn't we die?" Seff said sadly, this thin little voice a whisper of despair in the big ocean noise. "These memories will be worse than death. This stink is worse than dying!"

"We didn't die." Nate savored the words and the wonder of it. "We didn't die."

"Or did we?" Seff said thoughtfully. "Could this be why no one wants to die? Because it's this *smelly?*"

Nate shuddered. "Even death must be better than this. Dying must be better than this horrid smell. Anyway, I don't feel dead." He shuddered. "I feel terrible, but I can feel. This smell is too real for death."

"I stink, therefore I am," Seff said with a gleam of a chuckle.

Nate felt his wonder at their survival return. His beloved friend was beside him again. Even the horrid stench was proof that they were alive. "If this were death," he said, struck by a sad thought. "Then our parents would be here to meet us. There is no one here but us, so we must be alive."

"Even the dead wouldn't come near a stink like this," Seff declared, shaking himself so hard that sand sticking to him rattled against the sheltering driftwood branches. "The living certainly won't let us near them. We can't go home like this. This is worse than death! We're trapped out here. That must be why no one else who got swallowed ever came home."

Nate had been wondering about that, too. "Only until the stink wears off," he said to Seff.

"How can anything this awful wear off?"

"At least we don't have to be afraid of the fog creatures anymore, Seff. I don't want to go through that ordeal again, but we know that they can't kill us. No one knew that before." New information to bring to the village. If they could go home.

Seff, with his usual resilience and dancing emotions leaped upon this with delight. "We have discovered something important, haven't we, Nate! I will finally get to paint the Mystery Of The Fog – from the inside as well as the outside!"

The two laughed together. Nate felt again his respect for Seff's spirit.

Seff stared off across the beach to the creatures playing in the waves, crouching on the sand on their strange, extra set of limbs, slapping at one another with clawed hands and gnashing their teeth in mock battle.

"I am going to make some wonderful creature paintings one day," he said with a happy sigh.

The fog creatures clashed on in their mindless play. Sea-sprites wheeled and screeched overhead. Seff and Nate watched them cavort about in their wave-drenched games until the afternoon grew chill. The creatures one by one slipped back into the sea. The pound and surge of the green-crystal ocean went on forever. The beach stretched onward in a line to the horizon. At last, they were alone.

"We have got to try to wash this off," Nate said in a very small voice, disgusted with the thought even as he said it.

"My tongue would wither and fall off!" Seff protested. "Anyway, there's disease in this stuff, I'm sure." Seff shivered with dread as he crooked his slimed tail. "We really might die if we tried that."

They drifted along the beach, disconsolately dragging their filthy tails in the clean, white sand. "We could scrub ourselves like pots," Nate suggested.

Seff agreed. They scrubbed themselves and each other with handfuls of sand. They rubbed the hard crystal grains against their skins until it hurt as much as the stink.

And still they stank. Their silky hides glowed with new skin iridescence, but they stank.

"That's it," Nate said finally. "That's all I can stand."

The sun was setting, a giant gold-green circle sizzling on the edge of the ocean. "Tomorrow," he said. "Tomorrow we'll try something else."

They found a driftwood shelter high up on the beach, coiled their tails into the tangles of its dead branches and fell headlong into sleep, huddled together and wrapped up in their oversized stench. Nate awoke briefly in the first pale reaches of dawn. The last stars of morning were sinking into the sea. Wavelets sucked and pulled toothlessly at the trunk of their driftwood piece stuck in the sand. Bubble-packed foam-spiders were clustered on the flat span of each wave's leaving. They blinked with fierce, jeweled eyes. Nate did not think about where he was, but the impact of memory struck him with the full weight of that awful smell, gagging him abruptly.

He sobbed, and flung himself back into sleep, clinging to Seff. They slept until the sun was an unforgiving brightness high in the sky.

The Smell of Success

"Nate! Nate, wake up!" Seff's excited voice cut through the blissful unawareness of sleep.

"Go away," Nate mumbled, squeezing his eyelids down tighter against the brightness. A hideous stench overwhelmed him. He could not put away the memory. "I am awake."

Seff pulled Nate free of the driftwood shelter with eager hands, clearly delighted by a discovery that had all his attention. He led Nate over the beach to sand dunes that stood between the flat expanse of the shoreline and wild reaches of marshland. Nate did not ask. He just let Seff pull him along. The rush of air in his face was almost soothing, since every other breath was free of the smell.

Seff had found a stand of thorny wild bushes in a hollow among the dunes. The branches of the small, twisted bushes reached up to them like open arms, voiceless. The bushes were dense with ribbed leaves and loaded with fat, shiny berries as black as moonlight.

"They're delicious!" Seff exclaimed excitedly. "I've never seen them before, but they're wonderful! You couldn't get a better breakfast, really." Seff drew himself in among the leaves, wrapping his tail around a twig to hold himself in place. He pulled off a handful of the fat, shiny fruit. "Here," he said, offering them to Nate.

Nate had no interest but he took the berries rather than argue. He could hardly taste the sweet fruit over the stench in his nostrils, nevertheless, his beleaguered senses slowly acknowledged the crisp refreshment. He began to feel some spirit rise in him. "At least we won't starve," he mumbled to his friend as he picked a handful for himself. Juice dribbled along his face and dripped from his chin, staining his fingers.

"No one's ever known about these," Seff said cheerfully. "I wish I knew how to paint a taste!" Berry juice stained his face, hands and chin. His smile was bright and heartened Nate.

Nate took another handful and stared at the dark juice stains, thinking to himself sadly that this was now even more mess to clean up. The fruit inside him, however, and the bright noon sun warming him made the stink seem less awful, or perhaps he was adjusting.

"Do I look as silly as you?" Seff said with a giggle.

His reddish-hued skin was stained purple, even the tips of his ears and whiskers. Nate held up his own hands, dark blue to the chin, and laughed. "I hope so. I wouldn't want to look any sillier than you do. They really would think we were fog creatures if they could see us and smell us at home!"

"We could sure stir things up a bit, couldn't we?"

"It might be fun at that!" They both began giggling then, imagining the comedy of panic they could create among their little village group. These giggles turned into laughter as they regaled each other with images of who would exhibit panic the most hysterically. Their terror and grief was released in a wild merriment of sound, and laughter spun them up into the air, high above the booming surf. They bounced into each other and clung together, quivering with mirth and swirling about in the clear air.

As they began to calm, they let the sea breeze puff them skyward, high into the sunlight. The view from this vantage above the ground was new. They had never strayed this far from the village before. Nate and Seff had no way of knowing how far they had been carried in the creature's gizzard. Swamps, dunes and beaches here were much like their village ridge, with differences like fine, black berries offered by a voiceless bush.

They entwined their tails together and continued drifting, content to let the wind carry them while they gazed around at this new scenery. The rippling band of dunes leading up from the beach melted into a marsh of reed stalks bending and flashing in the sun. Further inland, wildmoss hills rose up, crowned by a ridge of trees. For a time as they drifted toward it, Nate studied the distant forest, hoping to see treehomes and another village. The groupings were irregular, the hill uncultivated. He had to conclude finally that it was a grove of trees as wild as the moss. The raised ribbon of land varied only in width. In some places the beach was a stretch of white sand curving out to long, shallow tides. In others, the waves lapped into the marshland and stirred the tall reeds. The ocean was green and vast, spreading away to the green horizon on both sides of the land, and surf slapped and boomed along the shore.

On the other side of the wildtree ridge was another such broad slope of wildmoss leading down into a similar stretch of marsh, dune, and beach as could be seen on this side. That was all there was to the land – beach, dune, marsh, wildmoss, wildtree ridge, and on the other side of the ridge, wildmoss, marsh, dune, beach.

Nate turned in the air to look behind them. The same pattern went on and on, a long thin strip of land rising out of the cold green water. The sea was unbroken to the horizon, cut in half by that single, narrow line stretching out of sight on either hand.

There was nothing else to see anywhere, even from their great height. The world was mostly ocean, just ocean. The land that had seemed so adequately secure when he was safe within his treehome was, in reality, a thin strip of sand, marsh, and trees. It stretched across the horizon perhaps, but only as this narrow ribbon that did not seem enough to hold back such an enormous expanse of water.

Nate contracted in a cold shiver of fear, a reflex that made him lose altitude abruptly, diving downward in a wide, swooping curve. Seff kept his tail firmly wrapped around Nate's so that he slowed their descent. Thus linked together, they made a leisurely glide down toward the beach.

Nate was still shivering with the fright he had given himself. The sight of that green water rushing by below filled him with cold dread, as though he had seen the ocean devouring the world. He was grateful that he could float. As dearly as he loved his treehome, this view from above showed that no anchor was truly safe. The endless water pressed in all around. He carried the comfort of his beloved treehome inside him in his perfect memory, but that memory was his only security.

The fog creature had wrenched him out of the world he had known and shown him the wonders of a world of new memories, new visions, new experiences, the stuff of life to be added to his lifelong collection. This would have to replace the physical security he had felt before. If the sea were going to eat the world away, then he wanted to see it all, store all of it safely away inside himself, to have it even after it was gone.

These bouncing emotions were wearisome. Nate clung to Seff as they stabilized their flight finally above a tiny tide pool, hovering over the shallows while Nate apologized for having lost control so suddenly.

"It was scary up there anyway, Nate," Seff said easily. "Don't feel bad. We've gone quite a ways by now. Let's go over to the higher ground to see if there are berries here. They were *good.*"

Nate held up his juice-stained fingers. "We haven't cleaned up from the last batch yet." He rubbed his tiny palms together. "It's dried on pretty good now, too. I hope," – he did not finish because the thought that they might have added a second irreversible stain to themselves was too grim.

Seff had the same thought, for he lowered himself to the surface of the shallow waters of the tide pool below them at the same time that Nate did. The two splashed the salt water vigorously over their hands and face, shuddering at the cold touch. The dried berry juice washed off easily in the salty bath, staining the waters with clouds of purplish dye. Tiny fish swam up to taste it.

Nate and Seff washed and splashed, and splashed and washed, until the pool was stained with purple, and they were clean.

They were *really* clean.

Nate hesitantly sniffed at his fingers. "Seff! Could it be?" He started splashing and washing in earnest, ducking his head and dipping as much of himself as he could against his own natural buoyancy. He was made to float, and he was reassured by how strongly the water resisted him. The ocean might swallow the land, but it could not swallow him.

Seff watched for a moment without comprehension, a

puzzled frown curling his whiskers. He understood abruptly and with a joyful whoop, dove down and began to apply the salt water as vigorously. They splashed, and scrubbed, and rinsed, until they were exhausted, and the water was murky with hints of creature. More fish came by for a taste.

Seff and Nate then propelled themselves up the beach to find another clean pool. There they went through the process again. Once they had done as much as they could, they soared up to the sweeter air above the ridge and paused, afraid to breathe but sniffing gently, tasting the air around their once-odorous selves.

They smelled the sharp tang of sea-brine, but they were clean.

"We can go home now!" Seff whispered with as much fear as joy. "We're free!"

"Yes." Nate looked up to the slope of unknown wildtrees and the pale green sky above. Nothing was familiar but the sky itself and the wide, green sea. They did not even know in which direction home lay along the ribbon of land.

"Yes," Nate said to his friend. "Now we can go home."

A Whiff of Magic

They slept in the branches of a wildtree. She had no hollow interior to offer as a chamber and was unable or perhaps unwilling to speak with them; nevertheless her top twigs folded around them with the instinctively protective nature of hardwood trees. Nate lay awake for a long time after the stars came out. He gazed at the gauzy patterns of light in the dark, finding only a single corner of pattern on the bright horizon ahead that matched any pattern in the sky he had ever seen. Nate floated, face upwards, gazing at the stars until they had twinkled him to sleep. He awoke the next day still wondering about that single row of familiar lights low in the sky.

They set off following the ribbon of land as it stretched on through the ocean, following it in the direction of that row of stars, now lost in the day sky. They traveled close to the beach, letting the air currents push them steadily along. The land did not change, and the ocean was changeless. Only the arc of the sun marked their journey.

The next night another wildtree sheltered them, without answering their questions. The land was tall and broad, a solid wall standing between the waters. Wave-washed streamers of seaweed festooned the beaches. There were more berries of moonlight black to delight Seff.

Nate had to admit these were bigger and juicier. "And our fingers and our faces are even stickier!" He held up his juice-dripping hands.

"And even purplier!" Seff exclaimed.

They both giggled at the word. When they had eaten their

fill, they went down to the beach to wash.

While there, they saw a swarm of the fog creatures rise up out of the ocean and wade in toward the shore. A family of a dozen or more leaped up with delighted calls and trills to one another, playing in the surf and snatching at foam-spiders, catching fish in their teeth. The young were tiny, barely able to keep their jawed heads above the shallow waves.

Nate and Seff both shuddered at first sight. Neither of them could really be as afraid anymore. The memory of the experience would always be awful, but they could also never forget that it had not been fatal. They puffed themselves up into the air, well out of reach. They learned the fog creatures did not float. They crawled along the land like mobile plants or gigantic insects. Nate and Seff were true airborne floaters, with intricate interior hydrogen release-and-absorption systems to maintain buoyancy, and a body designed for controlled drifting. The fog creatures were anchored, somehow, to the ground. They could not catch the two Hupp floating high above them. They did not even look up.

The appendages that gave these creatures such a monstrous appearance to Nate were those ground-reaching limbs. Nate had never seen the like except on insects. Insect legs were tiny, thin, dry things. Plants connected themselves to the earth with roots dug into the ground. The thick, flexible limbs on which these beasts traveled were unique. They reminded Nate more of fish. Seff agreed with him, but he pointed out that fish were also floaters, just in the water, not the air. The fog creatures' unique limbs made them quite at home in the surf, diving and splashing and chasing each other like children at play in the breezes. Nate wondered if they were really insects. There was nothing else insect-like about them, and most insects floated. Animals float and plants have roots. Even fish floated in the water. Nate did not know where to place these creatures in his world view, so he simply watched them leap and play in their mysterious way.

Their pearly gray skin glistened in the ocean spray. Scaly knobs like mushroom caps covered the upper part of their bodies. The salt water changed the color of these knobs from gray to bright red, like a burst of wild flowers blossoming along their backs. They barked, and chirped and trilled in strangely gentle voices, hugging each other with their heavily clawed forearms as they scampered about in the waves. Seen from a safe distance, with fear of them overcome, they were entrancing.

Nate and Seff hovered, watching eagerly. Nate admired their awkward grace as they snatched at foam-spiders and guzzled fish. He watched them on the shore below and stored away the images of their mindless, carefree play. Curiosity about their nature had quite replaced a lifetime of fear. The memory of that fear would never fade, but Nate had learned in childhood to distinguish memory from the reality of the moment and the potential of the future. The emotion of curiosity was clear. He found the sensation most pleasant, distracting him from the hugeness of the ocean and the wild, strange landscape.

Sunset gilded the horizon and the first stars came out in an aquamarine sky. The creatures waded out beyond the waves and disappeared under green waters. Nate and Seff hung there in the sky watching until there was no trace. The sea turned into black glass reflecting the stars overhead. The land was a stripe of deeper black below, and the beach a barely visible line of white.

Worst Contact

The next morning Seff and Nate continued following the endless curve of sand. Seff chattered happily about the paintings he would do of the fog creatures at play in the surf, thrilled by their harsh beauty. Nate understood. The puzzle of where they were in the world had much of Nate's inner thought, but he listened closely to his friend's conversation about pigments and pages and moss-whisker brushes, and what petal-oils would make creature-skin shine and how to make waves look wet. Nate was relieved to hear Seff's happy preoccupation. The two drifted on together, each glad for the other's company.

Nate noticed that the land was narrowing and flattening, as though sinking into the sea at last. The trees thinned until only a single wildtree leaned over the edge of a rocky slope falling down to a stony beach. They stared down in dismay at the seascape, fearing they had reached the end of the world.

Huge, gleaming cliffs stood in an arc along the beach, enclosing a scene more chaotic and confusing than any they had ever witnessed or could have imagined. Dozens of figures swirled and struggled on the sand. Most were fog creatures, bellowing with rage as they surged out of the water to charge a line of silver-skinned creatures who stood side by side in orderly formation to meet them.

This was a new kind of creature, smaller than the fog creatures charging them and shiny as a full moon in the sky. They stood on ground-anchoring limbs just like the fog creatures. Lances of light flickered out from their claws and raked through the charging fog creatures like fingers raking through mud. With that, Seff and Nate realized what was happening below as the nightmarish scene resolved into an awful reality.

These new mystery creatures were killing the fog creatures.

The ugly smell of creature filth was harmless compared to the ugliness of that battle scene. The creatures died in helpless rage, died in heaps, died bleeding across one another with their big jaws snapping feebly at their own blood. They died clawing at the rocks. They died trying to catch the vicious killing-light in their teeth, bravely, stupidly, but they died.

Seff and Nate drifted forward dangerously close, frozen with horror, before they realized they had to get out of sight. These new creatures were *killers!* The two scudded about, breathless with the sudden change of course. They puffed themselves furiously back to the single wildtree on the cliff and the cover of its tangled twigs and tiny leaves. The screams of the dying creatures went on, stung through by the whine of the killing-light as it worked. The screams grew thinner, until a last champion charged and was cut to pieces. A silence fully as dreadful as the screaming fell over them.

Seff and Nate huddled together, trying to remain invisible, not daring to speak. They kept turning to one another, eyes wide. Nate could not bear to look full at the memory-image of the scene, but he had to understand what was happening. The strangeness of the events and the players was too much to look away.

"What kind of creatures *were* they?" Seff whispered finally. "Those shiny little ones who were killing our fog creatures – what were they?"

Nate closed his eyes and began to study the memory picture, comparing the two kinds of creatures and their mysterious, bloody game. "I don't know," he answered at last, very quietly. "Look at them closer, though. Are they really the same?"

Seff fell silent as he put his artist's eye to his view of the scene in memory. "You're right," he said thoughtfully after a long moment. "They are kind of shaped the same, but they don't have tails, and they came out of those big shiny cliffs, not out of the ocean. They're not like *anything* else at all, Nate!" He opened his eyes wide in sudden excitement.

"They're *completely* new!"

Nate had not paid attention to the memory image of the shiny creature briefly glimpsed climbing out of the shiny cliff. He closed his eyes and looked at the memory more closely. The strangely shaped objects piled to the side had looked to him first like towering cliffs fronting the beach. He had dismissed them in his closer scrutiny of the killing. These cliff sides, however, were as unique and out of place as the creatures themselves. They were shaped more like flowers or seedpods, grotesquely huge, looming over the dunes. They had mouths in their sides, big, square mouths.

However good a perfect memory might be, Nate needed to see those peculiar formations more closely and for real. Was it just the angle at which he had glimpsed them, or were those enormous shiny things resting on simple tripods of spindly stalks? Nate had learned to let curiosity replace fear. The lesson was as unforgettable as the stink he had learned with it. Those shiny new creatures were unknown in his world. There were not even legends to explain them. Did these unexplored places hold demons? Nate had never been of a mind to believe in such things, but the scene they had witnessed on that hard beach was *evil.* No matter how much he may have feared the fog creatures in the past, he did not like seeing them die so helplessly.

Seff was of the same mind, for he reached to part the leaves and peer out. "What was all that about? Don't you want to know, Nate?"

Nate did. They floated out of the wildtree's nest, quickly lowering themselves to float down out of sight among the wildmoss stalks to the edge of the beach.

The fight was over and the scene was silent. Corpses lay in heaps along the sand, bleeding violet blood in thick, slow drops. Openings big enough to admit an entire treehome had appeared in the sides of the shiny cliffs. The killing-creatures were dragging the corpses up along the beach and tossing them in through these. Teams of the shiny creatures were lined up along the shore, bending and tossing in orderly fashion to move the dead. Others were wading out into the water to draw in the floating bodies that the restless waves were threatening to carry away. Nate was reminded of watching spiders feeding in their nests and of sticky plants that drew in butterflies, yet he had little in his experience to compare with this monstrous, grotesque feeding.

From this new angle, he could see that those huge, silvery cliffs *were* resting on impossibly slender stalks. There were six such giant pod-shapes, towering upwards and arranged in a semi-circle on the beach. Nate had begun to think of the fog creatures as a natural part of his world, lovely in their own context. There was nothing of his world or lovely about these shining killers. He and Seff watched in silent horror until the last stiffening corpse had been dragged inside. Then the shining killers climbed in and the openings closed behind them.

The strangest thing of all happened then.

The huge, cliff-sized pods drew in their impossibly slender stalks, hovering impossibly over the beach. They floated upward, slowly, impossibly high into the pale evening sky, faster and faster as they rose, disappearing at last with a final, momentary gleam of sunlight in the upper air.

Seff and Nate stared after them in astonishment, awestruck. The evening twilight deepened to glowing aquamarine and the first stars came out. Still the two of them just stared, expecting the giant things to fall, expecting anything, with no idea of *what* to expect, completely baffled by what had happened.

The strange things did not return. The strip of beach lay still under the ceaseless slap of waves. The breeze brought occasional hints of the stinks of death, but the ocean was already washing the beach clean.

A Distant Shore Near Home

They flew on, following the narrow land dividing the vast green ocean. The stars rose up from the horizon and sparkled in the twilight, close to the water. The night sky grew thick with stars. The sea glowed like black glass. Two moons rose and chased each other hastily through the dust of starlight.

After the racing moons had set, lights came out just under the surface of the glassy ocean beneath them, peculiar patterns of phosphorescence writhing in the dark water off shore. The lights were incoherent but visually tantalizing, huge circles and crescents and arrows, whispers of glowing color. Seff and Nate flew all night, watching these strange shapes silently form and change in the dark ocean. They used as a guide the single line of the rock wall that continued on into the night ahead. The wild lines danced on below.

A clear dawn glowed on the strip of rock and glinted in the foam of the surf breaking against it. For a moment the ocean blazed with new light. They flew on, close to this remainder of land, and saw nothing alive but foam-spiders clinging to the wet rocks. They flew the whole day. The land went on in this precarious way between the green waters. Another such night, and the glowing lines moving enigmatically in the dark water became the dream orchestration of their weariness.

Another brilliantly glowing dawn greeted their sleepy eyes with the welcome sight of broad highlands on the horizon, with a beach and a marsh on either side of a tall ridge topped with trees. They picked up speed, soaring onward.

When they reached it, they saw that the salt marsh below

was netted by the fallen seed pods of fluffball plants, coated with a gauzy drape as though gift-wrapped. This was a sign that the land was wild. No villager would let so much fluff go un-harvested. It was just too useful, and this looked like good, strong fiber. The wildtrees on the ridge were semi-domesticated. They were greeted by stuttering, astonished murmurs of delight from the trees. The trees told them in their slow way that no one had ever before been blown to them from the sea. They had not had visitors from inland in much too long.

One tall treehome welcomed them in. She had furberries and chew seeds stashed away for visitors. The tree offered these with lazy pleasure, already lulling herself into the contented peace of a treehome with guests. Seff and Nate were glad to accept, and felt much of their spent strength flow back from the meal. The treehome was happy to fold them up in her fingers and let them join her in a sun-warmed afternoon nap that gently slid away into a night's deep slumber, recovering from their long, sleepless voyage.

Before they left the next morning, they asked the treehome how long it had been since anyone had visited her. The guest chamber at her top was quite small, which made her voice seem a bit insectlike, and thin. "Moss End has been just plants for more seasons than this one can count," the treehome muttered after long cogitation. That explained why the chamber had grown such thick walls, and was shrunken inside. A treehome craves the warmth of life-forms in that chamber. Without them she must insulate her heart with her own shell. "Most kind of little ones to stay here and be one with treehome."

"What happened to the ones who used to come here?" Seff asked, slightly alarmed.

The treehome gave no answer, since she did not know. They thanked her, promising to visit again, and set off.

The world below them as they flew looked less strange and fragile. Although of the same pattern of a continuous narrow land between two oceans, it began spreading wider and raising its central ridge up to a loftier reach of land, more like that on which they had been born. Stretches of meadows with wildflowers waving at them appeared between groves of trees and bush, varieties they recognized and could name. They began to feel the rush of hope that their little village grove might be nearby. Day after day they flew without recognizing any landmarks, sleeping in wild groves and trying to unravel the dialect of plants that had not spoken with animals in many seasons.

"They go. They go." A grove of wildtrees mourned inexplicably, unwilling to explain. They closed up the speaking lips over their hearts. There was no treehome to tell them more, so Seff and Nate traveled on.

On a chill, cloudy afternoon, they found who it was the wildtrees mourned. A high arch of land, almost a hill on the ridge, looked from the distance to be a village grove, with large treehomes standing in neatly staggered rows along the crest. They flew to it eagerly, calling as they got close. A pall of silence was all that they heard or saw as they arrived.

They clung together, suddenly afraid, as they halted in the center of the line of towering trunks, turning slowly to look at the disarray of branches and twigs. The ground was brown, dry and blasted, with only the moldy remains of gardens melting down into wildmoss. The treehomes were dead, every one of them. They had been dead for a long time, with whitened twigs and cracking bark crumbling around their knees. The speaking lips over their guest chambers were withered and drawn back in grimaces, with emptiness dark in their gaping mouths. There was a sense of terror here as great as the creature killing, yet nothing moved or threatened. The silence itself was an assault.

"They go," Seff murmured, echoing the wildtrees' sad voice. "But *where* did they go?"

"*Why* they left bothers me more," Nate said. He was peering intently at details around, trying to make some sense of what evidence was left. "This is a nice place for a village, a very nice place. Why would it be abandoned?"

"Because the treehomes had died," Seff whispered, shuddering visibly at such a terrible possibility.

The two clung together, staring around in cold horror, trying to grasp it.

They both missed their own treehomes with a fierce and pained intensity, fearful that their beloved partners would suffer such a fate. The treehomes had sheltered them and their parents and their parents before them since the beginning. No one in the village had ever known a treehome to die. Their apparent immortality was accepted without thought or question. It simply was. Animals died. Plants withered away in their cycles, but treehomes simply added another layer of growth now and then, topped off a layer of twigs when bored with them, budded branches when so inclined, and flowered with sudden, wild abandon. Their placid personalities and dull sentience went on unaltered.

"Don't touch anything," Nate whispered suddenly. "We must get away! Quickly!"

Seff did not argue, and they soared away. They could study their memories of the place for clues. Being among these horrible corpses of trees felt much too dangerous.

They hurried on, fearful now, rushing over the land with their ears scooping the breeze in frightened gulps, racing over meadows and wildtree groves and beaches. The setting sun threw shadows across a landscape they did not know.

New Faces, Old Fears

For several more days the land went on like this, broad, safe between the wide ocean, with salt marsh flowers and sweet blooming reeds. They flew over the central ridge, afraid now that they would find more killing-creatures on the beaches. They talked endlessly about the many clues they had seen about the death of the treehomes, but neither could agree with the other about signs that the creatures had killed the trees with their burning light. The trunks were unusually blackened – from death or from the heat of the light? The images they remembered did not really make that clear. Neither had ever thought about what a treehome would look like in death. It had been an unthinkable thought until confronted with the reality.

The next sight of treehomes cresting the ridge filled them with dread, and they floated up toward the grove with pounding hearts. Ahead of them were nearly thirty treehomes rising up grandly from a surrounding grove of blooming wildtrees. Neat gardens were planted in every clear space. Wildmoss softened the ground among the shaded tree roots. The treehomes were alive, and flourishing. Here and there they could see people tending plants.

Seff and Nate flew in among them with glad hearts, calling hello.

They were met with cold suspicion and silence. All but one of the villagers who had been out gardening whisked away into their treehomes. The one who remained hovered in the sunlight between the trees, his arms out and folded in front of his mouth in a gesture of challenge. There was a cold light in his eyes. He would not give his name when they greeted him and introduced themselves.

"No one has come from that direction of the land in years," he said carefully. "What village is your home?"

"We call it Stand Alone," Nate said. "It is a long way from here still, I believe." He pointed to the far horizon. "We did not come from the village there at Moss End," he added, pointing back in the direction from which they had come. "We saw what had become of it, though, when we went by. It's terrible."

The villager agreed. "We don't want to let that happen here."

Seff and Nate both exclaimed in horror. "We are not responsible!" Nate said. "We saw what happened there, but we did not do it!"

The villager relaxed his stern face a bit, looking them over more carefully. "You do have the colors of Stand Alone, and your names sound right for that village. Why do you sail in here from the other end of the world?"

"We were swallowed by fog creatures and they dumped us out somewhere in the world where we had never been. We are trying to find our way home. I am glad you know of Stand Alone. Perhaps we are no longer quite so lost. What is this place?"

"Swallowed by fog creatures!" he said, disbelief clear in his face. "What nonsense do you tell me?"

"Oh, I assure you that they are quite real, sir. Have you ever seen the strange creatures on your beaches? Yours is a fine, wide beach."

"Yes, I have myself once seen them climbing on the beach – and I saw them being killed with light, and the bodies devoured whole."

This was most alarming news. "When did you see this?"

"Months ago. We keep guards up always now, to warn us if they return."

"You have not sent your guards out far enough along the land," Nate said, addressing the villager most seriously. "My friend and I witnessed a terrible killing of creatures on a beach in a distant part of the world – and only a few days ago!"

This news was taken with calm, stern silence. Nate wondered if he were just trying to hide his own fear. "What proof have you?" the villager asked quietly. "I do not know you, and I do not know how those demons might work. Have you perhaps been sent out before them to choose victims?"

"What a horrible thought!" Seff exclaimed, clutching his little hands in distress. "You don't suppose they can really do that! I thought they only hunted creatures! Oh, Nate!"

He turned to his friend, eyes wide with alarm. "What if they go after our village! What do they want?"

"They want the fog creatures," the villager said to him. "Moss End was burned only because the creatures climbed up the ridge to the village trying to escape the killers." He looked back and forth at them as though deciding something about them. "We call them Haters here. They hate everything that gets in the way of killing fog creatures."

"How horrible!" Seff gasped.

"I saw them kill," Nate said. "I understand why you cannot trust us. We mean no harm, and you have given us the hope that our home of Stand Alone does indeed lie before us. If you will forgive us for having alarmed you, we will continue on our journey."

Seff looked over at him with admiration at this polite speech.

"Trust or no," the villager said gruffly, "you bring news the rest must hear. If the Haters have returned, it does not matter who brings the message. It is the warning that is important."

Nate agreed.

"My name is Tapper," the villager said to them. "Welcome to the village of High View."

Tapper went around to the various treehomes of the High View council to call them out. One by one they popped out and followed him, a half-dozen somber-faced individuals of browns and dark blues. Nate noticed that these villagers had eyes the same color as their skin, something which he had never seen. It gave them each a most unusual and exotic appearance.

They listened attentively to Nate's accounting and asked no questions until he had finished. The news was taken with so serious an air that Seff and Nate felt their own horror and outrage renewed. They hovered a long while silent in the bright sunlight among the trees, each trying to grasp the enormity of the danger and the unknown nature of these killing beasts, the "Haters."

"The Haters only want the fog creatures, so if they do come here, they will be chasing fog creatures, not you." Nate kept his voice calm. He could see the alarm in the faces around him. "The best thing is just to stay out of their way."

"But what if they come here?"

"They follow sound, so make noise to lead them away from the village," Tapper said. "I've told you that before. Once the Haters have the fog creatures, they leave."

"But you could get swallowed if you get one to chase you!" a young one exclaimed excitedly.

"So, if you do get swallowed, stay calm," Nate went on explaining, ignoring the disapproving looks of some parents in the back row of listeners. "Try to take a deep breath before you go down, and hold your breath as carefully as you can. Pull in tight, like dipping underwater."

Seff slipped away while Nate was talking. The littlest kids, caught up in the story, were shrinking themselves in with the shivery imagination of such an adventure. Their eyes, as mysteriously colored as their parents', were wide with excitement and delicious alarm.

"As soon as you're out," Nate continued, "keep moving until you get free of the pile and can breathe."

"Maybe we should try to push our way out of the creature faster," one eager young boy suggested. His friends giggled. He was, however, quite serious in his suggestion, and he shushed them angrily.

The children began whispering together about the adventure of passing through a creature. These children had seen their village elders afraid, fearful every day, never speaking of it outright yet referring to it indirectly in every decision. These two travelers from the sea were heroes. Seff and Nate had braved the dangers their parents had been in terror of facing.

Nate looked around at the circle of serious faces. "You have to hold your breath until free of the creature's body," Nate resumed his accounting carefully. "That is what you must focus on. It is very dark in there, I can tell you that. I don't know how you would figure out which way to swim.

"And letting its body push you out might be safer," Seff said as he came up the slope toward them. "Safer than using up your inner breath swimming the wrong way inside it by mistake."

He floated up to join the group, his hands full of tiny moss-whisker brushes and leaf-wrapped smears of colored petal-oils. His prehensile tail was wrapped around a roll of dried leaves selected from the wildtrees down slope. He had quickly gathered enough supplies to make just a few hasty sketches of their adventures on that killing beach. He went on speaking as he set these down on the wildmoss under the trees and began to work. "I can tell you I was spun around and squeezed every which way, and there is no way to know where to go. I was too exhausted to fight my way free once I was out – if Nate hadn't dug me out, I would have suffocated there. I was nearly spent of inner breath."

"And here you see it," Seff said with a smile as he held up his first quickly drawn sketch of the killer-creature, the Hater. "That is what we saw." He showed it to the circle around them, turning slowly so that each could see.

Their strangely colored eyes widened. Some gasped, and the children crowded closely to see, reaching out with hesitant fingertips to touch the paint.

"Yes," Tapper said. He sounded sad. "That is what I saw. They killed the creatures on the beach, and then they climbed the hill, chasing them, and they burned the trees at Moss End, spraying their fire around until the flames were everywhere, and no one escaped."

"Except you," another in the crowd called softly. "You survived, Tapper."

"Because I flew away," Tapper answered, his voice and face stern.

Nate and Seff clutched each other in alarm. "This is terrible!" Nate exclaimed.

"We really have to get home," Seff said to Nate. "We have to warn everyone. We have to make them prepare."

"Yes, this is more important than berries and paintings of sea creatures," Nate said. Tapper's story had renewed his sense of fear and dread. What if his beloved treehome should end up like those at Moss End?"

Nate and Seff were eager to continue on. The entire village of High View turned out to say farewell, holding hands and tails together in a long chain, waving as a multi-color streamer floating above the tree tops to watch Nate and Seff as they set off. They were visible for a long while, a bright ribbon waving on the horizon.

Golden Fish and Purple Berries

The band of rocky land beneath them grew wider as they continued on, a solid bulk rising up between the green seas. Wildtrees covered rolling slopes of wildmoss. Nate and Seff floated close to these ridges. Once they had flown along for a time, the winds rose with the sun. They were forced to cling to stems and outspread leaves in order to guide themselves safely down the slope closer to the relatively quiet air at the swamp's edge. They continued their journey at this level, glancing up often to the windy slopes.

They both began to long for sight of another village. There were not many people in the world, but Hupp had never before seemed such an empty place. The land flowed on and on. Wild treehomes grew in various spots, thick-skinned and dull-witted, waiting for villagers to refine them, but they had no words. Nate and Seff were the first to have reached them. Both were homesick now for their own treehomes, longing for the comforting surrounding that was a part of their deepest selves, and now dreadfully afraid for them in their hearts. Neither spoke of it, but Nate could see that Seff was as worried as he. They spent less time sightseeing as they traveled, despite the newness of the landscape. They had seen wonderful things on this journey, yet they were eager for its end.

The beaches were wide here, rimmed with tangles of bleached driftwood like toy villages. Foam-spiders blinked at them from the fingers of twigs and root. Tiny golden fish swam in the narrow tide pools between beach and marsh. These fish tagged along in swarming schools beneath Seff and Nate as they floated over. They kissed the surface of the water from below with their little fish mouths as though whispering to them in their flight. It made them both lonelier than ever for home and friends. They clung to each other as they flew, silent in their determination to move the world beneath them.

Berry bushes grew close to the driftwood tangles, the same black berries that had revived them when they awoke from being swallowed. They paused for a time here, cheered by the berry bushes' silent offering and enjoying the sweet newness of the dark berries' purple flavor.

"I wish we could grow these at home," Seff said. "They're so good, and I could get a wonderful color from them to paint with."

"Massay would know how to get them to move to our village," Nate said thoughtfully. "I know he would enjoy the challenge. We must tell him about these, and ask him to try."

They laughed together at the idea. "What fun old Massay would have at that!" Seff exclaimed. His face and hands were stained dark purple by the berry juice, and his eyes were shining. Nate began laughing helplessly, struck by the enormity of their journey and discoveries, all the wide world explored – with only juice-stained hands as the proof!

They decided to stay the night here, sleeping in the nest of driftwood, their village for the night, so that they could fill up again on the berries before continuing. The sunlight did give them some nutrition, energizing an inner layer of their stubborn latex hides, a lean kind of meal on the days of dry rock and sand. The landscape was, by and large, generous. These rich, fat, shining berries in luxurious clusters were a feast. There was nothing at home, not even in Massay's generous larder, to match them.

When they washed their faces and hands in the long tide pools, more golden fish came in thick numbers to swim, open mouthed, through the purple-stained waters. Seff and Nate hovered there, giggling, until the slight tide had pulled the little pool and the many fishes back into the sea. Night fell with stunning colors, drawing lights out of the ocean in patterns as unfathomable as the patterns of stars overhead.

They were awakened in the darkest dark of the night by a soundless rush of air that tossed them both about in their driftwood nests. They opened their eyes to a bewildering excitement of lights glowing and dancing around them. The beach was lit with an eerie glow as bright as moonlight. Nate's first confused thought was that the glowing light patterns in the ocean had taken on solid form and swarmed up on the sand.

Once they had calmed down enough to look more carefully at what was happening on the beach, their confusion was replaced by cold alarm. Giant silver pod-shapes as big as towering cliffs had appeared out of the night and now sat crouched on the sand. The beach was shining with the eerie glow that they shed. Nate and Seff recognized them with a cry. "The Haters!"

"They will kill the fog creatures again!" Seff whispered, anger and despair in his sigh. "I can't bear to watch that."

"If only there were some way to stop them." Nate spoke more to himself than Seff, but his friend was immediately taken with the idea.

"Maybe we can," Seff said.

Nate could hear in Seff's voice that an idea was forming. Nate knew that particular note of thoughtfulness. "They can burn down treehomes, Seff," he said patiently. "They are much more dangerous than the fog creatures."

"But we lived through that," Seff replied reasonably.

Nate had to laugh. He knew Seff so well, and already knew what they were going to do. "You want to know what those giant pods are, don't you?"

Seff smiled at him, his eyes bright in the reflected light. "Don't you?"

Night Lights

The beach around the glowing silver things was still, as though shocked by their presence. The eerie light was quiet but as they slowly drifted closer, a faint buzzing or humming sound like insect song could be heard from inside.

Nate and Seff clung to strands of dry seaweed pushed aside by the tripod feet of one of the giant, gleaming, mysterious things. They clung there for some time, peering up at the lights. The tension and fear was so thick around them that they were both on the verge of giggles and laughter. They kept hushing one another, and sliding under seaweed fronds to hide from their own audacity. They were so close to the enormous, curved shapes that the excitement of its mystery was overwhelming. They thought only of how to get inside.

They calmed down finally when nothing happened, and began to explore the enormous, enigmatic things.

Nate finally dared to touch one, expecting a variety of horrible things. It was as cool as the night air, and completely smooth. It was harder than the hardest wood or stone, and buzzed under his palm like a singing insect. Nate knew of no substance like it.

Seff was entranced. "I wonder how it takes paint," he whispered to Nate, making them both break out into uncontrollable giggles once more.

A huge mouth in the shiny thing abruptly split open, lapping the sands with its shiny tongue. Nate and Seff gasped in astonishment and alarm, puffing themselves into the night, then as one, they dove toward the opening and dashed inside.

They were immediately swept aside by the swoosh of air as a pair of the dreaded Haters came out. Nate and Seff let the air currents puff them high up into a far corner of the thing's mouth, feeling numb with horror and nearly condensed with fear. They grabbed at each other and clung, their giggles gone.

The two Haters, however, did not notice them but went out onto the beach, striding down the tongue to the sand.

The outer mouth snapped shut, trapping Nate and Seff in the inside chamber. They hung in the upper corner, clinging to one another. Another mouth opened in the opposite corner, ejecting two more creatures before snapping shut itself. These two did not notice Nate and Seff. They went on with their own mystifying activities. Nate noticed that these creatures were shaped the same as the dreaded Haters, but they were dark, of mottled colors, soft looking and not at all shiny.

Just as he was beginning to wonder what different kind they might be, a completely different answer to the puzzle was given. They opened places in the wall and drew out limp, shiny skins that dangled like beams of tangled light from their hands. They pulled these shiny outer skins over themselves, converting their dark and unfamiliar appearance into the gleaming perfection of the killers as seen on that terrible beach. Having done this, they made the outer mouth open again and they went outside, walking down the tongue to the sand and striding away on their strange, shiny legs.

Before Nate and Seff could recover from the sight of this transfiguration, the inner mouth closed, then the outer one, leaving them inside. They clung to each other and drifted with the air, trying to understand this utterly different place.

"It's a little like the inside of a treehome," Seff whispered finally. "It's straight and flat and shiny, but doesn't it feel like a room?"

Nate had to stretch some to change his impression of being inside an insect mouth. Seff's idea, once stated, gained greater meaning as Nate thought about it. After some looking and thinking, he said in response. "A room, but more like the inside of a solid bubble."

"Yes, a solid bubble," Seff said, that light in his eyes as thoughts of paintings took over his focus.

Nate went back to studying this new place. It smelled odd, as though the air were thin, and crisp with salted sea-winds. The flat, shiny walls smelled as nothing he had ever smelled. They waited to see what was next.

The two Haters returned, with the pale dawn light following them inside. The mouth closed behind them. They peeled away their shiny skins at once, as though eager to be free of them. These were stashed away again like crumpled leaves. The inner mouth opened again to let them inside. Nate and Seff slipped through at the very top, silent, terrified they would be noticed. The two Haters were making noises to each other and did not look up.

Their sense of terror did not last as long this time, overrun by curiosity.

Nate and Seff remained in the air high above everything, silent, further overwhelmed by the complexities around them. This strange place was of flat, shiny surfaces and curved tunnels branching off on either side, stocked with unimaginable objects set about in incomprehensible positions. The light was the same cool glow.

They drifted along behind and above the two dark Haters as they walked on. The elation of adventure faded into the complete astonishment of this other place, this alien inside, this collection of rooms like no room or hive or inside they had ever known or imagined. The thrill of its different reality was overwhelming, burning away fear finally, leaving only a hunger for understanding. The Haters made noise with their legs as they walked, a rhythmic clicking. It was a soothing sound, like the gentle buzz of this shiny place, and added to their curiosity. They drifted after.

Another mouth opened, and the two Haters went into it. Treehomes had only the one mouth. Chambers inside were separated by arched breaks in the wooden membranes. The image of mouths inside mouths inside mouths took a moment of adjustment, but they were both recovered enough to whisk inside.

There were more Haters in this room, each dark and unshiny. They made noises to each other, meaningless chatter mixed with raucous hoots that might have been laughter. Nothing they did made the slightest sense to Nate and Seff, who watched in complete fascination, trusting to their perfect memories for later review, thrilling now in the wonderful newness.

There was nothing in Nate's experience of his world to compare to this. Even the strange fog creatures playing in the surf on their outrageous legs were familiar compared to the sleek, straight, flat, shiny *otherness* of this place. Tiny colored lights glittered on dark surfaces, flickering in meaningless dance like the patterns out on the dark ocean.

It was delightful. Nate and Seff studied every surface, every gleam and flash and blip. They were both quite enchanted. They focused on the place and not the Haters, until suddenly they noticed that the creatures had fallen silent. The faces were turned up, looking directly at them. Nate could see clearly how ugly their faces were, with tiny, pale features.

"You let a bug in here, gentlemen." This noise from the Hater was terrifying, and quite dashed Nate and Seff's amusement. The Haters' voices were loud and harsh, the vibrations so strong as to be almost tangible in the air. Nate and Seff hung in place, limp with dismay.

"Ship command – lights up on the bridge." The shadows in the high corners that had shielded them melted away in a glare of white light.

"Those aren't bugs."

"Those aren't bugs," Nate echoed back, driven by sudden panic. He thought they were roaring at him, and he thought he was roaring back at them, an act of frightened defiance.

This got a reaction. "A talking bug!"

"A talking bug!" Seff echoed, suppressing a giggle, his eyes alight.

There was a long silence below as this was considered. "Hello there, little fellow."

Nate and Seff answered this back in chorus. That raucous sound like laughter went around the group. When that had fallen to silence, Nate tried roaring again. "Those aren't bugs."

"Wow. There is so much money in this."

"Shut up. No more talk. Everyone out."

"Wow. There is so much money in this." Seff took a turn.

Nate and Seff watched in amazement as the group filed out. With the Haters watching them in the bright light, they did not dare follow after. The mouth shut behind them, leaving Nate and Seff floating alone.

"What was that all about?" Seff said. "Did we frighten them away with those noises?"

"I'm just glad they didn't kill us they way they killed the fog creatures," Nate replied. "How will we get out of here?"

They began to explore. There was so much to see, so many textures and patterns glowing with self-importance and utterly incomprehensible. Seff was eager to paint it all, as though he could explain it to himself somehow by tracing it through his fingers. There were deep cracks and gaps here and there. They took turns squeezing into these, hoping to find an exit on the other side. There was no exit, but they knew where to hide once the Haters returned. They were left alone for a long time, but slid themselves into hiding as soon as the mouth opened up again.

A bright light was shined in at them, making them squeeze their eyes shut and draw in even more tightly.

Nate and Seff did not echo back the creature's noises this time, not being certain they liked the results. They were not really afraid, not yet. Nate was actually annoyed that he and Seff were interrupted in exploring this fascinating structure. He rather hoped that if they just remained hidden, the Haters would go away. He and Seff would leave then, he assured himself.

The Haters made their mysterious noises again. "We can't get them out of there without hurting them. And the Commander says he wants these things alive."

"He didn't tell us how to keep them alive."

"No, but he made clear what would happen to us if we don't."

Whatever these noises were, they were met by a lengthy silence.

Nate was almost ready to slide forward and peek out of their hiding place, thinking they might have left, when they made noises again. "The lizards come ashore to eat from those berry bushes. Let's start with the possibility that these little guys were here for the same reason. One of you bring in a bowl full of those. We'll leave that in here, and watch on the security monitors to see if they eat them."

Nate waited for a long time, listening to the silence after, before daring to look into the room. The Haters were gone. Seff shoved at him from behind, "Let me out of here! This is like being swallowed!"

They floated free into the center space of the bridge, looking around carefully.

"Look at that," Seff called, directing Nate's attention to a bowl set to one side on a broad shelf. "Those are berries – the good kind!" He pulled Nate along behind him as he floated over to the bowl.

Nate was as much alarmed as surprised. Why would these Haters have collected the fruit? He hoped it was a sign of friendship. He had seen them killing. He knew how dangerous they were.

Seff was already stuffing berries into his mouth, with juice running down from his whiskers. Nate watched him anxiously for a moment. There seemed no reason not to eat a few. They were so delicious, even in this place.

They ate as much as they could as they hovered over the bowl, solemnly licking their fingers and whiskers and drips from their tails. Even the juice was good. The little meal made this place seem less forbidding, almost friendly. When the group of Haters returned, however, both Seff and Nate whisked away out of sight, pressing themselves back behind a hard, cold wedge that had rings of colored light flashing rhythmically across its surface.

The creatures, however, did not try to get to them, or even shine their light at them, seemingly content to go about their mysterious activities. Nate began to wonder what could possibly happen next.

Here There Be Pirates

The giant man with the big voice patiently lifted the protesting men, one in each arm, and held them up in the air. Crushed thus in the giant's casual grip, each dropped his weapon, too stunned to struggle. The big man had moved with serene swiftness, sweeping them aside as if they were pebbles in a wave. Even his partners were alarmed by his impervious charge.

"Burke, will you quit doing that!?" Ray Harris, behind him, exclaimed. "I'm the one you fall down on if they shoot you!"

Rokey's long whiskers were drawn up in a smirk. "Leave him alone, Ray," he said as he padded into the control room. He confronted the men cowering back from the giant Burke. There were six of them, Earthmen, each dressed in tan deck-overalls with a company logo patch and their names embroidered on the sleeves. Each man had the nondescript look of mercenaries, interchangeable, disposable.

"You gents will just have to be patient," Rokey said to them. "The boys get very excited."

Ray retrieved their weapons and examined them. "Toys," he said impatiently and stuffed them into his jacket pockets. He was very stylishly dressed for hijacking pirates, in a sleek, black suit with hat and boots.

"Ask them," Burke the giant said with his big voice.

"Our boss would like to know where you gents are getting your dinosaur parts," Rokey said to the men they held at gunpoint. "You've been peddling a brand new variety of alien animal. It's getting you some dangerous attention, the kind of attention your employers will not like."

"We just haul cargo," the eldest of the group said. He did not meet their eyes. The name on his sleeve was Jarokov.

"I'm sure," Rokey said smoothly. "And we are not interested in your cargo, Jarokov, only in where you got it. Understand?"

Ray was at the instrument panel, hurriedly studying the controls. It was a small ship, designed to slip in and out of ports unnoticed. Ray linked into their board and began asking questions, with clearly increasing irritation.

"Scubb!" he snarled finally, drawing his fist back as though he might hit the board. "It's deadlock erased just like the rest of them," he snapped. "We won't find it here, either."

The pirates chuckled, relaxing a little.

"OK, gents," Rokey said amiably. "We'll just be on our way."

"Fine with us," Jarokov muttered.

"What's that?" Burke asked, pointing to something high up in a corner, just about on a level with his towering height.

The pirates gave nervous starts. "Nothing," one muttered.

Ray reached up and unhooked the object Burke had noticed. "It's a cage," Ray said, holding it up to peer inside.

"Those are personal pets!" Jarokov tried to protest.

"Isn't that cute," Ray said dryly. He was still trying to see past the wickerlike sides.

"Isn't that cute," echoed back from within the cage.

"Talking pets, no less," Rokey said, suddenly interested.

"Hello there, little fellow," the pets in the cage said in unison.

Ray looked at the men with hard, cold eyes. "Your 'pets' just got liberated."

"That's personal property!" Jarokov again.

"If they turn out to be legal property, we'll get back to you." Rokey said with a smile and a wave of his gun. "We'll look you up."

"You'll need their food supply," a younger man, labeled Albertson, said grudgingly, earning fierce stares from his partners.

"Good thought," Rokey said pleasantly. "And where might that be?"

"Shut up!" Jarokov snapped angrily. He took his own

advice when Ray aimed the gun his way.

"It's in the galley freezer, in quickboxes marked 'berries.'" Albertson made a face at his partner as he said this, then added pleadingly, "I like them little guys. I don't want them to starve."

"I might let *you* starve!" Jarokov said.

"Hold them," Rokey said to Ray as he went out to find the ship's galley.

The men left on the bridge stared at each other in silence until Rokey returned. He was carrying a stack of plastic freezer boxes under each arm. "You keep a well-stocked larder, gentlemen," he said to the pirates when he returned. "That will take good care of you while you wait for your employer to come find you." He gestured to Ray. "Ray, if you would be so good?"

Ray changed the setting on his laser and sprayed a line of cutting light across the controls. A curtain of sparks and smoke rose up from the beam. In a flash, the ship was floating dead in space. Burke's glare kept the pirates in place.

The three men, with Ray carrying the little wicker cage, backed out of the smoking bridge and left. The pirates leaped to fire equipment, cursing wildly as they set about trying to save their navigation controls.

Pleased to Meet You

Ray and Rokey stood with Whytock in his jumbled bedroom. He had placed the cage on a side dresser so that it sat in front of the mirror at eye level. Rokey peered in eagerly. The little aliens did not immediately come out when Whytock opened the door on their cage. They were pressed into the dried seaweed that lined the bottom, peering out from behind the fronds. One of them was moaning softly, a frightened, whispery sound. The men could see them only enough to tell that each was about the size of a human head, with long tails. One of them was orange and one was green. The colors were bright, glistening like flower petals.

Whytock was thrilled by their discovery. He paced about in front of the cage as if preparing to give a great speech. He had his ever-present cigar held tightly in his brilliant smile, but out of deference to the little aliens, it was unlit.

"I knew you gentlemen would find wonderful things for me!" he exclaimed happily. "This is totally new!"

"This is totally new," was repeated by one of the aliens.

Ray and Rokey gave each other knowing, guilty glances. They had once before been through an experience with "talking animals." Ray had nearly died. They both carried on their consciences the responsibility for some surprising results. Neither one wanted to be responsible this time.

Burke returned then, carrying a silver tray with two long stemmed, crystal bowls, one with water and one piled high with dark purple berries. He had thawed these carefully and they looked as ripe as though freshly picked. He set the tray beside the cage with a solemn gesture and stepped back, folding his hands behind his back.

They waited silently, watching the little cage.

After a few minutes, Rokey said thoughtfully, "If they were lured *into* that cage by those berries, I wouldn't be surprised if they don't want to trust the bait a second time. Perhaps we should leave, so they can get used to having the freedom of the room."

"Good thinking," Whytock said. He took his silver-headed walking cane from the back of the desk chair, and twisted an ear of the silver animal head slightly. "Personal security – full scan on my quarters," he to the silver animal face. "Maintain fix on moving objects in wicker cage." He twisted it back into place with a click, grinning around at them. "Shall we retire to coffee and dessert while we wait, gentlemen?" he said casually. "I don't know about our little guests, but the sight of those berries has given me an appetite."

They followed him out. Ray noticed that Whytock had shut down the holusion of his sister Wysteria dancing. Burke lingered a moment behind them, staring forlornly at her empty corner of the cluttered room.

Whytock led them to a much larger, more professional looking kitchen unit with less comfortable chairs and with a lot of monitor readout screens. The largest screen hung above a counter and four tall stools. They settled onto the stools and Whytock, again using his fancy walking stick, had the security camera feed from his quarters directed to this monitor.

Burke prepared and served out a variety of exotic pastries and fancy liqueurs. They had gotten as far as big mugs of hot coffee and whipped cream when the view in the monitor screen showed the little aliens at last emerge from their seaweed cover and float out of the cage.

The orange one went to the crystal bowl of berries at once, anchoring itself there by wrapping its long, thin tail around the stem. It was a face with a tiny mouth and big bright yellow eyes. Wide ears at the top of the head were on either side of the raised ridge of a vent, or gill, that ran from the middle of the faces to the back of the body. There were long whiskers on either side of its mouth. Although it seemed to have no other appendages, once it had anchored itself with its tail, tiny little hands popped out from under its chin, hands with six, multi-jointed fingers. It began putting berries one by one into its mouth. Dark juice spilled along its curling whiskers and dripped from its chin.

The green one was identical except for color, and appeared to be shyer than its fellow. It floated, with a gentle bobbing, in the entrance to the cage, looking around at the room. The orange one called to it finally, and they made noises to each other. The green one drifted over and twined its tail as anchor around the stem. Its own little hands popped out from under its chin, and it listlessly ate a few. They made more noises together, thin, wispy sounds that only Rokey could hear clearly.

The orange one untwined its tail and went over to the bowl of water. They exchanged more sounds, and the green one joined it at the rim of the water bowl. They each drank deeply, leaning forward to the water's surface, sipping at it as though kissing the surface. Together they carefully washed the dark berry juice from their hands and faces, showing that the long whiskers on their faces were prehensile, curling and uncurling independently.

Once they were clean, they twined their long tails together and just hovered over the silver tray, making their little whisper noises back and forth and peering around. They floated up to the mirror above the dresser, peering into it and discussing what they saw. The green one turned this way and that as though trying to see its profile reflected. Clearly they recognized themselves in the mirror, a recognition that was considered a reliable sign of sentience. They were also not very impressed with their reflections, as though familiar with their own faces.

Whytock once again linked to the ship's computer with the silver cane piece. "Specialized command, main system – analyze sounds from the life-forms in my quarters."

A smaller, secondary monitor screen below the main one changed to a readout of graphs and 3-D sound patterns flowing in and out of each other. Rokey knew what it represented, but not what the data meant. This screen flashed rapidly through a variety of displays. Then the computer's liquid voice spoke from the air around them. "Seventy-eight percent probability that it is non-ritual communication between sentient individuals. Language forms unknown."

Ray and Rokey were not surprised. They had been through this before. This was simply confirmation of the mirror test.

Whytock sat up with a cheer, startling everyone. "Wonderful! We have guests, gentlemen!" He exclaimed, smiling broadly. "Ambassadors of a new world! Mr. Burke – the champagne!"

Talk to Me

Knowing the aliens were people they could talk to was not the same as knowing how to talk to them. Rokey knew of educational programs for just this kind of situation, but such things were half a galaxy away – and out of reach for him now, anyway. He complained to Whytock that experts were needed for this job.

"You left Wozur because of those experts, Lord Rokhmyr," Whytock countered. He spoke very seriously, more soberly than they had yet heard. "The very officials who should be helping these people are pocketing profits from their world on the black market. That's why I am out here doing this myself. I can't begin to guess who can be trusted."

"You trusted us," Ray said.

Whytock nodded. "Yes, I trust you."

Rokey sighed, rubbing his palms together slowly. "I'll see what I can work out."

While Ray scanned the intricate structures of the ether for the intradimensional crack through which the pirates had come, Rokey scanned his personal database on board the *Shadow* for the bits and pieces needed to put together a universal dictionary. SpeakEZ, the interstellar language, had evolved from the need to communicate across a wide variety of cultural styles and prejudices, and most of the basics were there. He just had to assemble a presentation that he could work with while attempting to communicate with their new guests.

The little aliens continued to explore Whytock's room. Whytock sat for hours at the kitchen counter, watching them through his security cameras. His cigar smoldered forgotten in his fingers, and he smiled dreamily. Burke came in regularly to check on him, but Whytock was as enthralled as a child with a new game.

The two aliens stayed close together as they drifted around the room, sometimes twining tails as they floated about. They opened everything they could open, talking to one another excitedly about each thing they found. They explored Whytock's wardrobe as if the garments were caves, eventually turning his silk shirts into a playground. Whytock was reduced to helpless hilarity, rolling about in laughter as he watched the two discovering that they could slide through the silken sleeve like a tunnel. They would wiggle down into the collar as it hung in the closet, and bundle up tight to slide down the tube of the sleeve, zipping out of the cuff with a swirl of tail and hands. Even without a translator, it was clear the noises they made were giggles and laughter. Whytock was delighted. Burke stood by and watched, too, although not as hilariously as his boss, a smile cracking his granite face.

"Well, if they have to have a sponsor to be safe in civilization, they couldn't get one better than him," Rokey mused to his partner.

"I wouldn't mind having him as a sponsor myself," Ray added. "By the way, when you were negotiating us into this, did you happen to get our fee settled?"

Rokey gave him an embarrassed grin, feeling a twinge of guilt as he spoke. "Actually, I was more concerned with getting out of Club Sargasso at the time. Pirates make me nervous, especially ones who enjoy piracy so much."

Ray had to laugh, yet his eyes looked coldly at Rokey. "Leaving with Whytock is not exactly like disappearing, old man. If I recognized the *Reach*, you can be certain that others at the Sargasso did. The *Tamaroan* and Lord Jak are not so easily evaded."

"Nor will Johann van Zandt forget us so quickly," Rokey said with a sigh.

The two men sat quietly contemplating the potential disasters awaiting them.

"One problem at a time," Rokey said finally. "First, I learn how to talk to balloons."

"You'll manage," Ray said as he stood up to leave Rokey to his work. "I've seen you talking to rocks."

"I get results with rocks," Rokey replied. "I'm not so sure about balloons."

Rokey's most difficult internal debate had been whether to stand or sit when first addressing them. He was, after all, a comparative giant to them. He had, himself, had dealings with alien beings as much bigger than he as he was to these two. He knew what effect that could have on even an educated mind.

Ray came up with the solution in his usual, blunt approach. "So float," he suggested simply. "They float. Maybe they expect other people to float."

So Rokey entered Whytock's room riding on an antigravity platform that had little attitude-control air jets. It was just large enough for him to sit on cross-legged. It made him a bit dizzy at first, and he had to practice with the platform's minimal control system. He was rather pleased with himself by the time he was actually underway.

Rokey left the door standing open when he floated in to Whytock's room to meet the aliens face to face. Whytock had assured him that the ship's security system would be able to track the aliens anywhere in the ship. Losing them was not a concern. Rokey felt it was important to demonstrate that to the aliens that they were guests here, not prisoners.

Their first response was to dash across the room to Whytock's closet and to hide in his silk shirts. Rokey could imagine Whytock's laughter, watching in the monitor. Rokey did not pursue them. He simply remained floating in the center of the room. After five minutes or so, he could see them peeking out at him from a shirt cuff. Their gold-yellow eyes were wide, as much curious as afraid.

Rokey was encouraged. "Hello," he said softly.

They emerged a little more from the cuff. Their prehensile whiskers were straight out in front as though testing the air. Rokey had the computer play back a section of their own voices in their own wispy language, then he waited. They drifted up closer to him, their tails entwined and their hands tucked inside under their chins.

Rokey began the first lesson. He floated slowly to the silver tray and anchored the floater to the wooden dresser. He faced the two, and taught them the first word always taught in first contact, the one thing that was universal to life. He dipped his finger in the water in the crystal bowl, looked directly at the aliens and said clearly, "Water." He picked up the bowl, spilled a few drops on the dresser and touched them. "Water." Then he drank a sip, still meeting their eyes. "Water." He set the bowl down and waited.

The two hovered, watching him. "Water," each one repeated. Their little voices were thin but clear. Rokey felt an old, forgotten thrill returning. He had been a teacher for a long time and exile had forced him to put away the pleasure of it. He smiled to himself happily and settled into his task.

He touched the water again. "Water." He touched his own chest, raising his hand to brush his fingers across his forehead. "Rokey," he said. He spilled a few drops again and, pointing first to himself and then the spilled drops, said slowly, leaving clear gaps between words, "Rokey spills water."

"Rokey spills water." They repeated this together, and began drifting toward him.

Rokey sipped, looked at them over the crystal rim, and said, "Rokey drinks water."

"Rokey drinks water." They seemed eager now, and floated up beside him, hesitation showing only in the way their long, rubbery tails were wrapped about each other.

Rokey put the bowl down. They swooped over to it. "Water," they said in unison, touching the surface with their tails. Then they gave their own word for water, a single fluid syllable that reminded Rokey of something ancient and wet. The green one then popped its hands out, and touched Rokey's finger, peering up at him. "Rokey." Then it patted its own head. "Nate." It pointed to its orange colored companion and said, "Seff."

"Nate. Seff," Rokey said happily. The aliens responded with happy giggles. The game was on in earnest. Hours later, with the computer filling in gaps and helping Rokey to keep his place, they had a basic vocabulary down. They were able, at last, to start a conversation.

Nate and Seff carried their side of the conversation in SpeakEZ. They picked up on the vocabulary and concepts with astonishing swiftness, never having to hear anything twice to remember it. Only the computer could keep up with and repeat their wispy, fluid words. Rokey knew the computer was learning their language faster than he was. He kept an active vocoder file running so eventually these two could have electronic translators made. Nate and Seff became fluent in SpeakEZ so quickly, however, that the vocoder was needed only for archive. Having a stash of words, however, was not yet enough to know what questions to ask the aliens. "Where do you come from?" got only a classic, proto-world response, "The grove of Stand Alone."

Rokey reflected rather sadly that this name fairly aptly described the aliens' situation.

"What is the name of your world?" he asked them.

Rokey had to explain that one a little more before they understood that he meant their name for the ocean, land and sky that contained them.

"Hupp," Nate answered after he and Seff had conferred for a moment in their own language. "I think that is the name you are looking for." He hesitated on this. "It means Place Of The People, but we are the Hupp, too. I do not yet have words in your SpeakEZ to explain why it is both, but it is."

"Hupp," Rokey repeated carefully. "That will do very well. Meaning both at the same is perfectly understandable in SpeakEZ. You'll find it happens a lot. My world is called Wozur, which makes me a Wozurn. The rest of the people you will meet on this ship are Earthmen, from a world called Earth. It helps keep us sorted."

Then he had to explain "sorted," but they quickly grasped "this from that." Nate and Seff whispered together for a few minutes, and Nate said in SpeakEZ to Rokey, "How can you be so different from us? We have never seen people like you, or like the ones who took us. What is a world? And what is a starship? Where are we? Will we get to go home?"

Rokey reminded himself that there was a long road between words and understanding. He sighed gently, wondering where to begin.

"A world is where you live, the place that contains your home. The stars you see in the sky at night," he began, then stopped. "Do you know what a star is?"

Both gave the ear-flick that Rokey had come to recognize meant, "No."

"The lights up in the sky at night?" He pointed upward in automatic gesture, even though they were under a ceiling, not a sky.

"Oh, yes," Nate said. "What about them?"

"Each speck of light is a sun like the one in your sky during the daytime, the one that lights your world."

They both seemed astonished by this and exchanged wide-eyed looks.

"What did *you* think they were?" Rokey asked.

"Lights in the sky," Seff replied simply.

"They are very, very far away," Rokey went on. "That's why they look so small."

"That must be *very* far," Nate said. He seemed impressed.

"Many of those stars have worlds, just like your sun has your world. I am different from you because I come from one of those worlds so far away from Hupp that you couldn't possibly see it."

"Do you touch the ground?" Nate asked. "The ones who took us were anchored."

Rokey decided to reply by demonstration. His knees were getting cramped on this antigravity seat anyway. He unbent his legs slowly, powered down the floater, and stood up. He was afraid they would be alarmed, but they were only curious about his bare toes.

"No shirt?" they asked, pointing. They had learned the word for Whytock's silk-shirt playground, but Rokey had forgotten to mention pants or shoes. Rokey wore neither and usually only thought about them when Ray complained about needing new ones for himself.

"No shirt," Rokey echoed. "I have fur that stays on me."

"What do you call," – Nate floated down to touch Rokey's knee. "These things you touch the ground with? What are they?"

Rokey could see why they could be curious. He had no tail, either. "Legs," he said, and gave a demonstration of how they worked, carefully naming each part and the kinds of movement legs made.

Nate and Seff were fascinated, talking to each other in the

own language and finally breaking into giggles. They liked his ears. They stationed themselves atop his head and each took an ear, exploring the folds and whorls of fur with their tiny, tiny fingers.

It tickled, but Rokey stifled the impulse to flick them away. "Hold onto my ears," Rokey said to them. "I'll take you to meet my friends. They don't have fur, but you mustn't draw attention to that. They can't help it."

Once introductions and initial nervousness had been worked through Whytock explained, "We want to stop the men who put you in a cage from taking anymore of you or other animals from your world."

Nate and Seff responded to this with considerable excitement. "Yes!" Nate said clearly.

He and Seff began to chatter together rapidly in their own language.

Nate was the one who finally broke free and floated up closer to Whytock's face. "We were swallowed by a sea creature, but it did not hurt us. It carried us to a far place in our world, and left us there. I have also seen them," he searched for words in his newly learned vocabulary of SpeakEZ. "Falling in a way that was most difficult to see. We were taken by those men when we tried to find a way to stop them. It is good to learn that we have found you to help."

Ray pointed out that first he had to find the way back to their world.

"I do not know the way," Nate replied. "I do not even know how to tell you where it is."

"We have to find a way to ask you how you got here that will show us the way back," Rokey said. "This could take a while."

"The pirates never have any destination codes programmed in their navicomps, not even erasure traces," Ray said. "They have to program the navicomp somehow. It has to be done as you hit speed for the jump or you'll miss it. They have to have the numbers somewhere."

Nate asked what "navicomp" and what "numbers" were.

That took quite some time. Ray wandered off to study the engineering data-crystals he had stolen from each of the many pirate vessels they had stopped, boarded and examined in search of the source of the not-dinosaurs. Little Nate and Seff were all he and Rokey had gotten out of their hunt so far.

Rokey interrupted Ray's morose mood a few hours later with an hail on the intercom. "We got it, Ray!"

"Got what?"

"Get back here, Ray. Seff and Nate heard the numbers being called in by voice code – they can recite the entire string!"

"Well, isn't that cute," Ray said to himself as he got out of his bed, scattering data crystals. "All we had to do was ask them. Who would have guessed that?"

Trusting to the Numbers

"How can you remember a string of numbers four-hundred and thirty-two figures long if you didn't even know what a number was?" Ray tried to keep suspicion out of his voice.

"I heard them," Nate answered simply. "Rokey asked me if I had seen anything on their bridge that looked like numbers. I had not, but I heard the sounds of number names."

"You can remember that many sounds in order? Even though you didn't know what they meant?"

"I know now."

"It's worth a shot, Ray," Rokey said. "It's the closest thing we've got to a lead."

Rokey had not yet figured out Nate and Seff's particular native talent. He was getting a glimmer of an idea about it. Their language skills were even more remarkable than memorizing a string of numbers. Together, they suggested a unusual capacity. He wondered how to test it.

"Well, let's go up the bridge and put some numbers in," Ray said grimly. "But if even one's wrong, we'll end up in the East River somewhere this side of Nowhere."

Rokey and Whytock followed after, with Nate and Seff nestled between Rokey's ears. They seemed to like it there. Rokey was getting used to it. Mr. Burke stayed in the galley to make lunch.

Once Ray had the recorders going and the navicomp on, he told Nate to start with whatever the pirates had been saying just before the numbers began.

Nate began without hesitation, even getting the two pirates' vocal tones and inflection. "Are you two half-wits ready to go now? You were scheduled to jump an hour ago. I had to take care of those little animal things, sir. We had to get a food supply for them. All right, but they better be as good a catch as you claim. Talking animals, and cute? I think so, sir. You ready for coords to get out of there? Yes, sir. Online, sir."

Nate then patiently recited the four hundred and thirty-two numbers he had heard the pirates speak into their controls before leaving his world.

They were impressed by Nate's careful recitation. He even managed the monotonous tone of the computer voice reading out the numbers. Awkward as such a download might seem, Ray understood the encryption process of putting in coordinates by hand. He had recently used the system himself for the jump to the world where the *Tamaroan's* children were hidden. Jak had written the coordinates on a piece of flammable paper, and they had burned it once they were through the window. Electronic recording leaves traces, no matter how thoroughly scrubbed away they might seem. Living brains, however, erode information in a completely reliable way. Erasure leaves no mark. If the ships that were carrying the contraband dinosaur products exited the system with no electronic recording of the window coordinates, there would be no possible way to trace the route.

Ray took another day, but only because he could not make himself believe that the numbers Nate had given him were accurate. Even he had to admit, finally, that once he had done the math and the scan of space, there was the window.

"That window is not listed on any chart anywhere." He complained to Rokey. "This zip-system is a well kept secret, but even so, the other windows in this space have been listed for a long time, some of them for centuries. No one ever found *this* window before."

"No one ever *reported* finding this window."

"If it's a real window," Ray muttered.

"Ray!" Rokey exclaimed. "You're the one who did the math and the scan. You just said the window is there!"

"Yeah, I know." Ray did not sound happy. He was, in fact, seriously displeased. "But there shouldn't be an intraspace window there just because someone recited a string of numbers, Rokey. I found the window myself, but I just don't believe it."

Rokey decided to share with Ray his theory about Nate and Seff. Over the course of waiting for Ray to complete his calculations, Rokey had been discreetly testing the two little Hupps. "I think their mental talents are more than just good native intelligence," he said. "I think they have a unique capacity for memory. I've been noticing things. I am beginning to believe you can really trust those numbers. You found the window."

"I found the window," Ray agreed sourly. "Did you ask them about the memory thing?"

"Well, no. It didn't seem discreet."

Ray made a face, half smile, half grimace, and stood up from his instrument panel. "Well, Professor, I ain't the gentleman you are. I'm going to ask, because I don't want to jump through a window that might not be there."

"You've done it before and lived," Rokey said with grin.

Nate and Seff were in the garden talking with Whytock as he strolled about. They were asking the names of the many plants and sculptures. Whytock, clearly, was delighted by the exercise. He had an anecdote for every object, and Nate and Seff listened intently.

"I'm just about ready to secure the jump," Ray interrupted, speaking to Nate. "Are you quite certain that you didn't remember wrong or forget even *one* of those numbers? It could mean our lives."

"What is 'forget'?" Nate asked politely.

"It's the opposite of 'remember,'" Ray snapped. Ray did not have Rokey's patience.

Nate paused thoughtfully, hovering a few inches from Ray's face. His golden eyes almost closed as he searched in his mind and heart for a way to put his own understanding into the as-of-yet limited SpeakEZ vocabulary he had.

"In my experience, Captain," he said at last, "the opposite of 'remember' is the active moment now, things happening directly, before they have become memory. We have words for this ourselves, but I cannot find any match for it in your SpeakEZ, not yet."

"You don't have a word for not being able to remember

something, or losing a memory?"

"I do not know *how* to not-remember, Captain." Nate said. "Such a thing is not possible. Do you experience this 'forget?' Is it possible for you *not* to remember? Is this a skill you could teach us? I know it would be considered a boon by many."

"I know a certain smell I would like to have no memory of," Seff said with a giggle. "But what a silly idea! To lose a memory. How would you do such a thing? Where would you put it? Where would it go?"

Ray and Rokey looked at each other in surprise. Ray grinned. "I guess I'll trust that I'm seeing the window out there that I'm seeing."

He shook his head slowly as he walked away. "Buckle up, gents," he called over his shoulder. "It's time to go hunt dinosaurs hunters at home."

The Painting and the Lady

Once they were safely on their way in the intraspace window to the Hupp system, Ray brought up yet another sticky point about navigation and finding places. "Given the bit of luck that your planet is the only water world we find when we come out of this window, we still have to find one, small village on an entire planet. Any suggestions?"

Ray brought up this point at the end of a particularly sumptuous dinner. Rokey realized that his captain had brooded over this during the entire meal. An uncomfortable silence fell. Mr. Burke rose quietly and began clearing emptied plates.

Whytock was the first to respond. "I'm sure you'll think of something," he said with a casual shrug. "You're very clever that way."

Ray nodded. "That's why you hired me. But I'll need something to go on when we reach the planet, even a postcard would be helpful. Planets are big, big places," he said dryly, "with lots and lots of little places scattered all over them."

"I'm sure these two can give you considerable detail," Rokey said.

"We think about it all the time," Nate said with a sigh. "We would be happy to describe it in all the detail you need!" He and Seff began whispering to each other in their own language.

"You never know what details will help," Ray said.

"Let's move this to the library," Whytock suggested as he rose from the table. "I have a good holusion recorder there. We can start assembling a picture from their descriptions."

He took them to a spacious library off the same corridor as his own room. There was an oak paneled fireplace in one wall and antique books on shelves up to the ceiling. Big, comfortable chairs and couches were scattered about on richly made carpets. Rokey chose a chair upholstered in bright geometric patterns and went over to settle in. Ray followed after, sprawling across a couch beside him.

There was a life-size portrait of Wysteria above the fireplace. Seff noticed this at once and puffed over to it with an eager cry.

"It's so big!" Seff exclaimed as he hovered in front of it. "It's so big! It would take a lifetime to do something so big!"

Whytock strolled over to stand beside him, arms folded as he regarded the portrait of his sister. "Actually, it only took a few months. The artist was in love with Wysteria because, of course, everyone falls in love with Wysteria at some point or other. He kept the painting going for as long as she could stand to have him around. I think he did catch a decent glimpse of her, cold and utterly beautiful."

The portrait was in white and tones of silver, pale Wysteria in her glass-bead gown, standing in a wintry landscape with ice crystals making a crown in her flowing hair. Despite the imperious coldness of her pose, the artist had managed to catch a flash of warmth in her mouth and eyes that was the same as the brilliant dazzle that Wystan showed in his smile. Rokey thought he rather liked the look.

Seff reached out hesitantly and touched the portrait, caressing the brush stroke texture with his tiny fingers. His eyes widened and he turned to Whytock. "What is this? What do you call this? What is your word for this?"

"That's a painting," Whytock said, smiling at Seff's gush of enthusiasm. "It's a portrait of my sister, Wysteria."

"Painting," Seff repeated to himself, staring up at it in wonder. "You have this, too. I did not know how to ask you if you had painting. I do this." He turned to face Whytock, clasping and unclasping his hands eagerly. "I do this!"

"You paint, like this? You paint at home?"

"Yes!" Seff exclaimed, clapping his hands in delight. "Paint! I can paint, and I am the only one who does!"

"It's true," Nate said. "Seff is the first one to do this in our world. He made it up himself. At least, we never heard of anyone else doing it, and no one in our village had, either."

"They didn't really like it much," Seff said sadly. "Nate was the only one who understood."

"This all got started because Seff wanted to paint the fog creatures," Nate said to Rokey. "Only we didn't know what they were then. We thought they were monsters in the fog. We went looking for them so Seff could paint them, and instead we got swallowed."

"I'd say that you did find some monsters, though," Rokey pointed out.

"But I never got to paint the sea creatures," Seff said sadly. "My paints are at home, with Tree."

"Seff has lots of paintings," Nate said. "He even made a painting of me. I have it in my treehome."

Rokey looked over sharply at the little Hupp floating beside him as the full implications of this began to sink home. Everything the Hupp had said about their world had sounded pre-technological and most primitive. He had worried, because it made protecting them more complicated.

"Is that important?" Nate asked innocently.

Rokey felt a strange tightening in his chest, struck by just how important it was. He saw that Whytock was looking at Nate with the same serious expression.

Ray was the one who spoke. "I'll say it's important, Nate. You can stir up all kinds of excitement in high places if your people have Art."

"Oh, we don't have that," Seff said with disappointment. "All we have are my paintings."

The men laughed, making the two Hupp exchanged confused smiles.

"It's just language," Rokey explained. "Paintings are the same thing. Painting is Art."

"I wish I could paint my village for you," Seff to Ray. "Then it would be easy for you to find it and take us home."

"It sure would help," Ray agreed.

Seff made a painting gesture and asked, "What is your word for the tool to paint?"

"Brush," Whytock replied.

Seff touched the portrait again. "The brush that did this

must have been very big. How could he hold it?"

Whytock held out his own human hand, fingers spread wide, as answer. Even his delicate hand was much larger than the Hupp's.

Seff flicked his ears, turning back to the portrait. "I see. And your legs anchor you so that you can move the brush easily. Painting must be very common in your world."

"I wouldn't say common," Whytock said thoughtfully. He took a cigar from his pocket and then hastily re-pocketed it when it lit up. "But it does exist."

"Have you ever painted?" Seff touched the portrait again as he spoke, his eyes devouring every stroke and color.

"Not since childhood, but I remember it well." He folded his left hand into the small of his back, and with his right made gestures in the air of using an imaginary paintbrush on an imaginary easel. "There may even be a few of my scribblings left in the attic at home."

Seff hovered, still touching the painting.

"Oh! I've had a thought," Whytock said brightly. "Let me show you how my computer's artkit works. You never know, you might just like it!"

"Your computer can do painting?" Seff sounded incredulous.

Whytock shrugged. "No, it just provides the tools so that you can paint anything you want. It isn't as messy as chemical paint."

"I like the mess paint makes," Seff said in a small voice.

"Your computer seems to do quite a lot," Nate spoke up. He had been hovering at Rokey's shoulder, watching Seff's encounter with Wysteria's portrait with silent intensity. This close to him, Rokey could see that Nate's eyes were troubled.

"Computers surprise me all the time with what they can do," Rokey said. He smiled over at Nate. "But they always mind their manners."

Whytock lifted his walking stick and twisted the ear of the silver Anubis head. The ruby eyes lit up. "Library desk, please, with paint program active," he said to it.

The first greenish glow of a holo-suite activating poured out of the fireplace, focusing sharply into a hologram of a desktop console shaped in front of Whytock within easy reach. He leaned over and studied it carefully, arms folded and tapping his chin absently with his fingertips as he mumbled to himself.

"Ah! There it is!" He jabbed at the imaginary console, and a trio of rainbow-colored globes formed above the desk. He put a fingertip to one and it followed his hand as he directed it up toward Seff.

Seff drew back as if afraid. "What is that?"

"That's how you select the color you want to paint with. It's the same thing as your pots of paint."

Seff frowned, his ear tips folding forward. "How is that possible?"

Rokey wondered if perhaps Whytock might be giving the Hupp too big a dose of technology at once. It nagged at his conscience that they were interfering with a young society and a pre-technological one at that. He said nothing, though. What was there to say? Put the paints away?

Seff touched the ball with a fingertip and seemed surprised to feel nothing. "It's not there!"

"It's made of light," Whytock explained. "It's really just a way to tell the computer what color you want. When you've selected, just say 'this.'"

Whytock searched the desktop and then tapped at it. A floating oval of opaque white appeared, about a meter across and flat. Seff was startled and drew back.

"That represents the canvas," Whytock said. "You touch that with your finger or your brush, whichever, and the computer makes a mark on the canvas in the color you choose with that." He touched the color sphere. "This. There. I've just chosen red. Red's a good place to start. Touch the canvas," he said to Seff.

Seff reached out hesitantly and touched the opaque oval. A red dot appeared, bright against the white. "Oh," Seff said softly. He reached out more eagerly and traced a circle round the dot with his fingertip, and giggled as it appeared in the same bright red as he drew it. "And I am not really touching anything, so I don't need an anchor!" Seff was clearly enthralled now. He put both little hands out against the holo-canvas, and solemnly studied his red handprints as they appeared. "Wonderful!"

He leaned close to the color sphere. "I just touch the color I want and say 'this'?"

Whytock indicated a silvery spot at the top of the sphere. "Touch it there, with one finger on either side, and it will follow your hand until you let go. You can position it wherever you need it."

Seff tested this carefully. The sphere of light was nearly as big as his entire body. He maneuvered it up to eye level and studied it closely. "Where to begin?" he whispered. His face was beaming.

"The village?" Ray suggested. "Preferably viewed from above, which is how I will be looking for it?"

"Oh! Of course!"

Whytock showed him how to tell the computer to store the image, and clear the canvas for the next piece. Seff was enchanted. He reached into the color sphere to the greens, selected one and began. He used his fingertips as brushes. After only a few moments the outlines of the patterns of the treehomes in their grove and the land around them were clear. Seff's eager sketching gestures pushed him through the air out of reach of the paint surface, and he dissolved into giggles as he tried to grab at the nonexistent canvas.

"I guess he needs an anchor after all," Nate said, with a look of fondness on his face.

A Good Map

There was no way to know how long the intraspace journey would last, since this was an unknown crack in space. They braced themselves for a long haul. Some cracks were months in duration. This one turned out to be two and a half weeks, long enough for Seff to paint the scenery of their entire journey as well as dozens of paintings of the sea creatures at play in the surf. These were displayed around the library where he worked. The men came in often to watch Seff painting. It never lost its touch of magic.

Mr. Burke provided the next clue in the hunt for the little village grove of Stand Alone. "Atoll," he said out of the blue as he was watching Seff at work.

Rokey pulled himself up to one elbow to look over at Burke. "What do you mean?" he said sleepily.

Burke pointed to the line of images across one wall. "Their land. Sun changes."

Rokey sat up to see more clearly. He had been struck most by the fragility of the landscape, its meager presence rising above the surface of a vast, green ocean. Seff had captured the nobility of his feelings for the land, but the insecurity showed, too. Rokey looked back and forth at the various scenes and the changing position of the sun to the line of land.

"I don't get it," Rokey said finally.

"Land curves." Burke pointed to one in the far corner, an aërial view. He pointed to another aërial view further along in the sequence.

Rokey studied the sun positions indicated. "I think I get it. Seff and Nate are still traveling from left to right, but the sun is on the opposite side now, which means they're actually going in the opposite direction from the first one – but they never doubled back."

"You didn't, did you, Nate?" he asked the Hupp.

"Not that we were aware of."

"You sure that's not just the different times of day?"

"Shadows," Burke countered, pointing to various examples along the row of paintings as he spoke.

"That is my favorite time of day," Seff said in answer. He had been paying close attention as Burke spoke. "That's the time of day I feel best, and I like the way the shadows look at that time in the morning. I almost always paint it that way."

Burke shrugged.

"Unless we missed something, we're looking for a really big atoll, one big enough to disappear over the curve of the planet from one side to the other." Ray agreed with this when Rokey demonstrated for him what Burke had noticed.

"Well, that ought to make it easier to find," he said. "I guess Mr. Burke does know a thing or two about planets."

They came out of the Intraspace window into the Hupp system without any problems. Six gas giants with complex moon systems filled up the outer ring, but second out from the sun, in an orbit that would have fit neatly in between those of Venus and Earth, was a rocky little world that matched the descriptions of Hupp, an Earthlike world with three medium-sized moons chasing each other around their LaGrange points.

Approach took most of a day, time enough for the *Shadow's* long range sensors to watch a half-dozen cargo loaders lifting up from Hupp to rendezvous with a larger ship in orbit.

The invaders of Hupp were there.

Walk Me Home, Sailor?

"Strict radio silence," Ray ordered tersely. The sight of those ships had a sobering effect. This was no longer a happy adventure with newly found friends. This was war. "We can't do anything that will let them know that we're here. They have more people to draw on than we do."

"Than we do just now," Whytock countered. "I can get quite a lot of help in a few months."

"That's why we're here," Rokey said. He was concerned about his captain's apprehension because he knew the kind of intensity that went behind it. If Ray decided he had to fight pirates, he would fight pirates. Rokey just did not want to be there if it happened. He did not want Ray there, either. "Radio silence is doable," he said. "Staying out of sight is not a problem."

Ray turned to look at him with a scowl. "The *Reach* glows in the dark. You call that *not a problem?*"

"I can keep her out of sight," Whytock said, with his usual confidence. "You should be able to slip in unseen with your *Shadow,* to take our guests home."

Ray turned his scowl to Whytock. "More magical tricks?"

Whytock smiled.

Ray shrugged and turned back to his dashboard controls.

"If there's any difficulty, both ships will take the window out of here," Rokey said. "And we meet back at Snugglers Notch."

"Sounds like a plan," Whytock said.

"May I make one request?" Nate said quietly. He and Seff were floating in the upper corners of the bridge, watching with wide eyes and flared whiskers.

"Sure," Ray said. "After all, this is your guided tour."

"Thank you, Captain Harris. Once we have found our village, I do not want to frighten my friends. I think the sight of this ship would be terrifying to them. Would it be possible to land out of sight, and let us go on alone? Once we have had a chance to explain everything to them, and warn them of the danger, then you could come along, and they could meet you?"

Whytock spoke up. "An admirable idea, Nate. We should have thought of that ourselves."

"Seff's paintings show a good-sized beach not far from your village," Ray said. "I think the *Shadow* can land there more easily than on a wooded ridge, anyway."

"Thank you. That would be very good."

"I'm looking forward to meeting all your friends," Whytock said. "But the *Reach* and I are going to stay out of sight and watch. That is, of course, until we have been to the University Index and gotten you officially registered and recognized." He beamed around as though he had already accomplished this. "After that, I intend to come down and meet everyone!"

"Shouldn't one of us go along with you," Rokey asked Nate. "Just in case you encounter the pirates?"

"We need to collect Seff's paintings," Whytock said. "Not only do we need to protect them from these invaders, but the paintings will have considerable influence in the registration process. We have to get the right status assigned to your people or the legal complications could cost us this entire enterprise."

"My paintings?" Seff said in surprise. "Why would the Haters want my paintings?"

"To destroy them," Rokey replied promptly. "They are proof that your people are not just talking animals. If the invaders file a counter suit, they can prove they've been in this system longer than we have. They could persuade the Index that they have discovered a world with talking animals, not natives. It could take years going through the courts to reestablish your claim. Meanwhile, they make a fortune, and your people get scattered to the eight corners of the sky.

Talking animals are quite a commodity."

"What is a talking animal?" Seff asked. "It sounds rather dangerous."

The men exchanged sad and guilty looks.

"A creature that has the capacity to mimic sounds and words, even though is not itself sentient," Rokey explained. "People ennjoy them as companions, someone to talk with who doesn't really have a mind of its own but who just listens."

"Someone they can own," Ray added darkly.

"But what is sentient?" Nate asked. "Are *we* sentient?"

Whytock threw his hands up in a gesture of frustration. "What is sentience! Hah! That is still the biggest debate in the galaxy, my friends! Hello, this is me – Is that you in there? Are you a person? Or are you just *there?* Do you recognize your own reflection? Do you, yourself, know who *you* are?"

"I know who I am!" Seff exclaimed.

"Well, then you're sentient," Rokey told him.

"That was easy," Nate said. "Why is it such a problem?"

Neither Hupp seemed to understand the nervous laughter that went around at that.

You Can't Go Home Again

Rokey usually enjoyed being outdoors. He appreciated the wide expanse of sky and ocean and bright sunshine as he climbed, despite the discomfort of the confines of the space-suit. His helmet filters did permit him to feel the lightly scented breeze and even a portion of the world's natural scents. He had to content himself with this simple luxury. Rokey agreed with Ray's arguments for wearing the suit, he just did not like the results. He also did not like Ray's blunt statement: "You shed. You want to leave fur all over their world?" Ray was curt, but rarely outright rude. It was a sign of the man's emotional state. He was worried for Nate and Seff, too.

The twitch and clutch of the suit against his fur was a constant distraction at a time when Rokey needed his attention on his feet. The slope was steep and the moss was slippery. The flexible boots gave him some footing but he was better at climbing barefoot, able to feel and grip with his toes. Rokey moved slowly, making certain of his balance before each step. Nate and Seff floated along beside him, guiding him to rocky places with better footing and whispering to each other in their thin, wispy language. They were excited to be going home at last, but their excitement was clearly subdued. There was something wrong, although neither could say yet what it was.

"We are not far." Nate gestured to the towering wedge of bare rock ahead, a rocky promontory between Rokey and the sky. "This would be a good place for you to wait," Nate went on. "Our grove is not far beyond this, but you would be visible to everyone. I will come back for you once I have explained to them who you are."

"Suits me," Rokey said agreeably. "I need a breather anyway." He scouted out a patch of reasonably flat rock where he could sit. "I'll be right here," he said, lowering himself to the stone seat.

Nate and Seff whispered nervously to each other, then clasped hands and spread their ears to catch the breeze. Rokey watched as they drifted away. He had his suit camera on them. There was nothing recorded yet of these two in their natural environment. Rokey knew that Whytock would be curious.

For the sake of Whytock's curiosity, Rokey recorded the details of the spot where he waited, with close-ups of the moss plants and flowering bushes. The moss was actually a complex tangle of a variety of species growing intertwined in lacy patterns, with intermingled shades of green. Tiny flowerets in different colors dipped and flicked as though winking back at him through the zoom lens. Rokey got just a hint of their exotic perfumes through the ionic filters of his suit. After a moment he realized that the bushes were waving at him, beckoning to him with tiny gestures of twig and leaf. It was not the breeze. They were aware of his presence and calling to him. He leaned over and gently brushed the leaf tips of the closest bush. The leaves caressed his fingers in return.

"Not quite a plant and not quite an animal," Rokey mused aloud. "I like this place."

Rokey made himself as comfortable as he could on the bare rock, assuming he would have a long wait as the two reunited with their friends and told of the great adventure they had been on. Nate and Seff, however, came puffing back over the ridge after barely twenty minutes. They were clinging to each other like frightened children and their eyes were frantic.

"They're gone!" Nate called as soon as they had caught Rokey's attention.

Rokey sprang to his feet. "Gone?"

The two dashed up to him, their ears wide and stretched back behind them, and they wrapped their tails around the loops on his helmet. "Everyone!" They chorused. "They're gone!"

"The grove is empty," Nate said. "There is no one left."

Rokey immediately scrambled up and over the wedge of rock to the top, pausing there to look out across another long, mossy slope to the grove of Stand Alone. The treehomes were big, several meters high, with broad trunks and luxurious masses of multihued leaves. The trunks stood in a neatly staggered line along the crest of the land, with moss and flower beds at their feet and their crowns mingled overhead into a single, dense canopy. It was a peaceful scene made sinister despite the warm sunlight. It was too peaceful, the stillness of a cemetery. The open entryways of the treehomes looked like mouths frozen in silent screams.

Rokey hurried across the intervening slope as quickly as he dared, sliding occasionally in the thick moss underfoot. The ground was more nearly level once he reached the trees, nevertheless he walked carefully, mindful of where he stepped. The gardens had already been disturbed. It was clear that many heavy feet had trampled through heedless of the plants. The imprint of spacesuit boots was plain. Broken branches littered the ground, dried white like fallen bones.

With a terrible sense of certainty, Rokey knew what had happened. The pirates had raided here. From the look of things, raided several weeks ago. He had come too late.

Rokey walked through the grove recording everything, focusing his growing sense of outrage into the cold necessity to be as completely correct as possible. There were interstellar courts to which the Hupp could ultimately resort. Evidence would be crucial. He made his voiceover commentary terse and even-voiced despite his desire to shout and scream obscenities. He liked Nate and Seff, and he liked their waterlogged little world. His rage seemed a civilized emotion in the midst of this ravaged and mournful place.

Rokey realized abruptly that there had been witnesses to the abductions. "What do the treehomes say about this?" he asked.

"So far all they can say is that everyone is gone," Nate told him. "The trees are cold because there are no people in their chambers, and so they have begun to go into deep sleep. It may not be easy to wake them."

"They're very upset," Seff put in.

"They're afraid," Nate added. He sounded frightened himself.

"I'm afraid," Rokey said matter-of-factly. "Why shouldn't they be?"

Nate and Seff were heartened by this, and they guided Rokey over to Seff's treehome. "After what you said, I was so afraid that they had taken my paintings," Seff said, "but they're still here."

"The pirates must not have seen them," Rokey said. "Otherwise they would have destroyed them. Those paintings are your people's legal proof that you are *not* just talking animals."

He sighed with a sweep of oversized relief. He had felt a flash of alarm about Seff's painting collection as soon he saw the boot prints. Proof of sentience was such a delicate matter, and so heavily influenced by interstellar economics.

The entrance to Seff's treehome was about two-thirds of the way up the trunk, more than a meter over Rokey's head. He set the command priorities on the ladder belt so that it lifted him up slowly until he was at eye level with the entrance and he could see in. Seff puffed inside at once, floating over to an intricate pattern of woven bark and inner-rootlets that was the back wall of the chamber. He embraced this like a long-lost friend, talking eagerly in rapid words of his wispy language. It was a long speech.

Rokey peered around the chamber, recording everything with the helmet lenses as he looked. It was a natural-seeming hollow in the center of the tree, about a meter and a half across, with smooth walls stained deep twilight blue except for the back section. Shelf-bracken grew in regular patterns, and these were piled high with a variety of tiny objects that Rokey assumed were Seff's painting supplies.

The paintings themselves, however, were the dominant feature of the chamber, a riot of images piled casually everywhere, flowers in wild bloom, shiny bugs, green surf on the beach and hundreds of miniature portraits of the villagers of Stand Alone, painted on pieces of smoothed bark small enough to fit into Rokey's palm. They smiled at him from every corner. A single piece the size of a dinner plate was a painting of the entire grove, each treehome in exquisitely tiny detail, with the villagers floating among the branches like little jewels.

The row of sketches that made up the "note" that Seff had put up for Nate and that had started their amazing adventure was still in place, the message still as exciting in its possibilities. Seff's style was almost photographic in its realism, with light and shadows so realistically rendered that each was like a little window onto a scene, the three-dimensional illusion perfect. Seff's art, however, was not just in realistic rendering but in careful selection of pose and action, lighting and color. There was a vigorous joy in each, a sunstruck brilliance that was clearly Seff's own point of view on his world.

Rokey recorded everything in the highest resolution for which his suit recorder was capable. How many civilizations had records of their first art, the very beginnings of their culture, recordings of the workshop of their first artist? The Hupp were unique, a child-race catapulted to interstellar status by the accident of memory and abduction. If Rokey and Whytock handled this right, then every generation of Hupp, with their perfect memories, would get to see where their culture began, the actual moment and place where their civilization was born. Not another people in the entire sky had this kind of treasure.

If there were any Hupp left after the pirates got through with them.

"We better start packing these up," Rokey started to say, but he was interrupted by a low, thrumming voice that rang through the entire body of the tree. He could feel the vibration in the wood where he leaned against the rim of the entryway. He guessed at once that it was the treehome talking.

Rokey triple-checked that the suit audio-recorders were on and could handle the signal, then he just hung there in the entryway listening. He could not make out any distinctions that sounded like words in the slow, heavy voice, but the sense of grief and confusion was clear. The voice went on for a long quarter of an hour and more, fading off at last into a sighing hum before it fell silent. Rokey was eager for a translation but waited while Nate and Seff conferred hastily together in their own language.

"Tree does not see with light," Nate said, turning in the air to float up close to Rokey's helmet, peering in at his face. "She feels warmth, and she says that beings so warm they glowed like sunlight swarmed around the grove. They grabbed the people out of the trees, caught them as they tried to fly away. They even reached into the treehomes and took those who tried to hide. They stayed until they had taken everyone, then they went away. That's all Tree can say. They made no warning noise. They just appeared."

Rokey wondered how many other villages had been raided this way, and he felt a stab of despair. If this situation got out of hand it could result in the wholesale slaughter of the entire population of Hupp. Rokey needed to talk to Whytock, and he was suddenly deeply grateful that the strange little trillionaire had involved himself.

Seff picked up the nearest painting and gazed down sadly at the face smiling up at him. "I was so afraid for my paintings," he said. "It never occurred to me to worry that my friends were in danger. I can make new paintings, but how will I find my friends?" He set that one down again and picked up another. "These don't seem so important anymore."

"Don't say that," Rokey said to him. "Your paintings are beyond worth, Seff. They are the first true treasures of your world, and they are going to make you famous in places you can't even imagine. You will be more famous with every generation of your people to come, and with a people like yours, that's a lot of remembering!"

Seff took this news with a brief smile, but he sighed as he looked around at his work. "My people do not think much of my paintings, Rokey."

"They will when they find out how much help you can bring because of them." Rokey saw Nate's face brighten as he said this.

"You see, Seff," Nate said. "Haven't I always said that a time would come when people understood?"

"We should start packing these up," Rokey said again, gesturing through the entry toward the paintings. "I've recorded everything in situ, with the two of you here as identifiers, so someday you can put everything back exactly where it was, but we can't take the risk that the pirates might come back and decide that it's safer for them with this evidence destroyed."

"Why do my paintings threaten them?" Seff sounded angry.

"As proof that you are not animals," Rokey reminded him. "That proof changes them from pet dealers to kidnappers and murderers. The Law may be fuzzy on pet dealers, but it's very clear about kidnapping and murder."

And especially about genocide, Rokey thought to himself. He did not say that out loud. Instead, he said, "On top of that, this is pre-contact art. You can't imagine how much some museums will pay for pre-contact artwork. Sell off a few of these to the right people, and you'll be rich enough to buy an entire army to protect your planet."

Nate's little face scrunched up in an unhappy expression. "Wystan has tried to explain this thing about 'rich' and 'money.' He seems to feel it is most important, but Seff and I haven't really figured it out yet."

"The more he explains about it, the less I understand it," Seff said, with his soft giggle. "He says I will never have to worry about it, but then he goes on explaining anyway!"

Rokey sighed, hearing his own breath too loudly inside the confines of the suit helmet. "He's right, both times. You don't have to worry about it, *and* someday the crazy things he's said about it will make sense, but you don't have to worry about forgetting any of it, so I wouldn't bother thinking about it much until then."

"Yes," Nate said somberly. "There is much we need to think about now besides old memories."

Rokey activated the clever little "packaging package" that Whytock had prepared for Seff. It unfolded from his belt like a bird awakening and spreading wide its feathers. Seff had, of course, given the exact count of his collection and the size of each piece, so that Whytock's curious little portfolio was custom designed. Rokey had no idea where onboard the *Reach,* nor how Whytock had manufactured it so perfectly to spec, but he had to admit that Whytock was definitely playing "stupider than he really was." The man was a constant surprise.

Nate and Seff handed each painting out to Rokey as the

anti-gravity ladder-belt dangled him in front of the entryway, and Rokey carefully placed each priceless miniature into its prepared slot. Even though they worked efficiently, they had hundreds of paintings to pack. They worked through the afternoon.

Rokey had the distinct feeling that he was robbing a museum. As such things went, this place was the Hupps' first museum and the first of many things. Seff's little seedpod bowls of plant-oil colors were the beginnings of chemistry, the crucible of alchemy, the birth of discovering the universe.

As the bright treasures of Seff's artwork passed through his fingers, Rokey felt a heart-deep pang of regret that these people had been so savagely interrupted. The greatest adventure of any world, any culture, was that of its own childhood. It was being ripped from them by a contest between a pirate gang's greed and a rich man's altruism. They were suspended between opposites, and Rokey felt already the strain of maintaining the delicate balance of their future.

Each and every bowl and brush and bark canvas of Seff's painting supplies were also packed into the surprisingly capacious portfolio. The interior of Seff's treehome was left bare, with only the lichen shelves and the curled-up twigs of his sleeping rack in the far corner. The portfolio did not weigh much, but it was as wide as Rokey. Nate and Seff helped Rokey secure its clamps to the back of his spacesuit, then he powered down the ladder-belt until he was securely returned to the ground. The portfolio strapped to his back was unwieldy and he stood with his feet spread and his spine held very straight. The fur on his arms was so pulled and twisted by the suit sleeves that his arms hurt. He wanted desperately to get out of this spacesuit and comb down his stirred emotions.

"What about the portrait in your treehome?" Seff said to Nate when this was done.

"I am not happy about taking it away from Tree." Nate half-turned from them, unable to meet eyes with either Rokey or Seff. He paused, and turned back to face them. "I have no reason to believe this, but through all the things that have happened to us, I have felt that Seff's painting of me was. . ." Nate paused, and his face showed emotional distress. "I find it difficult to explain, but I know that as long as the painting of me is safe with Tree, then I will get through whatever happens."

Rokey was amused. "You know, Nate, that isn't so strange. I myself have a similar belief. There is a holusion of me back at Rokherton University that delivers the same series of lectures every semester, so I do understand. I feel the same way about that portrait of me. You feel connected to images of yourself. That's natural."

"But it is unsafe to leave it here," Nate said. His thin voice was plaintive, and the corners of his eyes drooped. "We must take it with us."

Rokey did some hard thinking. This was a brand new world, with so many things happening not just to an individual but to the representatives of an entire race. Nate's response to Seff's artwork was part of a new reality for these people. Whether it could be considered a superstition or not was simply unimportant. It was Nate's honest reaction to a last vestige of his own world, his old life. Rokey felt the need to respect that. The possibility that the pirates would find one painting among these treehomes was remote, especially since they were not likely to return to a habitat they had already stripped. The danger of them finding the painting, however, made those odds too close for comfort.

"The first thing to do is to record it in situ," he said finally.

Once Rokey was floating in front of the entryway to Nate's treehome, he had to peer in at just the right angle to see the painting. Nate had it hung beside the treehome opening. Rokey recorded the chamber carefully, and realized he had a plan that might work.

"I don't think you have to take the painting out," he said to Nate. "All we have to do is drape some moss or dried leaves over it."

"Yes!" Nate's relief made his entire being light up, as though his color had suddenly brightened.

Rokey lowered himself back to the ground, then found that he could not bend over to pick up anything suitable to cover the painting. He had a museum strapped to his back.

Nate and Seff started laughing when he explained, and their merriment became oversized in the stillness of the grove.

Rokey watched them clinging to each other and spinning about in giggling spirals, and he felt that same sadness rise up in him at seeing a child-world denied its childhood. These two were reeling between peaks of shock and elation, expectation and despair. He waited patiently until they had stilled their giggling fit and returned to hover in front of his face.

"Sorry," Nate said, almost bursting into laughter again. "We can't help it. Legs are funny. And legs aren't much help now, are they?"

"They have their moments," Rokey said with a mock expression of wounded dignity. "They just make it hard to balance sometimes." He grinned at them. "Let's get that portrait safely covered up, so we can get on with rescuing your friends."

"Do you think we can find them?" Seff said, putting himself close to Rokey's faceplate and peering in anxiously.

"We found you, didn't we?" That was meant to be reassuring but Rokey knew it was not much of an answer. These two had been surviving on sheer luck for so long it was becoming a habit. At least this time, Whytock and crew would know what they were seeking.

Nate and Seff puffed about purposefully for a few minutes gathering tiny handfuls of dried moss and fallen leaf. When they were done, Rokey floated up again to inspect it. He was relieved that his plan seemed to work. The chamber looked deserted, with windblown leaves piled by the entry.

"Excellent," Rokey said. "Now you and the painting are both quite safe."

Nate looked around the chamber and gave a wistful sigh. "I wanted so much to be here again, to return to Tree safe and see my world back in place. Yet now I feel like a stranger here, as though all this time, through everything, I've really have been remembering some other place."

"Travel will do that to you," Rokey said sympathetically. "Broadens your horizons so that you don't fit into rooms the same way anymore."

"I can change my size," Nate said. He seemed thoughtful again, considering Rokey's words. "But I cannot change my memories. That is where home is, I suppose."

He drifted to the back wall, to a pattern of woven root and

branch similar to the one in Seff's chamber, and he patted it gently. "Tree is quite asleep," Nate said. "I have been away for a long time, and her heart must be cold. I should wake her, just to let her know that I am alive, that I survived."

"Perhaps it is kinder to let her sleep," Seff said, floating up to him. "My Tree is very upset about everything that has happened. Having me return alive and well did not seem to help that at all."

"There is nothing she can do anyway," Nate said. "Let her sleep." He gave a rueful chuckle. "I wish I could leave her a note, but she could not see it."

"They will tell each other when the treehomes wake next," Seff said. "She will know you are safe. My tree will tell her."

"No more rock climbing with this thing attached," Rokey said once his feet were back on the ground. "I am going down to the beach, to walk back to the *Shadow* from there, and I want to record the tracks of the pirates' approach to the grove. Every bit of evidence helps."

It was slow going, even so. Rokey knew perfectly well that the protected portfolio on his back could get dumped in the ocean or left in a burning house without damaging the precious paintings inside. Nonetheless he kept his hand close to the emergency switch for the ladder-belt in case he stumbled. He had to do some backtracking along the edges of the moss slope to find a dry path through the marsh to the beach beyond, and Rokey was at last grateful for the spacesuit. The black, sticky mud in the marsh they crossed was not the kind that squishes nicely through the toes.

Wind and tide had erased most of the signs of the pirates' landing, although Rokey did find one clear impression of a landing strut on the high side of the beach, deep enough that its outline was still visible. Rokey recorded this from several angles on the hope that Ray could recognize the spaceship from its spoor.

They found other evidence of the pirates' presence.

Nate and Seff called Rokey away from the strut impression with frantic calls. He hurried over as swiftly as suit and baggage allowed. They were hovering low over the base of a dune, where sand-hugging moss raised slender blossoms. Rokey stopped short at the edge of the moss bed. There was a face staring up at him from the sand. It seemed a tired, haggard face, with the grayed eyes half-open and the lips pulled tight. Sand filled the lines of the face. One hand was up, fingers wide and resting against the sand as though caught in the gesture of pulling the face free. The filters in the spacesuit helmet prevented Rokey from sensing the more immediate evidence of death, and for a long moment he expected the face to speak to him from the sand.

"That's Massay," Nate said. "He was . . . he was important to us."

"They killed him!" Seff declared indignantly. "They killed him!"

"I'm so sorry," Rokey said. The rushing surf of the green ocean behind him seemed to snarl across the beach, hissing in anger.

"What can we do if they are willing to kill us?" Seff seemed bewildered, clasping and unclasping his little hands in front of his face.

"We must return him to his Tree," Nate said, forcing calm. "He has lain out here for too long already."

"Return him to his Tree?" Rokey asked. He worried for a moment that Nate was no longer dealing with the enormity of this loss, and had slipped into denial. What did death mean to these people?

"That is always what happens to the dead," Nate said, matter-of-factly enough that Rokey stopped worrying. "His Tree will expect that."

"What does the Tree do with the body?" Rokey asked.

"Every treehome has a deep chamber that seals around the body when someone dies," Nate seemed surprised that Rokey did not know that. "Tree takes it back, absorbs it."

"We'll bring Massay back to his Tree eventually, but proof of his murder will put those pirates in jail faster than anything else."

"His body will prove that?"

"Death always has a story to tell."

"Rokey, what will happen to you after you die?"

"Depends on where I die. If I'm at home, I will get a state funeral so big that the University will have to declare a world-wide holiday. With great ceremony, they will launch me into the Sun, to be dissolved in the light from which I came."

"And if you are not at home?"

"Smaller funeral, different sun, same results. Other than that I can't begin to guess. I'm past caring."

"That is not so different, really. We come from the treehomes, and we return to the treehomes."

"You come from the treehomes?" Rokey asked cautiously, not wanting to tread on too personal a ground, or too technical, either.

"Yes."

Nate did not offer more information. Rokey decided not to ask, not until later and not without a better recording system on. The issue at hand was getting Massay's body back to the med-lab onboard Whytock's starship. Finding out why this Hupp had died during the mass abduction would be important evidence. Eventually.

"We have to take his body back with us," Rokey said. That would not be easy. The portfolio did not have a body-bag space in it. He was about to say he could carry the small, deflated body. After all, he was wearing gloves, but Nate spoke up with solemn voice.

"I will carry him," he said.

"Oh!" Seff exclaimed. "I couldn't! It's too awful!"

"I am used to bad smells," Nate said to him quietly. "Bad memories, too. Massay was my friend, even if he frightened me sometimes. He would want the knowledge of his death to help the rest of the village."

"It will help the rest of your world," Rokey said. "All the villagers."

Neither Nate nor Seff, however, could get adequate grip to lift the body free. Rokey had to detach the portfolio and leave it standing while he knelt beside the corpse. Once Rokey had carefully, reverently, worked the stiff form loose, he held it out to Nate. The body was flat, like a deflated balloon, the rubbery skin cracked and fragile, the tough impermeability of that hide at last undone by death. Nate had some difficulty getting his stubby arms around Massay's flattened form, but he persisted until he had it secure. The dead face was turned to him as though offering comfort.

Rokey hefted the portfolio up with a grunt, and Seff helped get it back in place. It was not heavy, but his emotions were swaying. He strode off down the beach toward the *Shadow,* with Nate and Seff beside his face, clinging to his helmet with their tails.

Ray met them at the airlock. "I knew you'd want that suit off real fast," he said as Rokey climbed the ramp. Ray was grinning.

The grin faded as he noticed the corpse and the look on the Hupp' faces.

"Scubb," he said under his breath, and he quickly unlatched Rokey's helmet.

Rokey smacked his hand hard against the control panel to close the outer airlock door.

Seff unwrapped his tail from the loop on the helmet, and floated up to Ray's face. "They're gone, Captain Harris!" he cried. "The entire village is empty! They've been taken!"

Rokey's whole being flinched at the wash of death that hit his nose when the helmet came off. He said nothing, just turned around so that Ray could release the precious portfolio.

"At least, they didn't get the paintings," Rokey said. He twisted inside the suit to watch over his shoulder while Ray unlatched the case.

Ray carefully lifted the portfolio free. "Where do you want this?"

"Put it on my bed," Rokey said. He stripped the suit off, and dropped it to the deck. "And then get us out of here as invisibly as you can. We've got to get up to the *Reach.* I need to talk to Whytock but, now more than ever, we can't afford any communication signal that might be overheard."

Rokey put his hands up to Nate, who was hovering in the center of the airlock, tenderly holding Massay's corpse. "I'll take care of him for you now, Nate. Believe me, this is for the best."

Ray hurried out with the portfolio.

Rokey was just finishing up, scrubbing his hands clean, when Ray called, saying the ship was ready for liftoff. Rokey hurried up to the bridge and settled into his seat.

"Vertical-absolute on antigrav," Ray said. "Watch the fuel-cell backups. This will be a big drain, and the worst of it in the first three seconds. Both of us better keep our eyes on the scopes. Anything we can notice can also notice us. We have to notice them first."

The two men were silent at their work until the *Yankee Shadow* had risen into the sky and burst through the top of it into the star-filled dark of space beyond.

"We'll rendezvous with the *Reach* in about six hours, old man." Ray said. "You want to tell me what happened down there?" He did not look at Rokey, but kept his eyes on his instrument panel as he set in the course. Both men continued scanning the *Shadow's* long-range scopes as they talked.

"I've got it all in the suit-recorders," Rokey said. "It's a pretty place, and moist, even for me. I was actually glad of the suit by the end. But the pirates had already come through and they snagged the entire village population. Some time ago, too. I can't help believing we're too late. Grid! I hope I'm wrong!"

"Did the pirates kill the . . . the little guy you brought back?"

"Massay," Rokey said sadly. "His name was Massay. We'll have to leave it Whytock to find that out." He told Ray about finding the body on the beach.

"Are those two going to be alright?" Ray gestured over his shoulder, indicating Nate and Seff in the guest quarters.

"I think so. They need some time alone to react, to comfort each other. I think I'll stay up here until we're docked."

"We need eyes on the scopes right now, anyway," Ray said, pointing to Rokey's side of the display monitors. "You *know* what those men will do to the Hupp if they find out that someone has copped to them being here?"

Rokey caught his breath on a deep sigh. "Yes. They'll kill the entire lot of them, destroy the bodies and vanish like they've never been here, no witnesses, no evidence."

"Just don't say that in anyone else's earshot," Ray said, gesturing again, more meaningfully.

"I was thinking the same thing myself. They've had enough to swallow so far."

Good Grief

"They have a remarkable anatomy!" Whytock declared as he strode into the *Shadow's* galley.

Rokey looked up from his cocoa. It was cold. "Do they, now?"

Whytock flung himself onto the bench beside Rokey. His gestures were quick and fluttery, and he was clearly excited. "It is unmistakably the same DNA gestalt as the creatures we have been turning up on the dinosaur market. They are as closely related to each other as you are to a *kamarinann!* But they are certainly unlike any other form I have ever studied or read about. It is a unique life-code, not quite a plant, not quite an animal, and a lot of other things it will take *years* to identify!"

Rokey knew the primitive animal form on Wozur to which he referred, the *kamarinann,* but he was surprised that Whytock knew about such an obscure and now extinct creature on a world alien to his own. "Not quite a plant, not quite an animal?"

"Indeed! Isn't that *completely* fascinating!"

"So you have your confirmation for a case against the raiders?"

"Sewn up tight."

"With murder thrown in?" Rokey asked, referring to the question of how Massay had died.

Whytock shrugged elaborately. "That is more difficult to say. The medicomp's first analysis was full systemic shock. The body was intact, meaning that the gentleman wasn't injured in anyway. Their nervous system is most intricate, as you would imagine with minds like theirs." He tapped his own forehead as emphasis. "Their skin is an organic latex compound of astounding complexity, denser than anything commercially manufactured."

Whytock broke off with a grin and almost patted himself on the shoulder. "I have already filled in a patent document for them to register the formula. The Hupp should make a fortune once I get someone onto the process for growing it artificially. I am guessing their skin had to evolve such density in order to keep hydrogen gas molecules from escaping. They are not methane-floaters as I first thought, you know. It's hydrogen. And the internal hydrogen release-and-take-up mechanism they use for directed floating will take experts, not just computers, to unravel."

Whytock chuckled happily. "That's the first time my computer has had to admit defeat on analyzing anything, and I do believe she's sulking over it!"

"We will have to raise the general humidity in the ship," he went on. "They seem to derive the greater part of their hydrogen from the breakdown of water, and they get most of their water from the moisture in their atmosphere."

"They seem to have adapted pretty well."

Whytock sighed, suddenly serious. "That is the only hope I have for the rest of his people, that their remarkable adaptability will keep them alive until I can help them."

"This all takes so much time," Rokey said wearily. He pushed around the fur on his face with his fingers, letting the sensation override his rising sense of despair. "Do they have the time anymore?"

"We will evacuate the entire population, if that is what is necessary to protect them from this corporate monster, and keep them safe until we have them registered at Rokherton so that a police station will be set up to protect them."

Rokey nodded, but his face was troubled. "Let's hope that does the trick."

"But, of course, Lord Rokhmyr, you cannot go with us to Rokherton University, can you?"

"No. No, I can't." Rokey felt the rise of an old bitterness that he thought he had drowned long ago. He had been in exile for so long that his university life seemed from another time and space, from someone else's life seen in a movie. Even as he spoke, he knew he wanted desperately to go back. He ached to see the campus and his old life again. A vivid memory of the office he had once thought of as a fortress flashed across his mind. He had believed that his private fortress could keep out all the dark shadows of reality, but corruption had risen from within his own ranks. He could not go back, not for a long time. Being so sharply reminded opened a hurt he had put away years ago and thought he had forgotten.

"Take this straight to Hohlar," Rokey said, speaking more gruffly than intended. "I imagine you have the pull to avoid the lesser officials. He'll listen to you."

Whytock took his cigar from his lips and thoughtfully sniffed the glowing tip. Rokey could feel Whytock's eyes on him, despite the sleepy look. "I hadn't intended to speak to anyone else, as a matter of fact. I am greatly relieved to learn that we agree on that. Old Hohlar has a stiff spine, but sometimes that is just what is needed."

"The stiffest, but that's why he'll help. He is still Head Of Executive Action On Genetic Registration, isn't he?" Rokey asked Whytock. "He hasn't been retired or something since last I looked, has he?"

"No, still signing paperwork at lightning speed," Whytock replied. "That's why I had thought to go straight to him. I've had occasion to visit with him, and not that long ago. He sets an excellent table."

He paused, looking down at his cigar. "Would you like me to bring him a message?" he said. He spoke seriously, his usual bluster quieted.

Rokey thought about the possibilities, and thought about his old friend, Hohlar. No, the very fact of Rokey's continued existence was too dangerous for Hohlar to know. A web of government surveillance had Hohlar invisibly surrounded, thoroughly and secretly contained. The same web had almost ensnared Rokey, but he had chanced upon its invisible movement before it could close around him, and he had escaped. The same web waited for him yet. Better that Hohlar did not know he was himself a victim of it. Perhaps, by now, he had figured it out for himself, anyway.

"No. I think this should be your project alone," Rokey said.

Whytock nodded, and put the cigar back in his mouth to puff a cloud of smoke before his face.

We Have to Get Out of Here!

Locating the kidnapped villagers turned out to be deceptively easy. The *Reach's* fancy computer intercepted a radio message broadcast between the orbiting cargo-loader and a ground base on a small continent near the southern pole. The signal pinpointed the location precisely: "The captured animals are adapting well, and should be processed for transport and distribution."

The ground base responded that it would take a few days to get the animals packaged up for travel. Ray, Rokey and Whytock would have to do something soon, or else the Hupp would be scattered to pet stores around the galaxy. The ones who survived the trip.

Communications from the orbiting ship were chilling: "Those animals are worth more than ten million a piece, Jian. You remember that when you handle them."

"We ain't been thinking about much else since we got here, Mr. Richards, sir. Any luck on finding them first two that was stolen, sir?"

"Sacrifices had to be made for the sake of keeping a low profile on this project, Jian. Keep that in mind as you prepare the rest of them for travel, won't you?"

"Yes, sir, Mr. Richards, sir."

Whytock had reacted to the name "Richards" with a gasp, and he put his hand to his forehead.

"This is bad," he mumbled. He groped around for his walking stick, and was startled to find it on the bench beside him. He flicked the silver ear and spoke into the Anubis face. "Computer. Cross-reference the name 'Mr. Richards' with registration data we have on the suppliers and cargo ships intercepted in Operation Mystery Meat. Specify *Leroy Chrétien* Richards under all aliases where it appears."

"Working, Boss." The Anubis head spoke with the *Reach's* computer voice.

"Leroy Richards is someone you've encountered before?" Rokey asked Whytock. The change on Whytock's face from his usual stubbornly cheerful look was alarming.

"Not personally yet, no. I had hoped to keep it that way, but the more I investigate the illegal dinosaur market, the more I run into his name. From what data I could get, the extrapolation on his empire is that he controls between thirty and seventy percent of the entire interstellar black market on bio-products. He's terribly well-organized, and I suspect he has government connections at a very high level."

Ray and Rokey took this news with the dire solemnity it deserved.

"I told you," Ray said, shaking his head. "Didn't I tell you this was *way* too big for us?"

"If he is actually here, supervising this in person, he will also have a well-organized bodyguard."

"Heavily armed is what you mean, isn't it?" Ray said darkly.

Whytock nodded.

"It could be another 'Richards,' couldn't it?" Rokey said. His hackles were starting to lift the mane across his shoulders, and his voice almost squeaked. "I mean, it's a common enough name in some sectors. All it really means is that we're dealing with an Earthman."

He tried to smile. "Right?"

Whytock sighed heavily.

"Data cross-referenced, Boss," the computer announced. The light in the ruby eyes grew bright.

"Put it through to the monitors here in the *Shadow's* galley," Whytock said to the computer link.

The data scrolling across the closest screen was coded to some private system of Whytock's, and he began studying it with a serious expression. Rokey pulled himself up to his feet, and went to reheat his cocoa. Ray sat beside Whytock, arms crossed tightly across his chest, scowling at the data flow.

Finally, Whytock sat back with a sigh, shaking his head.

"His security is remarkably good. There is an eighty-percent chance that it is, indeed, Leroy Richards out there. At the very least, he has control over enough of the industry that was carrying Hupp bio-products to indicate pretty reliably that he is involved. One way or another, he is involved."

"You managed to keep this a big secret!" Ray said. Anger was clear in his voice and stance.

"I knew that the products were being sold to him, Captain Harris," Whytock said. "I had no way of knowing how deeply involved he was, and certainly no suspicion that he would be here, in the system, *himself.* Of course, this does explain why he has been so difficult to trace. This was a good hiding place for him."

He stood up, bracing himself with the walking stick. "We must be most cautious, gentlemen. Most cautious, indeed. Leroy Richards leaves no traces, no witnesses, and he makes no mistakes. He has destroyed whole species, ravaged worlds of their biological treasures. He will not be kind to those people."

"We have to get them out of there!" Ray said.

Whytock nodded. "We have to get them out of there. *All of them.*"

Rounding Up the Folks

It was Ray's turn to find himself down on the surface of Hupp, admiring the scenery outside and hating the spacesuit he was in. It concentrated the stink of his own fear. Ray Harris hated planets, especially at night, and most especially in an unknown wilderness, hurrying towards people who would kill him if they saw him.

He had brought the *Shadow* in low over the green ocean, approaching the coast where Richard's men had located their ground base. Ray landed the *Shadow* on a secluded beach amid low, rocky hills, several kilometers from the base and upwind. Richards might keep guards with noses as sensitive as Rokey's.

Nate was in a pocket on Ray's suit utility-belt, riding in grim silence. Ray was not happy that Nate had come along on the rescue mission, but his logic was irrefutable. "How else will they know that they're being rescued?" Nate had said, most reasonably. "You'll be just another big, scary alien to them. Someone has to explain why you're there."

Ray *was* glad that Mr. Burke was also along, almost invisible in the dark night. Ray could only see him because he knew he was there, a looming blackness in the night beside him.

Rokey had not liked that part. "No splitting up, remember?"

"We need Captain Harris' youthful endurance and military expertise for this operation," Whytock had said, reassuringly. "You, Lord Rokhmyr, will be onboard the *Shadow,* ready to whisk everyone away to safety at an instant's notice. Mr. Burke has had years of experience with planets. He used to live in the woods, you know! Captain Harris will find him most useful to have along."

Ray did find the giant man's presence reassuring. Despite his size and oak tree density, he moved silently, at ease with the darkness. Ray let him walk a little bit ahead.

The ground was hard. It was cooler here than at the atoll, and drier. The night was filled with the whispery sound of the wind.

After a time, Ray realized that Whytock had not exaggerated Mr. Burke's experience with planet-side trekking. The dark did not seem to hinder or slow him. He picked a trail through the difficult terrain as easily as though walking a familiar pathway home. Their suit radios were off, to be used for real emergencies only. Their helmets were equipped with "talking spots," discs set into the forehead and sides that would transmit vocal vibration between suits when in direct contact. The two men communicated with hand signals while walking. Occasionally, Burke would raise his hand, motion for Ray to wait, then he would disappear into the darkness ahead. He always seemed to reappear out the night silently, as if by magic.

Despite the dark and the unknown terrain Burke led them to the base with surprising speed. Ray hoped they could go back as quickly. When this was over, Ray decided, he would have to have a look at the inside of Mr. Burke's spacesuit, to find out what kind of mapping display it had. It made sense that Wystan Whytock's gentleman's gentleman would have unique spacesuit.

Burke motioned for a halt, and disappeared for some several minutes this time, long enough for Ray to get a fluttery sense of concern, but Burke abruptly leaned over him out of the night, to link talking spots. "Ahead three-hundred meters. Beside lake."

He turned and strode off. Ray had to stretch his long legs to keep up.

Faint starlight reflected off the lake surface, shimmers in the dark ahead. The telltales from a row of equipment banks gleamed more brightly, visible in a line along the shore. As they got closer, Ray could make out a big, Quonset-hut style building a hundred meters long, beside the lake. The telltales were shining through the lower edge of the arched roof, for the building appeared to be open on the sides, between struts anchored in the ground, as though it were just an arched canopy rather than a roof and walls.

Nate drew himself out of Ray's pocket and puffed up to a talking spot. With his mouth pressed close to the spot, Ray could hear him clearly, even though he spoke softly. "Let me go ahead and see where they are and to wake them. I must speak to my people, warn them that you are coming to rescue them."

"What if someone grabs you?"

"I will not let them," Nate said, and he was gone before Ray could respond to that.

Ray tapped Burke's shoulder and gestured to the talking spot. They leaned together. Ray told him of Nate's plan. Burke nodded, and the two men stood side by side, watching the building with anxious attention. Ray turned up the infrared filters on his suit view-plate as far as he could, in spite of the drain on the suit battery. He could just make out a glowing ball bouncing down the slope. Nate disappeared under the edge of the arched canopy, and Ray could not see him anymore. They waited.

The minutes were dragging past a quarter of an hour when his infrared monitor showed the glowing ball re-emerge. At the same moment, Burke gestured, pointing to Nate. The little figure hurried toward them, ears spread wide to catch the breeze blowing steadily away from the lake.

Nate caught himself on Ray's helmet, his whole body heaving as he tried to calm his breathing.

"They're *all* there!" he whispered into Ray's talking spot. Burke touched his helmet gently to the talking spot on the other side of Ray's helmet to listen. "Each group of villagers is locked in a separate place, behind some kind of tough netting. I've told everyone to be ready, explained what I can. If we can get the cage doors open, they will follow us out of there."

"What kind of doors are on the cages?" Ray asked, speaking in a low whisper himself.

"They are solid, but clear, and they slide open to the right. Each one has a number keypad at the side, and Tapper said that he has seen the sequence in which their captors pushed the buttons to open the door, but I am not strong enough to press the buttons! I tried and tried!"

Ray almost laughed, but this had become so serious. "Good work, Nate. We'll get them out in short order." He whispered to Burke. "Cover me. I'm going down there with Nate. When we come out, be ready for anything."

Burke nodded solemnly, anonymous behind the military-look of his fancy spacesuit.

Ray made Nate get back into the utility belt pocket. He began a slow, cautious approach, crouched low and seeking dark pools of shadow. The infrared view on his faceplate showed only the glow of the building itself. The ground between was black.

The glowing telltales cast a useful light. Ray kept heading toward the strip of floor he could see. The area was quiet. This close to the lake he could hear the small noises of the water and the shore. He could also hear the barely audible purr of the compression motor that kept the building inflated. It was really just a fancy tent, easy to set up, easy to remove, leaving little trace, a portable prison.

Ray realized that Nate had already proven that there were no motion detectors active around the cages. Otherwise they would have been in trouble by now. Nonetheless, Ray moved with painful slowness, caution drowning out the screaming anxiety threatening to rise in his throat and make him slash desperately at the rope struts and rip off the roof of the building to set them free at once.

He crawled under the low-slung edge at the end of the building furthest from the lake, creeping forward, his eyes adjusted to the dim light in here. Nate had popped out of the pocket and was floating beside him. He said nothing, clinging to Ray's helmet and pointing. Ray found himself in a corridor between fabric cage-walls running the length of it. The floor was tilted slightly downward toward the lake. It was difficult to see the structure of the cage, apparently of some fine mesh like insect netting. The keypad locks glowed, suspended in the dark. Ray could just make out the Hupp faces pressed close against the other side of each door, waiting. He could feel their eyes on him.

When Ray reached the first lock panel, Nate did not call out the lock code. He hovered close in, guiding Ray's gloved finger with his hands. The door slid open with a light snicking sound. The crowd of Hupp burst out. There had been many hundreds of them in that cage. They came out as a cloud. Nate had warned them, though. They came out silently. Their eyes were wide with fear, but they kept silent. They clung together, hands and tails entwined as needed, and followed just above Ray's head as he hurried from lock to lock.

Unoriginal or just cheap, the kidnappers had given the same the lock code to each cage door. By the fourth one Ray had it memorized. He went from lock to lock, hastily jabbing in numbers. Nate gathered the many escapees together, keeping them smoothly in a group above Ray's head. The narrow corridor filled up with floating bodies and entwined tails dangling.

When the last cage was opened and everyone was free, Ray ran back up the corridor, closing each door and locking it once more. He hoped finding the empty cages locked would slow them down. It was important to keep their kidnappers confused about how they had escaped. Ray reached the section at the far end where he had come in. He went to his knees without breaking stride to crawl out under the edge, forcing calm.

He scrambled to his feet once he was outside. Hupp by the thousands were pouring out through the gaps around him and on either side, rising silently into the night, clinging to each other with hands and tails. Their ears were spread wide, vents puffing, silently. Ray did not know any way to safely hurry them along. He could only stand and wait, holding the gap in the tenting open wide. He realized, as they puffed past him, that this was an entire world of people. More than twenty tense minutes went by before Nate signaled to him that the last of the Hupp were free.

Ray hurried up the slope, away from the lake and the rows of cages in the big tent. He could hardly believe that they had gotten away with it. Nate was clinging to the helmet loop closest to a talking spot, waving to get his attention.

Excitement made Nate's words tumble out on top of each

other, and his eyes were shining. "They tell me that their captors sleep in another building, on the other side of this one. There are twenty-four of them altogether. A guard will be around for a check very soon, that is the routine. We must hurry."

Ray had an inspiration, and tapped Burke's suit for his attention. "You go on to the *Shadow* with them now. You can move faster than I can in this dark, and you can find your way back better than I can. I'm going to sabotage the compressor so that the tent starts collapsing. That will distract them long enough to give us a good head start. I'll track your footprints in infrared, so don't worry about me finding my way back."

Burke nodded solemnly. He put a gloved hand out to Nate, who had been hovering close to Ray's face so that he could hear their conversation.

"I will make sure that everyone stays together," Nate said. "We will hold onto each other and to Mr. Burke, and his legs will hurry for all of us!" He giggled, a response to tension that Ray had noticed before. "Legs are good for hurrying!"

Burke strode away, his long, long legs making good on Nate's claim about the value of legs. The cloud of Hupp was a huge mass surrounding him and high over his head, a great cloud of frightened faces clinging tightly to each other in the dark. They disappeared swiftly into the night, the last ones trailing like loose ribbons.

Ray crept down to the lake shore, making a wide circle around the tent-building with the cages. From the lake shore, he could see the second tent-building that housed the guards and staff, a few meters off and at right angles to the cages. There was a single spotlight shining over the main entrance. The rest of the building was dark. Ray sneered, disgusted despite his relief. Evidently these people felt safe here, hidden by the secrecy of their location.

He let the purr of the compressor motor guide him. Once he reached it, he risked a quick flash of light across the housing to look for weak points. A second flash across the top showed the intake where air was drawn in.

Ray knelt, groping about on the ground for rocks until he found one that felt to be the right size. He shoved the rock into the intake vent, pushing it in hard, scooped a handful of dirt and pebbles in on top of that, then he immediately hurried away from the shore.

The tent-buildings were hundreds of meters behind him when he heard the first alarm bells sounding from the distance, followed shortly thereafter by angry shouts and called orders. Ray picked up his pace, focusing his attention on the hard, stony ground ahead of him. He ran, at once astounded and dismayed by how swiftly Mr. Burke had run before him, pulling the floating cloud of Hupp along with him. Ray did not catch up with them until he saw the single tail light of the *Yankee Shadow,* perched in the dark on a rocky slope of beach. The ramp was down, and the entry was open, waiting. The Hupp were streaming in.

It took more than half an hour for all the Hupp to get through the airlock into the ship. Ray was staggered by the numbers. He had been aware of many eyes in the dark during the rescue and of a mass of faces pressed together, but the actual count was far beyond his expectation.

They crowed the ship's corridors and filled up every space, clinging to each other and whispering together in their soft, breezy language. Nate and Seff floated from group to group, encouraging and explaining, already busy with language lessons of his own. Ray began to hear words in SpeakEZ here and there. He heard his own name, and those of Rokey and Whytock and Burke, echoed from group to group in their wispy voices.

There was only room for the three men on the bridge, with Burke perched uncomfortably on a pull-out seat beside the entry, his knees drawn up close and his head nearly brushing the instrument panel behind him. He was still in his spacesuit. He had taken the helmet off and held it in his lap. Liftoff was silent. The men did not speak until the little world of Hupp was fading behind them.

"Well, that wasn't so bad," Ray said at last.

Not So Good, Either

"We've been copped," Rokey said tersely, pointing to the flare of warning lights across a side panel. "And these guys really *are* pirates."

Ray's hands flashed across his controls. "Top-speed, Rokey," he ordered. "Never mind not being seen. We've got to get out of this system."

"The *Reach* has better armaments," Rokey pointed out. "We need to get to her first."

"She moves like a lump of mud!" Ray protested. "They'll catch us without breaking a sweat. That's the whole fleet on our tail!"

"The *Reach* slings some mighty powerful mud. Whytock's got enough weapons to take out a whole fleet, Ray. Especially with us doing the shooting."

Ray calculated distances and time, cracking his knuckles with a hard, sharp sound.

Rokey flinched, but said nothing. He knew what the gesture meant.

"Put everything into speed, Rokey," Ray said. "If we don't need fuel-cells for the window-jump, we can run faster. Radio-silence is no help, now. Signal Whytock and tell him to start acceleration for the window and be ready to match our speed so we can dock before the jump."

Whytock congratulated them on a successful rescue. He said nothing about their pursuers except, "Standing by."

Another tense hour went by, then two, with the fleet behind them. At last the radio crackled on. "You are trespassing in private space. Stand by to be boarded, or we will fire."

The *Yankee Shadow* sped on, gaining more velocity with each second, but the Richard's fleet was swiftly closing in. Fighting while accelerating toward half the speed of light was awkward and often self-defeating. Ray knew the rules and possibilities. He knew he could keep the *Shadow* just out of range until safely docked within the giant *Reach*, and he knew that once they made the jump window to intraspace, they were safe.

He also knew that Richards and his fleet would still be behind them when the *Reach* came out on the other side.

Take a Number

"They did capture everyone known on Hupp," Nate said. "Everyone who was known by anyone is accounted for." He did not sound as triumphant as this information might suggest. "Three hundred and four died during the capture, and another twenty-two died in the cages." His ear tips were drooping over, and his whiskers trembled as he spoke. "None of the dead have been returned to their trees. Their bodies, I am told, were destroyed. That is very sad."

This news was met by shocked silence. Whytock stood abruptly, clasped his hands behind his back and paced around his chair, then around to the front again. He sat down, stood again, and began to pace back and forth with short, measured steps.

"How many have survived?" Rokey asked.

"Ninety-seven hundred and five."

"You learned your numbers well, I see," Whytock said, interrupting his pacing to stand face to face with Nate as he floated before them.

"It seems to be an important thing to know," Nate replied. "When we counted each other, I taught them each the number-names in SpeakEZ, as well. Everyone will, of course, remember what number they were in the count. That will help us to be organized in the future."

He almost smiled. "Some thought the number-names sounded very silly, and the younger ones liked that. We have alien names now, and we've become new."

Whytock sat down in his chair again. His heavy black eyebrows were arched almost to his hairline in astonishment.

"Rokey," he whispered. "What have I done?"

Rokey had been a teacher for too many years not to recognize the emotion. He smiled at Whytock, his whiskers spread wide. "You've started something," he said.

Nate went on. "I gave Massay the number-name of 'Zero'." He was speaking very seriously, clearly having thought about this a lot. "He is gone, but he should still be counted. Even though he is dead, he is the beginning of the count. Is that the right thing to do? Did I correctly understand what zero means, a place-holder for something that is not there?" He looked around at the solemn faces of the men. "I thought Massay would be pleased."

"I think he would be," Rokey agreed. "I would be, in his place – well, metaphorically speaking."

The Hupp were gathered in the garden at the center of the *Reach.* Whytock had set the atmosphere in the garden to higher humidity and raised the light level in there, using the frequencies of the Hupp sun needed by the photosynthetic cells in their skin. The illusion of distance and space was lost in the brightness. The great, open space, three stories high at the center of its domed ceiling, seemed small now and crowded, filled with floating people. They had collected into groups, village members keeping together, familiar faces clinging to each other. Some floated as couples, holding hands and tails entwined. Many were playing in the miniature waterfall on the hillside, riding the rush of water down the fall and swirling into the pond amid giggles and shouts.

Despite this, Rokey realized that the Hupp had simply been moved to a fancier cage. When would he be able to bring these people back to their village groves? Making them understand what was happening to them was not going to be easy.

"Will we ever get to go home?" Nate asked the men. He spoke quietly, as though he did not want the other Hupp to hear his question. "Will we return to our treehomes?"

"That is certainly our intention," Whytock replied, once he and Rokey had exchanged guilty glances.

"It is not safe now, though, is it?" Nate's voice had become a wistful whisper.

"Not just now, no."

"We intend to change that," Ray said firmly. "Terrans are responsible for this and Terrans should set it right."

Rokey looked at him in surprise. "When did you ever claim allegiance to your race?"

Ray met Rokey's gaze with a hard, unreadable look in his green eyes, his face serious. "We will get you home again, Nate," he said.

Our Separate Ways

Later that evening, however, alone with Ray and Whytock at dinner, Rokey did not feel the same certainty.

"Lord Rokhmyr and I have already discussed the difficulties that would arise if the *Shadow* were to travel with us to Wozur," Whytock said as he poured their wine, "nevertheless, it troubles me deeply that I would have to leave the two of you out there to face Richards' pursuit alone."

"The *Shadow* takes care of her own," Ray said with an automatic flare of pride.

Rokey understood the feeling. The *Shadow* was his home and she kept him alive, but the universe had become a much more dangerous place of late. He enjoyed the comforts of the *Reach,* comforts he had almost forgotten existed. He also knew that checkout time comes eventually even in the best of hotels.

"I'm going to miss you, too, Wystan," he said. "But it is more important than ever that you take these people to Hohlar."

"Yes, and it is more important than ever that we get some serious protection for that little world," Whytock said. "If we have to wait until Hohlar sets up a federal police station to guard them, we may find there is nothing left. I've been doing some serious thinking about that, and I have concluded that you have already found the right people to hire for private security."

He regarded Ray silently, puffing on his cigar so that smoke rose in lazy curls around his face.

Rokey had had this conversation with Whytock earlier, in

private. He had explained the many reasons why his young captain would resist this plan. Rokey did not like it much himself. There was just no time anymore to find people whom they knew they could trust. Under different circumstances, he would have preferred to take this problem to his old partner, George Humphrees. Unfortunately, Ray and Rokey had deliberately put as many light years as possible between themselves and George. He was further away than Wozur.

The two men sat quietly looking at Ray, who was staring down into his wineglass as though seeking the answer there, or else seeking a reason to say no.

"The *Tamaroan,*" he said at last with doomed finality.

"Well, only because George is too far away," Rokey said helpfully.

Ray winced.

"Do you think you can find them?" Whytock said.

"The question would be how long before *they* find *us,*" Ray said. "I'm sure that Lord Jak wants to know why we didn't wait for his messenger at the Sargasso."

"This will give you a chance to explain," Whytock pointed out.

"Won't it, though," Ray said glumly.

First Day at School

"Everybody walks at Rokherton U," Whytock said cheerfully as he stepped out the airlock. "They won't let you go to class until you can find your way to it! Learning to follow directions and to read maps is the first course they set you on."

Nate and Seff were tagging along, one on either shoulder. Whytock had a pair of matched brooches on his lapels, silver and gold anchor-shapes that the Hupp could wrap their tails around in order to be close to him as he walked. They found that this made conversation with Whytock easier. They had no difficulty speaking in their own language when deliberately puffing along, but the harder consonants of SpeakEZ demanded, literally, more air from them to speak. Letting Whytock pull them along gave them the air to talk to him. It also meant that they could afford to take in the sights and sounds of this strange new environment without fear of losing themselves.

"Doesn't anyone float?" Nate said, almost plaintively. "Is it all legs?"

"Not too many of the floating races can handle the atmosphere here," Whytock replied after a moment's thought. "The only ones I know of are from methane worlds. There is the Rokherton Aerie. That's for peoples who live exclusively on the wing. The University accommodates them at a campus high up in a mountain range west of here."

"But wings aren't floating," Seff said. "This strange concept of birds and feathers fascinates me, like us but so different. Will we meet some birds?"

"Once we're in the Park, yes, I should think we will see some. Whether any of the winged people are on this campus, well, that I couldn't tell you. When we're done with our business here, I will phone around and see if I can get you an introduction."

They were in a bright, open and sunny place; nevertheless, Nate felt uneasy and overwhelmed by the enormity of it. All he had ever seen of land was the narrow ridge of his atoll, a tenuous wisp of land in a great, wide ocean. The *land* here was the ocean, land from horizon to horizon wherever he looked, with trees in solemn rows along walkways filled with leggy beings rushing about their business. The flashing motion of all these legs as they walked, or in some cases, hopped, swiveled and undulated, seemed a windstorm of movement, like branches thrashing against the ground. It unnerved Nate, distracting him from the rest of the strangeness here.

"There are flowers everywhere!" Seff exclaimed in delight, interrupting Nate's preoccupation with legs. "They can't be from Hupp, but they look just like flowers!"

"'A rose is a rose on any world,'" Whytock said, "and I am quoting Lord Rokhmyr on that."

Nate had not yet paid attention to the riots of color spilling from windowsills and lining pathways, spiraling around the tree trunks and posts. He had merely registered the colors. Seff's keen eye had identified them. Whytock paused so that they could float over to a hedge beside the sidewalk that was blooming in brilliant shades of orange and crimson. Whytock immediately thrust his face deep into a mass of flowers, inhaling noisily and exclaiming over their perfume. Close up, the fragrance was powerful enough to taste. After a few breaths, it seemed to fill Nate's whole being with flavor and light. He touched the bright petals, astonished by the rich, smooth, moist texture. The blossoms were more complex than any Nate had seen, the leaves of some heavier stuff. He immediately thought of all the things he could make using leaves as tough as these, far denser than the fibers produced by plants on Hupp.

"Who knew when we went into that spaceship that we would find flowers at the end of the ride!" Seff spread his little arms wide to take in the wall of blossoms. "I'd love to meet every flower on this planet!" he declared happily, with his usual exaggeration.

Despite the captivating perfumes and flaming colors, something about these thick blossoms began to disturb Nate. He drew back slightly to survey the hedge as a whole. The leaves at the top fluttered in the slight breeze. Other than that, the bush was as still as if dead. He realized that the leaf he had touched and the flower he had pressed his face into had not responded.

"They have no voice," he whispered to Seff, speaking in their own language. It frightened him in an odd way, to see a plant look so alive and yet not. "They aren't really like flowers at all."

Seff drew back beside Nate and looked at the hedge. "It's still very pretty."

Whytock took their withdrawal as a signal, and continued his walk. "That would make an interesting tour," he said, responding to Seff's exclamation, "because this place has a lot of gardens, a lot of flowers. They're mad about flowers here, come to think of it. The ephemeral nature of student life, I suppose," he finished with a sigh.

Neither Nate nor Seff understood what that meant, but they were getting used to that with Wystan Whytock. Whytock had a lot to say and not all of it was to the people with whom he was talking.

"Why didn't the flowers speak to us?" Seff asked outright of Whytock. "Do the plants here only understand SpeakEZ?"

Whytock laughed. "Your world of Hupp is a rare find, my friends, because plants don't talk much in the rest of the galaxy. I mean, they do in places, and I can introduce you to some as time goes on, but by and large the plants you meet up with will be like this hedge." He ran his fingers gently against a leaf frond of the hedge for emphasis as he spoke. "They don't talk, or move or respond to us. They just are."

Nate looked back at the hedge as they crossed the street, watched its flame-colored shape standing in sad, brilliant, deathlike stillness. He thought about the concept "sentience," and wondered if he would ever get used to the idea of plants with no heart. It seemed wrong, somehow. Despite the strangeness of beings with legs, these plants struck him as by far the most truly *alien* beings he had yet encountered.

Seff, however, with his usual contrariness, thought the novelty of such plants quite pleasant. He asked all manner of questions about how could they live. What purpose did they serve if they could not offer up their seeds and fruit in proper season?

Nate found himself wondering why he had not noticed this about the plants in the garden on Whytock's starship. Looking at the garden in memory, he saw the same frozen stillness he was noticing now, yet it had not struck him with the same sense of the living-dead. He realized after a moment that it was because of the permanent twilight of the place. He had, without thinking, assumed that the plants were asleep. Plants were much more dependent on the intensity of the light on which they fed. He had been confused by their strange familiarity.

It was vaguely disturbing, so Nate concentrated instead on the many legs thrashing around them as the alien students hurried to and fro along the streets.

"There's someone I know!" Whytock announced, turning to stroll across a circular, open space surrounded by stores with neon signs in the windows. Whytock had taught Nate to read SpeakEZ during the flight to Wozur. Nate found that reading gave him the same emotion that Seff's very first note had given him, a kind of jolting thrill that was as much surprise as delight. Nate read the storefront signs to himself, wondering at the arcane meaning of things like "Chemist," and "Bandoleer."

Seff began exclaiming about the neon fixtures themselves, getting excited over the possibilities of painting the light-drenched colors into a scene. Whytock interrupted him by stopping in front of a chunky column of rock standing on the curbside. It was about waist-high to Whytock and a dark, mottled gray with pale green lichen growing in circles on one side. The sidewalk around it was thickly coated with drawings, powdery colors in a hodgepodge of images. Some were messages. Some were merely elaborate initials. Some struck Nate as being like Seff's paintings, even though clumsy and distorted. The images blazed in the afternoon sun with the crisp colors of flowers and bugs.

"Anyone at home?" Whytock called pleasantly as he rapped on the top of the column of rock. He folded his hands over the silver head of his walking stick and waited politely.

There was a moment of silence filled with distant voices from the streets.

"Could you put it up to seventy-eight rpm, fellows?" Whytock said after a moment. "These are mere human life spans you are dealing with here." He struck a pose before the column, facing it with a smile as if waiting for the stone to speak.

"This one remembers Wystan Whytock The Second." A voice emerged from somewhere inside the stone column, a voice like granite clicking up and down a musical scale. "This one had branched already for many seasons when Wystan Whytock The Second came first among our memories."

Whytock gently breathed a cloud of sweet cigar smoke over the figure as if pouring a benediction.

The statue chuckled like beads rattling in a glass. "Life form readings of Wystan Whytock The Second do not vary greatly from those of last appearance. This one is pleased."

"And you haven't changed an inch yourself, my friend." Whytock exhaled another cloud of smoke across the stone being.

It gave that bead-rattle laugh again. "You breathe better than most life forms, Wystan Whytock The Second."

Whytock grinned. "I can afford the right catalysts."

Nate looked at the stone being with a new appreciation. A fine sheen of rainbow colors gleamed on its rough surface from the dust blown across it off the sidewalk artwork. No part of it could be seen moving when it spoke, but Nate was used to that with his treehome. Indeed, this person was vaguely reminiscent of Tree, making Nate feel a wash of longing and nostalgia. He had been away so long.

"What have you seen, Wystan Whytock The Second?"

Whytock answered only after thinking visibly for a moment, screwing his face up and puffing grandly on his cigar. "I've seen more than most and less than some."

The stone being found this statement quite amusing and chuckled with its merry rattle. "This one inquires after your sister, Miss Wysteria Whytock. She is still cold?"

"Frozen stiff, thank you." Whytock's smile faded from his eyes for a moment, but he caught himself and puffed a cloud around the statue. "We had a fabulous visit a few years back. She's as lovely as ever and just as stubborn!"

"Then all in Wystan Whytock The Second's life is as it was. This one is pleased at such stability."

"Oh, my!" Whytock exclaimed, "I do have some friends to introduce to you. Meet my friends Nate and Seff."

Nate and Seff each reached out and touched the stone in greeting. Nate was surprised to find it felt warm against his hand.

"This is Osmo," Whytock said, patting the stonelike being on the top. "He's a dear school chum of mine, from my old days on campus. He's a Noggins, you know, and I don't suppose you've ever met a Noggins before. No, of course not! But Osmo has never met a Hupp. Did I tell you that, Osmo? These gentlemen are from Hupp, which you've never heard of before because no one has! Isn't that wonderful?"

"Expanding horizons of this one's knowledge is prime goal in being," Osmo said solemnly. "Meeting new friends of old friend is pleasure beyond words. This one wishes knowledge of new world of Hupp and most fortunate inhabitants."

Whytock sighed, leaking smoke. "If only they were, Osmo. Their world is in some danger, and that's why we're here."

"Knowledge is power," Osmo said, his stony voice solemn.

"It's what we don't know that brings us here, Osmo! I wish we had time to fill you in on the details, but we've been months getting here, and minutes might count."

"Excitement is prime ingredient in meeting with Wystan Whytock The Second, as always." Osmo added that rattling laugh. "Now Wystan Whytock The Second journeys to the Index, this one guesses. Validation brings security."

"Osmo always was a fast thinker," Whytock said to Nate and Seff. "He doesn't get around much, but he thinks like lightning."

"No energy lost in unnecessary motion," Osmo responded.

"That's why you haven't moved from this spot in two hundred years!"

"Two hundred and forty-seven years," Osmo corrected.

"Two hundred and forty-seven years," Whytock echoed

without losing a beat. "Can you imagine how much he must know about this place!"

Nate felt by Whytock's tone that he should be impressed by this. Instead, it made him wonder what was really intended. He had no idea of Whytock's age nor what that meant. He knew his own age if he thought about it. It was just not something often on his mind. Whytock was in a hurry for some reason yet he seemed reluctant to leave Osmo and continue on, which was curious. Nate compared the man's face at that moment to memories of the trip here. He realized that Whytock looked strained despite his smile, as though the pleasure of meeting this old friend had renewed an old ache.

"Osmo's real name takes an hour to say," Whytock said to Nate and Seff. "But, once you've heard it, you know everything he is and everything he's done!"

"Name is longer now, Wystan Whytock The Second. This one has learned a few things lately."

"I'll bet you have!" Whytock puffed up another benediction of smoke. "We call him Osmo because he learns by osmosis," he explained. "A great study technique, just soaking it all in. A technique I've tried to soak up myself!"

"This one is indeed soaked in knowing and stewed in it!"

The two laughed together as if this were an old joke between them.

"Osmo has certainly soaked up this corner of the world," Whytock went on. "He's been here all these years studying sociology and ecology."

"The ecology of social systems," Osmo corrected Whytock. "This one studies the nature of artificially maintained ecologies."

"Candy wrappers and spacesuit exhausts, right?" Whytock chuckled.

"Yes. Patterns of street litter and stray pets. Many such systems."

"You must know this corner pretty intimately by now."

"Too well. All patterns have repeated now. Every four generations patterns repeat."

"There are lots more places to study," Whytock suggested pleasantly. "Why don't you change spots?"

"Choice of next location is issue of internal debate. Voting has not worked. This one is of many minds."

"I wish I could help," Whytock said. "Sincerely. How did you choose this spot?"

"Random selection."

"An excellent choice!"

"Random selection, however, only works randomly. This one is stuck."

"An interesting problem," Whytock conceded.

"This one throws caution to breeze and accepts fate. Wystan Whytock The Second has provided random-chance event that will serve. You seek Index in search of security. This one will accompany Wystan Whytock The Second and new friends to Index Park."

"That's wonderful!" Whytock tucked his cigar away in his pocket and applauded. "I applaud your decisiveness!"

"This one gives thanks for inspiration. This one weighs, in surface-gravity of Wozur, seven hundred forty-two otts. In excess of capacity of Wystan Whytock The Second to assist in move?"

"Why, no, not in the least!" Whytock exclaimed. His face lit with warmth. "You would do me the honor of letting me carry you to your next spot?"

"Shared memories of moment will sustain this one in absence of Wystan Whytock The Second and new friends, Nate and Seff."

Whytock rubbed his palms together happily. "This will be a great pleasure, Osmo. Just tell me which side you want facing forward and we're off to the Index Park and the next adventure in the ecology of social systems!"

He tilted his head to Nate and Seff floating beside his face, smiling happily. "Isn't this exciting!" he said to them. There were two bright circles of warm color glowing on his pale cheeks. The trace of sadness Nate had seen was gone.

Whytock knelt to get his arms securely around the Noggins stony form, cradling it like a child, and he rose with a grunt.

Osmo giggled. "Suit tickles!"

"You always were caging for a hug, as I recall," Whytock said. "Any excuse."

"Contrast of surfaces provides pleasurable data."

"There! You see!" Whytock laughed. "Any excuse!" He set off at a brisk pace, pulling Nate and Seff along beside him. As he walked, he gave Osmo a shorthand account of the adventure that had brought them together.

Nate listened with only half an ear. He would review it later in memory. People walking past were beginning to turn around and follow them. Doorways were opening with an excited flurry of hushed calls and dramatic gestures. Whytock turned a few more corners, strolling along purposefully as he continued talking with Osmo. There was a parade following them at a polite distance behind. Whytock turned onto an even wider walkway lined with towering trees. The parade poured in after. There was growing talk and giggling among the crowd, and more of them were pointing to Whytock at the head of the parade.

Whytock strolled on, oblivious to the crowd following behind him, deep in conversation with Osmo. Nate drew himself in so that he rode closely against Whytock's shoulder. He tucked his fingers under the jacket collar as though anchoring against a hard wind. He had never imagined there could be so many different kinds of aliens in one place, all thrashing their inexplicable legs against the ground as they followed after him. Nate felt the flash of the fear he had felt on the beach, watching fog-creatures dying in rays of harsh light. The faces in the crowd were each different yet alike in their strangeness, and too many of them were clearly focused on him. Nate pressed closer against Whytock's shoulder and shivered as if cold.

Whytock noticed this. He paused in his sentence to glance down at Nate's face. "What's up, my friend?" he asked cheerfully. He saw Nate's frightened gaze, and he stopped to turn around.

"Oh, my!" Seff exclaimed in delight. "Look at all the *people!*"

"Oh, my," Whytock echoed. He was not delighted. "Look at all the people."

"Will they hurt us?" Nate whispered. He was suddenly breathless with fear.

"No." Whytock sighed sharply. "Not until they start talking." He turned back and strode on, more briskly now and without speaking.

Seff drew in and peered around Whytock's chin at Nate. "What does this mean?"

"Newsmen and Newstalk," Osmo piped up cheerfully. "Pattern repeats. This one was Newstalk at last change of spots."

"I should have thought of that," Whytock said. He spoke as though only to himself and he did not sound pleased. "Leave it to me to get caught up in the history of it."

Nate felt a renewed rush of fear. "What will they do to us?" he whispered.

Whytock glanced down at him, smoothing the distressed look from his face. He smiled apologetically. "Nothing physical, Nate. Don't worry about that. They will cost us some time, and they will make it possible for the wrong people to find out that we were here, and why we were here. It means that we will have less time when we leave here to make this work for everyone."

That sounded most ambiguous to Nate. He was not always certain of what Whytock meant when he talked, especially when he explained things. "They won't eat us?" he said, feeling foolish as soon as the words were out.

Whytock did not laugh. "They will not eat us. Under different circumstances they would make celebrities of you, but this is just not the time."

Nate decided he would ask later what "celebrities" was. At the moment he was just relieved that he could put away the sharp fear that the crowd following behind instilled in him.

The fear came back for an instant when a tall, narrow, dark-clad being pulled ahead of the crowd and caught up with Whytock, striding along beside and smiling down at him. Whytock glanced up at him with a frown and only nodded, picking up his pace. The man's eyes were big and much too shiny. He blinked with a faint clicking sound, reminding Nate of sand falling.

The man matched Whytock's stride. "Good afternoon, sir. Good Afternoon, Osmo. Congratulations on finally making the decision. Where have you chosen as your next spot?"

"Index Park," Osmo said. "In passing, old school chum carries this one along to next destination. Random chance breaks tie vote."

"Index Park." The tall, dark man nodded solemnly. "An excellent choice. What would the other choice have been, if I may ask?"

"Docks." Cosmo chuckled in his bead-rattle way. "Park is better."

Whytock strode on without speaking. Nate wondered why this man in black seemed so dangerous.

Those glinting eyes scrutinized Whytock's face. "And what brought you to Rokherton today, sir?"

Whytock slowed a little, frowning up at the man. His black eyebrows drew down in a v. "I'm afraid I have to invoke alumni privilege and ask to be left out of this. It is, after all, Osmo's occasion, is it not, Mr. Whicker?"

The man looked pleased that Whytock used his name. "Indeed, sir. As you wish." His black eyes clicked at them.

"And no pictures, please, not of me," Whytock added.

"Certainly, sir." Whicker reached up and tapped the side of his head as though reminding himself of something. "And do you speak for your guests, as well?"

"Yes, he does," Nate piped up, suddenly afraid of being seen as an animal.

Whicker tapped his head again, and strolled along beside them without speaking again.

This conversation had led them at last across a wide boulevard. They walked under an enormous arch of stone into the Index Park. Nate was overwhelmed again by the extent of the land, yellow-green lawns rolling across hills as far as he could see. The land here was as big as the ocean of Hupp. This place, this world of Wozur, had all the solid ground and safety that his world of Hupp did not.

"There," Osmo said. "Water. This one will stand beside water."

Whytock carried the Noggins over to a little meadow of flowers beside a mossy stream bank, and he set him down in the grass at its center. The parade of people crowded around the little hollow to watch. There were a few moments of moving the Noggins first a little this way and then that way, until he was completely satisfied with his relationship to the trees and water, selecting finally a spot between a weathered, mossy up-thrust of stone and a massive tree.

Mr. Whicker stood slightly to the side, arms folded behind his back, blinking steadily as he watched. With each blink, his eyes clicked.

"Grass tickles!" Osmo exclaimed in delight. "First important data about changed location – sidewalk does not tickle! Grass tickles!"

Laughter went around the crowd, and a group of children broke free to run up to him.

Whytock knelt on one knee beside Osmo, pouring that benediction of smoke one last time. "Good bye, old chap," he said softly. "I'll be back to chat when I have this problem taken care of."

"This one will hold dear moment of reunion and look forward to next one! Please to bring new friends Seff and Nate when you return."

"I'd like that," Seff said. "I want to ask you about all those pictures on the sidewalk."

Whytock hurried off, slipping away to a path leading under the trees.

This path led them to a towering structure that Nate thought at first was a wide stone hill, until he reminded himself that he had first thought the pirates' spaceships were "shiny cliffs." He stared hard at the gleaming thing as they approached it, yet he could make no sense of it. Whytock seemed to be carrying them toward a froth of gigantic bubbles splashed up against a massive wall of natural stone, bubbles bigger than the biggest treehome, bigger than the "shiny cliffs" that had turned out to be spaceships, bigger than anything Nate had ever seen. They shone brilliantly in the sunlight, reflecting the parkland around them with rainbow sheen.

Whytock pointed to this enigma. "That's the Index."

"It's beautiful!" Seff exclaimed breathlessly. He reached out and squeezed Nate's hand. "Did you ever see anything so beautiful?"

"I can't wait to see your paintings of it," Whytock said to him. "I myself think it is quite the most beautiful spot on the planet, and this is a lovely world!"

"That thing will help us?" Nate had to ask. "What does it

do?"

Whytock laughed. "It's just a building, my friend. The people who will help us work in there."

"A building? What is that?"

Whytock thought for a moment about how best to answer. "A spaceship that stays anchored to the ground," he said finally. "People live or work in them."

"Like our treehomes?" Seff said.

Whytock nodded. "Yes, and the Index was even grown like a tree, although not organically. Do you know what nanites are? No, of course, you don't, and there's no reason why you should!"

"Are they anything like money?" Seff asked.

Whytock laughed at that. "They might as well be!"

"Then I won't worry about them, either."

Whytock allowed as how that was probably a good idea. He went up to the gigantic bubble complex and walked right through the gleaming mirror of its surface without breaking stride. Seff and Nate pressed themselves abruptly against him in alarm. The bubble wall turned out to be an illusion. There was nothing there.

Inside the enormous space of the lobby, the air was cooler and dryer, with only the slightest whisper of breeze. Hints of incense and flowers filled every breath. The bubble's walls were invisible from the inside. They appeared to be high above the parkland, standing under an open sky, with a spectacular view of hills and trees and gardens below. Huge columns in varying shapes and sizes stood in irregular patterns, a forest of carved stone rising high into the sky. The tallest, widest such column stood directly opposite the entrance. A receptionist's desk seemed to float in fog at its base. Similar desks were placed at different angles at the base of the other columns, each with someone busily monitoring data-flow. Every desk floated in curling wisps of fog, and fog swirled around Whytock's feet as he walked. Seff was enchanted, and exclaimed at everything. Whytock was pleased.

He took them up to the main desk in front of them. The receptionist paused the work screen in front of him and presented a pleasant, brown-furred Wozurn face to them. "Good afternoon, Mr. Whytock," he said smoothly. "What a pleasure to see you again so soon."

"I do seem to be turning up more and more often, don't I?"

"I trust your gentleman's gentleman, Mr. Burke, is well?"

"Better than ever, thank you. I realize I have arrived unannounced," – Whytock began.

"As you always do," the receptionist said, with no trace of resentment. "Therefore, Lord Hohlar has standing orders that you may interrupt him without hesitation." He leaned forward with a hint of mirth in his metallic eyes. "I do believe that he looks forward to your little surprise visits!"

The Wozurn then nodded amiably to Nate and Seff. "Go right in, gentlemen." He gestured to the broad, densely carved column towering behind him. "I've signaled him that you're here."

Whytock strode toward the column with confidence, and did not hesitate as he walked right into the seemingly solid stone. The two Hupp cringed down against his collar, but the illusory wall swept over them without any sensation.

They blinked in astonishment. They were no longer in an office in a sunny, open place of towering columns. They were standing on a vast, darkened plain of tall grass stretching away to the far horizon under a starry sky. A night-breeze, sweet with grass scents, tugged at the Hupp's wide ears. The entranceway behind them was a dull panel of backlit glass standing alone in the grass. In front of them was a softly glowing cup of light, like a fragment of radiant eggshell. A stone workdesk floated in the midst of the light. A Wozurn with white fur sat at the desk, his head bent over a screen. He flicked his ears in greeting as they approached and carefully signed out of the desk.

Then he stood and held his hand out to Whytock. He nodded solemnly to Nate and Seff clinging to either side of Whytock's face. A comfortable-looking seat unfolded itself from the front of Hohlar's desk, and Whytock sat down, resting both hands across the silver head of his cane.

Hohlar settled back into his desk chair. He and Whytock began to exchange words in Wozurn, so rapidly that Nate and Seff had to look back and forth at them, waiting for the cue from Whytock to speak themselves.

I Could Have Danced All Night

Ray and Rokey had filled the *Yankee Shadow* with crates of fuel-cells from Whytock's seemingly infinite supply. Room to carry cargo was, for once, less important than the option to skip through link systems in a flash of light. They were able to keep moving on a spiral course through the known links toward the Sargasso, hoping to keep Richards' fleet searching for them without leading them back to Hupp.

Eight weeks of weary tension and four link systems had crawled past. They could at last hope that they had gained enough lead to keep Richards' fleet circling around in the maze behind them. For a time, anyway.

Arriving at the Sargasso was almost like coming home. There was even a car to meet them at the door, with armed guards wearing face-shields and security headsets. "Mr. Ricmorran wanted to be certain there were no interruptions, Lord Rokhmyr." The chauffeur was very polite. His eyes were invisible behind the shield, but his smile looked genuine.

"Interruptions?" Rokey said.

"What kind of interruptions?" Ray said, standing just behind Rokey.

"Just the usual, Your Honor," the chauffeur said.

The news, when they got to the owner's office, was also "just the usual." Lord Jak was not a happy man, and Ray and Rokey were in trouble.

"But it's just the usual, ordinary kind of trouble with him, Your Honor," Ricmorran said amiably as he filled their glasses. "Nothing like what you seem to have just gotten yourselves clean of." He then proposed a toast to the brave crew of the *Tamaroan.*

Rokey downed his drink in two deep swallows.

Ray sipped, wincing at the fumes. "How long ago did Jak's man leave?"

"Lord Jak's woman, actually. It was that icy creature of his, Zabor. Don't turn your back on that one, Your Honor," Ricmorran added, pouring a second libation for Rokey.

"Zabor?" Ray queried. "What's wrong with her?"

Ricmorran's ears pulled forward tightly in a gesture of concerned agitation. "Nothing too ghastly, just so long as you remember to treat her like the Queen of Here and Beyond."

The two Wozurn laughed harshly then at what must have been a joke peculiar to Wozurn thinking. Ray did not get it, and just sipped at his drink once more. He found himself suddenly eager to be on the move again.

"Pirates," he muttered softly to himself.

Rokey caught the undertone of impatience. He finished the last of the second drink. "'With all of the width of the star-lanes between us,'" he quoted, smiling up at Ricmorran and using SpeakEZ for Ray's sake. "'The seconds, they fly by like years.'"

He pushed himself unsteadily out the chair. Ray was standing beside him once he was on his feet. "We had best be flying on ourselves, Ric," Rokey went on. "We may already be out of time."

"Zabor has taken some kind of dislike to your captain there, Your Honor," Ricmorran said with uneasy twitches of his whiskers at each word. He could not meet Ray's fierce eyes. "She left a team of assassins here to wait for him. I've got them under surveillance, but I'm not taking any chances."

"Assassins?" Ray felt a sweep of bewildered hurt. "Me? I hardly know the dame."

"I have not yet explored that question, Captain Harris," Ricmorran said to him. "As I said, I have them under surveillance, but I did not want to tip my hand with them until you and His Honor had gotten the message and were under way. Once the *Shadow* is safely out the window, I intend to round up the lot of them and ask some pointed questions."

"May I sharpen some of the points before we go?" Ray said. His flash of anger had settled into cold determination.

There You Are

The rendezvous point in space was as gloriously beautiful against the backdrop of stars and dust as it had been the first time. The fleet of *Tamaroan* fighters waiting there in battle-stance spoiled the view. The fleet-commander signaled them only that the *Tamaroan* would be in radio-range in two hours, and that the *Shadow* should make no move until then. Ray and Rokey sat in their bridge seats, waiting. There was no way to predict how Jak would respond, nevertheless they did a lot of speculating.

"This thing with Zabor is a surprise I can't quite figure," Ray said. "I got the impression back at the party that she didn't like me, but to go to the bother of sending assassins? I just don't get it."

"Motherhood is the source of some strange ideas," Rokey said.

"Assassins are *expensive,* too," Ray went on, then he stopped, caught at last by Rokey's words. "Motherhood?" Ray considered this for a moment. "What? She wants me dead so I can't tell anyone where her children are?"

"Maybe."

"You noticed, I suppose, that Ricmorran said that the assassins were after *me,* singular, just me, and not us, you *and* me, plural."

Rokey nodded, rubbing his face with his hands in an attempt to smooth away the agitation. "Noted."

"And you *do* know where they are, too."

"I know where the children are, yes."

"So, why me?"

Rokey leaned forward, peering out the front shield at the starfighters grouped around them and poised to strike, glittering like angry fireflies. "I'll do what I can to find out, son. Meanwhile, you keep your eyes and ears open and your mouth shut."

"Should I get out the uniform again?" Ray said darkly.

Rokey shook his head. "Not this time."

The *Tamaroan* arrived with hull lights blazing and her heavy guns drawn and ready. Ray let Rokey do the talking. He understood enough Wozurn to follow the dialog as Rokey and Jak snarled and yelled at each other over the radio. To Ray's great relief, he could also hear Briggs interrupting her husband with steady, insistent demands that he shut up and let Lord Rokhmyr explain.

Jak shut up, and Rokey explained.

When Rokey was finished, the connection remained open. The radio was silent while Lord Jak considered their story and the offer a job with the wealthy Mr. Whytock. A long, tense minute, then another passed, and he said nothing. Ray concentrated on the fighting ships surrounding the *Shadow* and tried to keep his breathing steady.

"This is not good for radio broadcast, Your Honor, even on an encrypted beam." Lord Jak's voice was calmer, suddenly thoughtful. "The docking matrix is opening for the *Shadow.* Briggs and I will be in the docking bay as soon as you are onboard, and we will board the *Shadow* to speak with you in private. We have much to discuss."

The fighters withdrew with perfect precision, regrouping into escort formation.

Ray and Rokey fired up the engines and eased the *Shadow* over to the *Tamaroan's* docking matrix, guided in by starfighters on every side.

Rokey had a big carafe of coca warming in the galley once they were fully docked and secured. He sent Ray out with a tray of mugs for Jak's guards standing watch outside the *Shadow's* main airlock and the two at the base of the ramp. Ray did not stay to chat. The guards would not quite meet his eye. Ray knew that with Wozurn this was a bad sign.

Jak and Briggs arrived in a cloud of anxiety, old, long-standing anxiety that saturated their fur and made them seem large and jagged in Rokey's senses. The three exchanged formal greetings, and Briggs spoke with jittery distraction. Rokey led them to the spacious galley, and they seated themselves while he set out the tray with the carafe and mugs. He poured the cocoa from an exaggerated height to make it foam up as it filled the mugs, and to draw out the aroma. The rich chocolate began at once to smooth away the bite of their fear-scent. Jak and Briggs both visibly relaxed as the fragrant steam filled the galley.

"There was no sign of any kind of trouble at the school," Rokey reassured them for the third or fourth time as he poured. "They even had good weather," he added.

Briggs put her hand on Jak's arm before he could pound the table, and she snapped, "We haven't got time for your nonsense now, Jak." Her Wozurn dialect made the word "nonsense" very serious in its implications. The blaze in her golden eyes made her determination equally serious. "Lord Rokhmyr has a plan that can save those little people *and* solve our problem, so let's cut to the details and start planning this operation."

Jak sagged back on the galley bench, looking over at Rokey with a rueful tilt to his whiskers, his ears drooping over. "Didn't I tell you, Your Honor? Most organized mind I ever met."

Rokey flicked his whiskers in sign of full agreement, feeling a rush of relief that he had these people as allies. "Where do you want me to stand, ma'am?" he said cheerfully. His ears were straight and wide, and he was glad he was wearing his Wozurn collar of status.

Briggs' silken fur rippled as she reached across the table to rest her hand on Rokey's arm. "The first step is to get our children, to take them out of there, to evacuate the place completely."

She pointed to the deck at their feet, a gesture that implied the *Tamaroan* herself, the giant starship in which the *Shadow* was parked. "We are almost at jump-speed now. We will be through the window in a matter of hours."

"In which case," Rokey said, his voice heavy and concern clear in his solemn cadence. "We have something else that must be unraveled."

He told them of the assassination team who had been waiting for Ray Harris at the Sargasso.

Lord Jak reacted with a pained, stunned silence, his eyes sick and getting sadder as he thought through the implications of this news. He sank down into his seat, staring at his hands gripping the cocoa mug.

Briggs spent thirty seconds in an impassive study of her husband's face, her own face unreadable behind the groomed, flame-red fur and her hooded eyes. Then she flicked at a jewel set into the outer edge of her right ear that was evidently a communications module. In a clear, commanding voice, she ordered a combat team on red-alert and ready to peel off before the jump. They were to set course for the Sargasso, with very secret, very specific orders.

Rokey leaned forward and rested his hand over hers. "Tell them to say that Lord Rokhmyr sent them to ask Ricmorran for the report. Tell them to ask nice."

Briggs' intense look broke into a flare of pleasure, and her eyes smiled. She relayed the message, then flicked the jewel again to sign off.

"We must get the children away from there," she said to Rokey. "I want to help the Hupp, but this is now more important."

She could not meet his eyes, and her long whiskers were drawn back tightly. "If it is not already too late."

They both looked over at Jak, who sat unmoving, staring inwardly. They said nothing. Grief was clear with his every breath and gesture. Finally, he sighed deeply and looked over at Briggs with reddened eyes. "I'm so sorry, Love," he murmured to her, using the most tender of Wozurn terms that was "my love, my kitten, my mate, my destiny, my other self, my source," expressed in a single, soft syllable. It was a syllable used only in private.

Rokey made himself notice that the cocoa carafe needed refilling. He got up from the table, picking up the carafe without a word, and went over the other side of the galley.

"Zabor is under full surveillance," Jak explained to Ray and Rokey carefully, almost apologetically. "As long as she doesn't know that, anything and everything she says or does will condemn her, but we have to find out how far her corruption has spread among the crew, who is loyal to her. If she knows that we have found her out, we will never learn. We could end up destroying ourselves with suspicion."

"There are ways of making *anyone* talk," Ray said coldly.

"She is the mother of my children!" Jak protested, almost whispering. He had diminished, somehow, in the last hours. The price of their exile had never before been so large nor so unwieldy.

"I will let her condemn herself, but I will *not* force the truth from her."

Ray caught the glare that Rokey was glaring at him, and he shut up.

"They haven't explained yet why she picked *me* to pick on," Ray grumbled once they were alone.

"We'll find out soon enough," Rokey said with clear dismay at the anticipated news. "We won't like it when we find out, but we'll find out. It will be awful news, and this thing will just get worse."

Ray got up and put ice in a pitcher and poured in half a bottle of Kaheer Water, swirling the pitcher slowly to chill the potent liquor. When Rokey talked so morosely, there was only one cure.

Rokey grinned tightly. "The Lord Rokhmyr's Squire knows his job well, he does."

"Yes, sir, Your Honor, sir," Ray said. He held out a glass, tinkling with ice.

"Just stay away from the Queen of Here and Beyond."

"You know it!" Ray said.

Ray did indeed avoid contact with the tall, icy Zabor. The many decks and corridors of the enormous *Tamaroan* made that easy. He guaranteed that he would avoid her by the simple expedient of staying in his quarters onboard the

Yankee Shadow during the flight through intraspace. The guests who dropped by to visit with him were delightful, bringing with them sumptuous feasts of the trader-ship's finest delicacies and most delicate finery. Ray even bothered to remain sober so that he could savor the experience.

Zabor, however, *was* onboard the starship, no matter how many decks and corridors there were between them. The dangerous mystery of her desire to kill Raymond Harris put the wrong kind of edge on the excitement. Ray knew, behind the fun, that he was under self-imposed house-arrest for his own protection.

School's Out

"I knew you'd come, Father. I just knew!"

The radio signal was faint, ragged with the jamming interference from the siege-fleet, yet the words rang with the clear, high-pitched sweetness of a child's voice.

"I knew you would come to save us!"

Lord Jak's howl of outrage filled the bridge, resonating through the wooden dais his throne sat on, a rage loud enough to drown out the blare of the battle-station alarms ringing through the ship.

The siege-ships had been sighted as soon as the *Tamaroan* dropped into space. The first line of fighter squadrons launched immediately, going in at high-speed to attack the siege-satellite systems. The power satellites brought by the *Yankee Shadow* at such awful cost were gone, replaced by spy-eyes, sky-shooters and massive ray-shielded siege-platforms. These created an extensive net around the planet that would not be easily sliced away.

Enemy ships began launching at the same time from the orbiting platforms, burning fuel in a race to intercept the *Tamaroan's* fighters.

Briggs remained seated at the control panel beside Jak's right hand, giving rapid orders into her headset while scanning the steady data-feed of the battle scrolling past on multiple monitors. Her eyes were bright red with fury, and the set of her face made her look like the real Queen of Here and Beyond.

On the planet below, the lands surrounding the school were burning, millions upon millions of acres pouring smoke into the sky, with millions of acres more blackened, decimated, smoldering and charred. The entire continent appeared wounded. The holo-projected view from long-range scopes showed that the force-fields over the campus remained intact, holding back the thick smoke of the burning land, but buildings inside the shielding had fallen.

A grim, difficult, busy silence reigned throughout the ship. The heartbeat pound of booted feet running across the decks to duty stations counter-pointed the voiceless hand-signals and flashing visuals on every monitor. The *Tamaroan* was at war.

"*Tamaroan,* you have Captain Raymond Harris onboard – *my* Captain Harris."

The radio signal from the siege-platform was strong and rang loudly in the bridge. "Return my dear boy to me. Bring him to me quickly, *Tamaroan.* If you keep my Captain Harris away from me much longer, I will drop a very large rock right on top of your children."

Van Zandt followed the demand for Ray Harris with a visual of the "rock" that he had towed into orbit, a two-kilometer wide mass of nickel and iron. The visuals he broadcast showed the hot, glowing modules of the engines he had installed in that rock, powered-up and ready to fire. These primitive nuclear engines would not only slam the asteroid into the planet with terrifying force, but would also themselves explode with dirty, death-dealing results.

Ray and Rokey recognized at once who was speaking. Both men felt the same body-blow of dismay and guilt. Apparently, without knowing or intending it, they had led the demented madman, Colonel Johann van Zandt, directly to the children of the *Tamaroan.*

Lord Jak sat forward on his bridge throne, resting his hands across his thighs, staring at Rokey beside him. Jak's whiskers were flared back, his ears twitching as though he wanted to lay them flat against his head and snarl. His eyes, however, were dark with pain, and he said nothing.

Briggs stepped up beside her husband, resting one hand

lightly on his arm, looking down at him with calm, clear compassion. Their eyes met for a moment.

Before Briggs could speak, however, Zabor strode onto the bridge with such vivid determination that it was as if she had shouted in triumph as she entered. She had an entourage of armed guards behind her, each carrying an oversized flame-thrower aimed at the bridge crew.

Ray and Rokey, in the same gesture, moved behind Lord Jak's throne so that he was between them and Zabor.

"I will *personally* deliver Captain Harris to Johann," she announced to the entire bridge. The diamonds in her ears flashed as she turned her head, looking back and forth from Lord Jak to Briggs. "I promised Johann that prize so many months ago."

"Those are *your* children down there," Briggs exclaimed. The Wozurn syllables were a cry of grief. "*Your* children!"

Hatred flared in Zabor's stance, the sharp intake of breath, the flash of diamonds as she laid her lovely ears back flat and hard against her skull, revealing harsh outlines of the revulsion, confusion and rage gripping her. "Yes, I am their mother," she said, biting hard on each word, "but they call *you* 'Lady Jak' and they tell *me* how much they love you. They can go to hell *with* you!"

Lord Jak had not moved, observing his once-beloved with sad, weary eyes. "Why, Zabor? There were easier ways for you to have what you wanted." His big voice was surprisingly quiet.

"This was the only way I could have *him,* to have Johann!" Zabor responded at once. "Johann will have no peace until he has this boy-toy captain in his bed, this little soldier-man he craves. I am the only one who can bring him that peace."

The imperious arrogance in her stance diminished slightly. She spoke with a hint of pleading, eye to eye with Lord Jak, father of her children. "Johann will finally stop wasting time chasing shadows. He will have time to be with *me.*"

"You know that I would have given you the freedom to go to him," Jak said, "if you love him so much."

Zabor seemed almost uncertain. Her whiskers flared out straight, then drew flat to her face, and she took a deep gulp of air before speaking. "This was the only way I could bring

Johann his boy-toy. I needed the *Tamaroan's* business as cover to lure him to Johann."

The arrogance returned and she added, with a sneer in her voice, "I needed the good and organized mind of Captain Briggs to find him."

"Little Wennofar and the boys," Lord Jak said softly, sadly, "you would risk *them?*"

She raised her flame-thrower higher, aimed it directly at Briggs. "Then let me take Captain Harris to Johann!" Her voice was shrill, harsh, loud and afraid.

Lord Jak shook his head slowly, with a terrible sadness in his reddened eyes. "No, my girl. Not this time. You don't get your way this time."

Her gun hand was steady, however uneven her voice. "I'll take Harris' corpse to him if I have to," she said loudly. "That will make Johann just as happy." She flicked an icy-hot glance at Ray, standing behind Jak, and added. "Johann can have him stuffed and mounted."

She drew herself up, regaining her furious composure. With a sharp gesture of her gun hand, she ordered two of her guards forward. She pointed to Ray Harris, standing behind Lord Jak. "Take him. Don't mess him up too much."

Ray had put his hand on his laser hilt the moment Zabor walked in, but he had not moved since. He knew that it was stupid to be the first one to fire for the wrong reason in a room full of guns. Zabor's guards could not win here, ultimately, in an all-out shooting assault. The death toll nonetheless would be appalling before they were done. A flame-thrower in close quarters was vicious enough. The use of them against furred opponents was intentionally evil. Ray could feel the outrage boiling inside, but he had learned through hard experience that he had to put that particular sear of outrage in the background. He kept his focus on Zabor, while listening to every sound, ready to draw, just as ready to drop to the deck and crawl under the throne if he thought it would help. Therefore he noticed the faint hissing sound overhead even before Rokey did.

Ray did not let himself react or look up. He stepped forward, free of Lord Jak's protective bulk, and said loudly. "No shooting, Zabor. I'll go quietly."

Every eye and ear turned from Zabor to him. Rokey put his hand out as if to stop him, then drew back.

Ray raised his voice again, to cover the faint hissing overhead. "I can't let these people risk their children. No shooting, and I'll go quietly."

Ray had been guessing about the meaning of that slight noise. He was therefore not surprised when he found suddenly that he was no longer standing but had sunk to his knees on the dais steps. He tried to raise his head to look around. He fell over instead. From the angled perspective of the floor he could see bridge crew falling into heaps before their stations. He tried to see if Zabor and her guards had also fallen. Everything stopped, seeing, hearing, thinking.

Ray woke up with a start, his senses abruptly alert and his head ringing with an odd, spiking pain. He was lying on the steps of Lord Jak's throne-dais. The bridge crew was once again busily managing the data-flow of the battle. Rokey was bending over him, and put a hand gently on Ray's chest when he tried to sit up.

"You have to let the antidote circulate for another minute or two," Rokey said. Concern was clear in his voice. He was lightly touching Ray's throat with his long whiskers, checking pulse and breathing. "Lie still."

"Who did that?" Ray spoke softly so that his voice would not make his head vibrate too much.

"Captain Briggs. It's some kind of emergency defense system she had secretly set up to knock out everyone on the bridge with sleeper-gas, then let her private guards come in and sort out the players." Rokey showed his amusement, eye to eye with Ray in a look that said volumes. "Jak's right about how organized she is."

"How long was I out?"

"A few minutes, that's all." Rokey told him. "Zabor and her people are on their way to detention," he added.

"So who kicked me in the head?" Ray wanted to know, even though it hurt to speak.

Rokey chuckled. "That sleeper-gas was designed for

Wozurn and Phridyan biology. You're just lucky it didn't kill you."

"Tell me that later when we're sure I lived through it." Ray gave another try at sitting up, and found the throb in his skull had faded to just a nasty ache.

Rokey swept Ray's throat once more as he helped him to his feet. "Your blood pressure is getting back to normal. Your head should clear in a few minutes."

"We have to get those children out of there," Ray said quietly to Rokey as he resettled his jacket.

"Briggs left in one of the transports going down after them." Rokey cast a glance to Briggs' empty bridge seat. "Other ships are launching to pick up the school staff."

"Van Zandt meant it," Ray said. "He'll throw that rock at them." The pounding ache was fading. His brain was not yet reset to fully awake mode, and terrible images of the kind of death that hovered over this world flashed through him, mixed with vivid memories of the children he had met when they delivered the satellites, their faces and their names, the naked arrogance of those young inheritors of their parents' exile. Without fur, the Wozurn children did resemble Earthling children. Ray had actually let himself believe that he had done something right, something good for them. Ray steadied himself by putting his gloved hand on the armrest of Lord Jak's throne.

The big Wozurn paused in the orders he was dictating to his adjutant, turning his head to look at Ray. His whiskers tipped forward in a gesture of query.

"Let me pilot the next transport that launches," Ray said clearly. He was trembling inside from the chemical assault, but he clung to his resolve. "I have to be out there, flying with those transports. There's no other way to stop him from destroying everything down there. As long as he doesn't know *which* ship I'm flying," Ray went on, "he won't dare shoot at *any* of them. He may not care if I'm dead or alive, but he doesn't want the pieces blown apart and burned."

Lord Jak nodded reluctant agreement, and snapped quick orders to his adjutant.

"The orderly to take you to the launch bay is waiting in the main corridor," he said to Ray. "Two transports have launched already. The escort teams are in launch position and waiting for you."

Ray strode off across the bridge at a half-run.

Rokey stepped up closer to Lord Jak on the dais. "I'll take one in as well."

Lord Jak shook his head at this. "No," he said in Wozurn. "I want," – he paused – "I *need* you here on the bridge, Your Honor."

The strain was clear. Rokey consented, and silently took Briggs' seat beside the throne.

"We must convince van Zandt that your squire really is flying one of our ships," Lord Jak went on. "My Briggs is out there. We have to convince him quickly, Your Honor. You can do that."

Rokey said, "I can do that," but his throat was dry.

There Goes the Neighborhood

The transport ship flew like the big, wide double-decker bus with lift engines that it was, wallowing into the atmosphere of the resort-school planet with a splash and sizzle of heated shields. The ragged clouds of smoke from the burning land obscured sight even high up in the atmosphere, leaving radar and sonics to guide them in. Ray had to concentrate closely on the unfamiliar controls. He pushed the transport into a steep descent to the campus below, and he could only hope that the escort fighters flying alongside knew how to stay out of his way.

Rokey's message to van Zandt had apparently gotten through. The enemy fighters changed tactics, no longer attacking the *Tamaroan's* transports or escort ships. The shielding over the school had been dropped to let the transports in, and van Zandt's fighters began to swoop in on ground-strafing runs. Laser-sparked chemical rockets exploded and burned with devastating fury. The transports' escort fighters were taking these attackers out one by one with coordinated precision. Enough fire was getting through, however, to threaten the people making the run from underground bunkers to the landing field and the transports.

By the time Ray landed, the campus was ablaze, pouring thick, choking smoke into the air. As he brought the ship in for landing, he could see figures, their faces hidden behind breathing masks, waiting in the billows at the edge of the field. They began running toward the transport as soon as the struts touched ground.

Ray had the outside security-eyes on and he stayed in the

pilot's seat, watching the screens carefully as transport crew members hurried people up the loading ramps and onboard. The engines were powered-on, ready to leap skyward the instant Ray touched the release. When the last of the people waiting on the field were onboard, the crewmen signaled the "all clear" and began drawing up the ramps.

Ray's sharp eye caught a movement in the smoke at the edge of the field. His hand remained steady over the release tab.

"Captain!" Someone yelled from the corridor. "We're loaded! Everyone's in!"

Ray searched hastily through the overhead controls, selected the portside comlink and shouted, "Ramp down – now!"

"Captain!" the protest was from the co-pilot this time. "We have to get out of here!"

Ray pointed to the monitor view of the landing field and the campus. The figure was partly visible now, stumbling toward them through the smoke, a lone figure with no breathing mask, hunched down under the weight of the limp body it was dragging along.

"Rescue team!" Ray shouted into the com. Unnecessarily, since three crewmen were already running down the ramp as it lowered to the field.

When the crewmen had these last two survivors safely onboard and the ramp was up, Ray released the engines and the transport roared back into the smoking skies.

The five transport ships were overloaded, with people crammed into every space and huddled in groups in the aisles and corridors. The engines were pushed to capacity as the heavily burdened craft lumbered skyward. Each pilot struggled with the need for speed and the effort of balancing the overload.

The giant *Tamaroan* was straining her own engines, racing to cover the deep-space distance to the transports. Van Zandt's fighters had regrouped into a single attack. Van Zandt had, indeed, ordered his fighters away from any ship that might have Ray Harris at the helm. He hurled them with renewed fury at the *Tamaroan* herself. Lord Jak's fighters were engaged in the battle over the planet and too far away to help, leaving only the ship's onboard guns as protection. She was taking damage.

Behind them, just out of range, van Zandt's flagship waited, shielded by the same hunk of rock with which he threatened the planet below.

A Seat for His Honor

Once safely docked with the *Tamaroan,* Ray remained in the pilot's seat, stoically enduring the stench of smoke, burned fur and flesh, the moans and cries. The *Tamaroan's* emergency crews were brisk and well-trained, yet the shock showed as much in their faces as in the faces of the wounded. There was a scramble as the returning ships docked, and parents began searching for their children amid the chaos. Frantic voices calling names added a fierce edge to the cries of the wounded.

The transport's monitors showed the pursuing fighter ships surging after the *Tamaroan.* Ray could feel through the soles of his boots the heavy vibration of the giant ship's massive engines as she raced toward the safety of the intraspace window. He watched in the monitors as the last of the *Tamaroan's* escort flyers returned and docked.

Ray flinched with a physical response to the sight as the last two flyers, trailing behind, were blasted to space-dust by van Zandt's pursuit ships. Ray had been running from van Zandt's so-called love for too many years. Too many people had died. Van Zandt continued to cling to the trail of the *Yankee Shadow,* a maddened, love-struck hell-hound flinging lives after him like fleas in the wind, slaughtering anyone who got in the way of his obsession.

Ray did not try to leave the transport bridge until everyone had been triaged and taken to safety. He could only get in the way of the real work. He was weary beyond words, drained by the encounter with the sleeper-gas and exhausted in every muscle as though he had carried the overloaded transport up from the planet on his back. Ray recognized the particular degree of fatigue, and knew it was psychological, not physical. If he tried to sleep, he would only twitch and stare, seeing dead faces in the blackness behind closed eyes.

When the chaos and anguish had diminished to the murmured conversation and soft commands of the cleanup crew, Ray finally relinquished the pilot's seat and went in search of Rokey. Ray was wearing the flight suit, and even he could smell the smoke in the fabric and clinging to his skin and hair. He was abruptly reminded of his condition when he entered the bridge. Everyone paused for a heartbeat in their work to notice him, to turn to stare at him, whiskers wide and nostrils flared.

To Ray's amazement, he saw Rokey seated on Lord Jak's bridge-throne, apparently in command. Jak's tall, gray-furred adjutant was standing beside Rokey, explaining data scrolling past on the throne monitors. Rokey looked up when he smelled Ray enter the bridge, and waved him over.

Ray strode over. "Did you stage a coup or something while I was gone?"

"Don't be cute, son," Rokey said with little amusement. "There isn't time. This ship hasn't reached the window yet. We're vulnerable."

"We?" Ray's amazement grew. "We? Suddenly, you're one of *them?*"

"I am as long my furry ass is parked on this thing!"

The adjutant interrupted Rokey with a polite demand for a decision on damaged docking bay doors. "Your Honor, can we make the window jump with that large a gap in the hull?"

"Don't you know?" Rokey asked him.

"We've never taken this much damage before, Your Honor," the adjutant replied unhappily. "It's in the projections, but we don't have any experience with it."

Ray stepped in. "The magshielding will hold over the gap, and you will be able to patch the doors once we're in intraspace, as long as you set the door and frame into the hull in one piece, with a fifteen-percent interior edge overlay to take the mag-bolting."

The adjutant looked at Ray uneasily, then said to Rokey, "Sir?"

"What he said." Rokey waved a hand at Ray. "He knows intraspace engineering better than I do."

"Better than most do," Ray muttered.

The adjutant nodded and dashed back to his post to relay the order to engineering, but he cast a worried glance over his shoulder as he ran.

While confirming orders and assessing damage reports, Rokey filled in the details of how he came to be in command of the *Tamaroan.*

"Jak made the mistake of going to Zabor in the holding cell, and he compounded the mistake by going in to see her alone."

"That was stupid," Ray agreed. "What did he do that for? To pardon her?"

"He wanted to know how much she had told van Zandt about the *Tamaroan's* defenses," Rokey explained. "He thought that, for the children's sake, she would tell him."

"She tried to kill him instead?" Ray said, taking a guess at what had transpired.

Rokey nodded. "She had more secret confederates in the crew, evidently. She put a delft-knife into his gut, then she and her friends escaped and jumped ship. We tracked them docking with van Zandt's command ship about twenty minutes ago."

Ray wanted to laugh at the enormous absurdity of the situation, but he felt the terrible sadness behind everything. Instead, he quietly asked what had happened to Captain Briggs.

"She tried to stop Zabor's ship from escaping."

Ray could not bear to ask the next question. He just looked up at Rokey.

"They got her to hospital in time," Rokey went on. "She'll live."

"So, meanwhile, you're in charge here?"

"On the Wozurn social scale." Rokey spoke softly, using SpeakEZ so that only Ray would follow what he said. "I outrank Lord Jak by some several degrees. I have been nominally in charge here anytime I was onboard."

"You sure kept *that* quiet," Ray protested.

"I don't like to take advantage," Rokey responded with a

glint of humor. "Besides, I was drunk most of the time I was here."

"You sure you're sober now?"

"I'm only sure that this is one messed-up situation!"

"Do you think Jak let her escape?"

Rokey sighed. "He could have broken her in two with his bare hands." He shook his head sadly. "He wanted her to escape."

"That's stupid," Ray said. He said it very softly.

"That's love."

"For Zabor? But he married Briggs!"

Rokey nodded. "He married Briggs. He worships her. He worships Briggs' energy, and her intelligence and skill," – he sighed again – "But he's in love with Zabor."

"He told you that?"

"He didn't have to. I know what fatherhood does to a man."

Ray took a long moment to digest this, seeing the bridge, the *Tamaroan* and their mission now with different eyes. He stepped up to the throne monitors and made himself focus on the damage-reports streaming past, and on the data for the ship's progress toward the window.

"Your Honor, I may only be your squire, but you need someone helping you who knows how to fly," he muttered. "So let's see where we are and whether or not we can get where we're going."

A Broken Heart and a Promise Kept

Lord Jak summoned Ray and Rokey as soon as he was conscious. They were met at the entry to sickbay by Sejan, the elder of the Jak's twin sons. He was young enough that he was not yet furred, and he wore a fresh set of green deck fatigues. He was almost as tall as Ray, muscled like an athlete, with his mother's clear, white coloring and diamond-hard blue eyes.

"You held the transport for me," Sejan said to Ray in SpeakEZ by way of greeting. "You saved my life. None of the other transport pilots saw me, and I was sure I would be left behind."

"You were trying to save someone yourself," Ray said to Sejan. "We heroes have to stick together."

The young Wozurn showed the signs of the ordeal, with burn marks on his face and ears and a haggard look in his eyes, but he had already learned his father's spirit of self-command. He saluted Ray crisply, then led them to the private room where Lord Jak and Briggs were recovering. Both men were dismayed by the Wozurn's ragged demeanor and weakened voice.

He was surrounded by the machinery, tubes and panels of the hospital unit and attended by an army of doctors, nurses and secretaries, no longer the giant in charge of his world. Briggs was in a similar ICU cradle across the room. She had not recovered enough to be awake, and Jak kept looking over to her as he spoke.

"You can't hold yourself responsible for what happened down there, Your Honor," he said sadly. "We were crazy to think we could just tuck our children away in a safe nook and fly on with our lives."

"They were safe there until I came along," Ray said. His inwardly turned focus on grief and guilt was blurred by the enormous rage burning just out sight. He was powerless to stop van Zandt, and there was no other target but himself.

"We were fooling ourselves, Captain Harris," Lord Jak countered wearily. "They were never truly safe there. It is only because of your suffering that our eyes were opened in time to save them."

Rokey felt his own guilt as a large and unwieldy addition to the decades of guilt and remorse that his self-imposed exile had already brought, a helplessness far greater than anything Ray understood. Rokey was powerless to stop the corruption and stagnation of generations and nations. These people were casual bystanders randomly victimized. This was only the latest outbreak.

Sejan went over to stand beside Briggs and stood with one hand resting over hers, looking down anxiously at her unconscious form.

Lord Jak continued, "Zabor is responsible. I refuse to let you carry her guilt. You warned us in time to save the children. She was willing to betray her own children just to help van Zandt trap you. She would have done that for something else she wanted. You warned us in time to save them."

Lord Jak gestured weakly to Ray. "You saved my son, Captain Harris. You saved Sejan, and I will always be especially in your debt for that."

He waved away a doctor who was protesting the changes in his blood pressure and the strain on his injured organs. "I called you here, Lord Rokhmyr, to reassure you that the people and resources of the *Tamaroan* are pledged to the protection of the world of the Hupp. What happened to our children does not change that."

His deep sigh alarmed the doctors even more, and he snapped at them with a flare of his usual command.

"We will go on now and establish a base in the Hupp system," he went on to Rokey, "and we will be the guardians of those little people for as long as they need us."

"It could be for a very long time," Rokey said.

Jak's whiskers twitched upward in a Wozurn smile. "Good."

The doctors insisted they had to let Lord Jak rest.

Rokey paused on the threshold long enough to look back at the injured couple, themselves diminished by the enormity of the fate that had fallen across their lives, and at the tall, proud boy standing beside them. Victims of love.

Ray's primary concern became the danger of leading van Zandt to Hupp. He brought the question up whenever he and Rokey were alone together and both of them were sober. Rokey gave him the same answer whenever Ray brought it up. The dark concern that drove Ray would not let go of him.

"That's why we're bringing the *Tamaroan* and her people to Hupp," Rokey repeated patiently for the fourth or fifth time, "van Zandt has done a lot of harm to Jak, very personal harm. Van Zandt's only hope for survival is to stay as far away as the galaxy permits."

"He isn't smart enough to figure that out," Ray said. Bitterness made the words sharp and mean in his mouth.

"Then he is a dead man, and those who sail with him are in peril."

"More of Jak's people could die in that fight."

That was a new verse to Ray's anxious refrain. Rokey had to pause and consider.

They were in the galley, sharing a sumptuous meal delivered by the *Tamaroan's* kitchens, a meal that was a late, late dinner for Rokey and an early breakfast for Ray. The usually peaceful ride through intraspace was giving them too much time to think, with no action possible. Rokey picked up the cocoa carafe and stirred it before refilling their mugs, using this familiar ritual as cover for the surge of anger and remorse he felt.

They sat in silence for another moment, then Rokey spoke. "Van Zandt became the enemy of everyone on the *Tamaroan* when he seduced Zabor," he said quietly. "We got caught in the crossfire of *their* battle, not the other way around. They saved our lives and, by giving them the duty of protecting the Hupp, we are saving their honor."

"People are still gonna die because of this."

Rokey sipped at his cocoa, but the richly scented flavor was no consolation. "People will die because of this," he said quietly.

Of Hearth and Home

The fireplace in Whytock's favorite den onboard the *Reach* provided the only light, glowing brightly as the stack of logs burned. The fire was only a hologram, unreal. A great many Hupp were drifting about, admiring it. Some were even floating inside the fireplace, looking out at their friends through the flames. This daring game had initiated a growing rush of giggles and teasing in their native tongue, mingling with the soft sizzle and swish of the holo-audio. The Hupp were fascinated by fire, having never encountered it or any need for it. Whytock was dimly concerned that they would misunderstand the danger, even though he was charmed and pleased by their innocent fun with the light and the patterns.

After all, he reminded himself, he could be quite sure that they would never forget that he had warned them that *real* fire was hot, destructive and a source of pain.

They enjoyed the fireplace holo-display anyway, and he let them.

Nate, settled beside Whytock on the sofa, did not join in the celebration of the flames. Fire brought back a renewed wash of fear that the dreaded "Haters" were ravaging his world, burning his treehome. Nate had a real name now for the "Haters," and he knew what and who they were. The enormous memory of that village of dead trees crowded out the more rational definitions. Tapper, the only Hupp who had survived that destruction, refused to be in the room with even a hologram of fire.

Burke came in with a rolling table layered with snacks for everyone, interrupting their reverie and the fireplace revelry.

Burke was greeted by a shower of soft, whiskery kisses rained down upon his face and head and shoulders as the Hupp floated up to him. They crowded closely around until he disappeared from sight within the happy cloud. The Hupp were very fond of the giant who had led them away from captivity. Burke's exact feelings were never spoken, but his face turned bright red each time the rain of kisses began. He closed his amber eyes with a sigh.

The cloud of Hupp settled around the snack table, which expanded outward into an array of shelves, trays, dishes and bowls, displaying the dinnerware which Burke had designed just for the Hupp. There were ornate handles on the stands to which they could anchor themselves, and tiny, tiny cups and platters. Whytock's luxury cruise-liner starship had enormous banks of growth vats that could reproduce any set of aminoes, proteins or sugars needed for an alien meal. Every dish, however, was based on the berries that Richards' men had gathered for their captives. No one complained about monotony in their diet, because Burke worked hard at creating a continuously varying menu for the berry-nutrients. The Hupp were always glad to see him.

"Exit two hours, twenty minutes," Burke announced to Whytock once he emerged from the cloud.

Whytock thanked him, then turned to Nate's little face hovering beside his and said quietly. "After all these weeks and weeks, you are almost home."

Nate could hear the worried tone. "You do not know what to expect, and that is a problem for you, isn't it? Not knowing?"

Whytock did not like what he had to say. "I want to be wrong about what I expect," he said after a moment's hesitation. "I have a problem with knowing just enough to worry and not enough to be sure."

"A perfect memory is little comfort in facing an unknown future," Nate said. "But I do remember that you saved all of us. I remember the feeling, and I remember why I trust you."

"You trust me?"

"Yes," Nate responded without hesitation.

"Trust is a very large thing," Whytock said softly, almost as if speaking to himself.

"It is large enough to hold onto and to feel anchored by."

"I will not forget that." Whytock flashed his brilliant white smile, "President Nate." He chuckled happily. "Have you gotten used to the title yet?"

Nate tasted the emotion of pride once again, dipping into the happiest, most puzzling memories of his life. "It feels new every time I think about it, or remember the election, because it is just too strange and wonderful to understand."

"You were made for the job, my friend!"

"I just hope," Nate could almost not say the words, "There is a world left for me to be president of."

They sat quietly together, both concerned for the future, yet glad that their friends could enjoy the last hour of the evening.

There was no way to know who would be waiting for them in the Hupp System until they jumped out the intraspace window and could see for themselves.

"Trouble, Boss." Burke's heavy voice was strained.

"Mr. Burke quite understates it," Tapper said as he puffed up to eye-level with Whytock. "That is an entire fleet of starfighters out there!"

The *Reach's* elegant bridge was dominated at the moment by the holo-display of the Hupp System. The planet was a distant orb against the face of the Sun. The view was dominated by the swarm of starfighters flying toward them in precise battle formation.

"We have put the ship on full defense-system alert," Tapper went on. He grabbed Whytock's collar with one hand to pull himself closer. The agitation was clear in his eyes. "But I have not learned anything yet of the fighting capabilities of this ship! I have only learned navigation!"

Whytock patted Tapper's tail with a reassuring gesture. "I haven't lost a fight yet, my friend. Let's find out first who that is out there."

Whytock settled himself into the captain's chair, careful not to jostle the Hupp clinging to his jacket. "There is always that one little difficulty with the watertight defense screens I have, you see, Tapper, communications can't get through, either. An EM block is an EM block, so our first real defense is to drop the screens and introduce ourselves."

He grinned at the anxious little face floating beside his. "Isn't that easy?"

"But doesn't that mean that they can shoot us? They shoot with long-wave radiation. I remember that."

Whytock nodded, made a gesture to reach for a cigar but interrupted himself. "I said it was easy. I didn't say it was altogether safe."

He told the computer to drop the screens, and hailed the fleet of starfighters hurling themselves at his ship.

"Whytock!" Rokey's voice was clear despite the static in the radio signal. "Status. I have to convince these people you aren't the lead ship of a federal fleet coming through."

"I take it that your expedition was successful?" Whytock was beaming.

Tapper was not sure what that meant, but he kept still.

"Yes," Rokey radioed back, "and we got here ahead of Richards. His men scrubbed away every trace of their base camp on the planet, and we haven't found any sign of them anywhere else yet. Ray checked out a number of village-groves. There doesn't seem to be any further harm done. The trees are asleep, but they're alive."

"This is all good news," Whytock said. "We may have arrived in time to set up our defenses."

"Are you bringing federal troops in?" Rokey asked.

"No. Government troops would just become another invading force. The President of Hupp has hired me as defense minister, and I am providing the guardians of Hupp, or rather, your most illustrious self has provided a defense team."

Rokey interrupted with laughter. "The President of Hupp!"

"Oh, yes! They elected Nate, unanimously! Didn't I tell you about the elections? No, of course not! I haven't had time!"

"Look!" Tapper exclaimed, tugging on Whytock's collar and pointing to the holo-display. "Look! They're turning back! They're not attacking!"

The fleet of starfighters were, indeed, changing formation

with showy precision. The giant *Tamaroan* was approaching.

"We must tell the President at once," Whytock said merrily to Tapper and Burke. "His army has arrived to escort him home!"

Nate peered anxiously over the edge of the entranceway to his treehome, afraid of what he would see even though Rokey had reassured him that his portrait was in place and all was well. A strange air of neglect hung over the village. Everyone had floated out the *Shadow* and puffed on to their treehomes without speaking. The gardens were overgrown, and they complained in their whispery voices as the Hupp went by.

Windblown leaves inside were piled about in untidy arrangement. Tree was soundly asleep. His beloved home was otherwise unharmed. Nate floated inside sure that he would burst with the enormity of feelings that swirled through him. He was home. They might not really be as safe here as they had thought before Contact, but it was home. This was his Tree, she was alive and well, and his friends were alive. He thought of Massay, victim of the pirates. He wondered who they would find to move into his tree.

There was the portrait that had inspired him to follow Seff's dream of art. It was intact, as shiny-bright and unchanged as a memory frozen in the air. Nate carefully removed the bits of leaf and lichen that he and Rokey had used to cover it, and he cleared the corners of the chamber. He could not make it look as it had before he had set out that fateful morning. Nothing in his world would ever look the same, even with a perfect memory of what had been. His emotions were also a color, a dimension and a flavor to every memory-image; his feelings about his home, his world and the universe around him would never be the same.

He drifted over to the sleeping twigs in the back and curled up in the once-familiar cradle of their tender grasp. It was only mid-afternoon and there was much to be done, decisions to be made. Nate cuddled within the embrace of his Tree and fell at once into a deep and dreamless sleep.

Safe in the Arms of His Beloved

"They're all napping," Rokey said with some surprise as the gravity belt set him back down beside Ray. Ray, with Whytock and Sejan, stood in the center of the village-grove beside the crate with the Hupp's first radio transmitter. They looked uncomfortable in their spacesuits. There was no longer a single Hupp in sight. The grove was quiet, with breezes sighing through the crowns of the massive treehomes.

"Everyone?" Whytock turned on his heel, surveying the village. "Apparently so. Should we be alarmed?"

"Perhaps that's their way of coping?" Ray suggested.

"That's certainly your way of coping," Rokey said to him as a tease. "You fall asleep at the slightest provocation."

"You're just jealous," Ray teased back.

"You know it."

Sejan broke in. Amusement at their banter was clear in his voice and face despite the partial screen of his spacesuit helmet, but he spoke respectfully. "I think this means they are communing with their treehomes, Your Honor. From what I've learned in talking with them, they have a unique relationship with their trees."

"The trees are sentient," Rokey said. "I've seen them in conversation with the Hupp."

"I have a theory about the treehomes," Sejan said. "I made Father let me come along because I want a tissue sample from Nate's tree so that I can do DNA analysis."

"What's your theory?" Ray asked him. He was grinning.

He could tell that Rokey wanted to launch into a lecture about his own theory, so he cut him off by getting Sejan to talk first.

"Lord Rokhmyr and Mr. Whytock did explain the concept of gender in language when the Hupp first learned SpeakEZ, and I know that Nate, at least, understands that the pronouns 'he' and 'she' and 'it' are referential. I talked with him about it quite a lot."

Sejan was evidently excited about his theory and he went on with growing energy. "I went over your computer recordings of their registration of names, and not a single one of the Hupp listed themselves as 'female.'"

The three men stared at the boy in outright astonishment.

"Not one?" Whytock said finally. "But they said we rescued everyone?"

"Perhaps we just didn't explain the concept correctly," Rokey said thoughtfully. "But you may have something."

"Do you see where my logic is going, Lord Rokhmyr?" Sejan's excitement showed in his eager stance.

"You're right that we need DNA from the treehomes to be certain."

"Live tissue?" Ray asked uneasily. "I'm not doing any wood chopping."

"Oh, no!" Sejan said hastily. "A leaf, or a fallen branch will do fine. I would just have to be certain that it is from Nate's specific tree."

"Getting one from Seff's tree would be a good idea as well," Rokey said, all professor now and enjoying the role. "It's that one there set off to the side. I'll show you."

He gestured to Ray. "You check Nate's tree and see if you can get a loose piece. And don't wake him."

Rokey and Sejan strode off, careful not to walk over any of the flowering plants.

Ray made a sour face at Rokey's back, clicked on his antigravity belt, and floated up to the entrance of Nate's treehome.

Whytock stood unmoving, arms crossed over his chest despite the restraint of the spacesuit. He tapped a control on his sleeve, and a faint wisp of smoke wafted through the helmet, filling it with lazy spirals.

"I'll just unpack the radio then," he said brightly to no one in particular. He stood there without moving, inhaling the sweet smoke filling his helmet. He was smiling.

Let's Talk

"This radio-thing is really quite a pleasant form of communication." Nate's voice, amplified to be audible throughout the bridge of the *Tamaroan,* made the little alien an enormous presence, actually even a touch presidential. "It feels as if I am in two places at the same time, both there with you and here in my home."

Rokey was seated on Lord Jak's bridge throne, still in charge of the starship and crew. Despite the discomfort of wearing his collar of rank, he was enjoying the role of starship lord and master more than he cared to admit, even to himself. "Some people do this just for fun," he said to Nate.

"I can well imagine," Nate replied. "I look forward to the time we have placed one in every treehome. It should be quite a conversation!"

"The kids are building them at record speed," Rokey said. "The conversation should start soon."

"This is not yet for fun, however, is it?" Nate said.

"It will be soon enough, President Nate. That's our job." Rokey signaled for Sejan to step up to the throne microphone. "Now that the radio connection with you has been established, we can warn you if anyone breaks through to the planet itself.

"Meanwhile, we have a volunteer for the post of special communications officer, someone who will be available for radio contact with you whenever you want." He nodded to Sejan.

"I will have a receiver in my ear at all times," Sejan said. He flicked one broad, naked eartip as he said this, flashing the diamond-flecked receiver clipped to the rim. "It is tuned to your transmitter, so you have only to speak my name into it."

"Sejan!" Nate exclaimed, "How delightful! I recognize your voice in this radio! We can continue our discussion now, even while you are in space far away."

"I look forward to it, President Nate," Sejan said.

"Be prepared, however," Rokey broke in, "for radio silence if we give the word. If Richards' people come back, that signal would guide them right to your front door."

"I won't let that happen," Sejan said quietly but firmly. He paused, then added, "Your Honor."

"We have an army up here to make sure it doesn't happen," Rokey said. "We also have a plan, proposed by the enigmatic Mr. Burke and the ever ready Captain Harris. We will signal you for silence if anyone does enter the System."

"I know you are expecting the starships of the men who were following you before. Do you know when they will come?"

"I know that they *will* come," Rokey said, "but there is no way to know *when.* In an hour? Next month? We are using every minute to prepare, but so are they."

"That is why they are dangerous men," Nate said.

Sejan stepped forward with a dash of his father's aristocratic assumption. "That is also why *we* are dangerous!" he declared.

"I certainly hope so," Nate replied in a most matter of fact tone. "I believe that is the reason Lord Rokhmyr asked you to come here."

There was a unanimous cheer of affirmation from everyone on the bridge.

Finders, Keepers

The giant, golden starship drifted in open space, her engines cold, her many ports and galleries dark, her brilliant hull scarred with time. A lone antenna light blinked erratically, the single sign of intelligent life in the entire system. The ancient ship was clearly abandoned, waiting for eternity or for the discovery of a moment.

The system's primary blazed nearby, close enough that the polar prominences were distinct shapes against the stars. The intra-dimensional threshold, the window in space that was the only entrance/exit to this solar system was invisible, imperceptible, close enough that any starships which arrived through that window would see the abandoned, elegant starliner almost at once.

"Why didn't we see her when we first scouted this system?" Fleet Commander Leroy Richards demanded of the lieutenant who had brought the derelict to his attention.

"She was probably on the other side of the sun at that time," the lieutenant replied, pointing to a portion of the readout on the carry-screen he was holding in front of the commander. "She's in a polar orbit, and we did not send scouts to the northern polar region. There was no need. She's dark, so none of our sensors would have scanned her. She just happened to have orbited around to this point when we entered the system."

"It's true we've only been using this system for the last decade or so," the commander said thoughtfully as he read over the screen. "We certainly could have overlooked her before now."

He handed the carry-screen back to his lieutenant. "What a bit of luck."

Leroy Richards sat hunched over in his command chair at the center of the main bridge level, watching the holo-display as his fleet approached the derelict starliner. He knew the value of this and that in the galaxy, and he knew that the bits and pieces of this antique monstrosity just might begin to recoup the losses inflicted on him in his latest project.

"No trace of the *Yankee Shadow* anywhere in the system that we can scan," another eager lieutenant reported. "There are no life-signs detected on the derelict, not even from this proximity."

"Harris may have only been stopping through to see if we were here," Leroy Richards said in speculation. "After all, we are only stopping by to see if the *Shadow* is here."

He studied the display of the dark, desolate starship. "Has Riley reached her yet?"

"They'll be docking with the derelict in twenty-three minutes, sir."

"Make sure the feed from their cameras goes directly to the bridge display."

"We already have the feed, sir." The lieutenant flicked his hand across his forearm control panel. The view in the holo-display switched to a close-view as Lieutenant Riley's shuttle approached a docking bay on the scarred hull. The doors of the docking bay hung loosely, as though they had been forced open at some point.

Richards watched in silence as the shuttle docked and Riley and his men disembarked. The landing bay was enormous, but photon burns scarred the walls, and the equipment racks were gutted.

Once inside, however, it was clear the invaders had been driven off before the ship was abandoned. She was a luxury liner of the first class, in excellent condition inside, filled with treasure and a treasure herself.

"I'm going onboard," Richards declared. He unbuckled the safety belt on his command seat and stood, beckoning the orderlies who awaited his command. "In fact, bring everyone. I think we are going to sleep in comfortable beds tonight!"

Lost in Amazement

"Ray had the idea of using a sub-sonic broadcast to keep them disoriented while the ship's computer leads them around," Rokey said cheerfully. "He and I went through hell and back once on a real derelict because of sub-sonics."

"How long have they been wandering around down there?" Lord Jak asked. He was still in sickbay, surrounded by medical machines, but he was recovering. His massive voice had regained some of its vigorous timbre. "It's been several days now, hasn't it?"

Whytock checked the enormous wristwatch face he carried tucked away in a pants pocket. "Ninety-four hours now. We have let some of the plumbing systems continue to function, but they have had nothing but water since they boarded."

"You sure that your ship's computer can keep them separated and going around the maze of corridors?"

Ray and Rokey both answered at once. "Yes."

"That was how Ray and Burke got the idea of luring them into those corridors in the hotel section of the *Reach*," Rokey explained. "We've been through it ourselves."

"And the sub-sonics are keeping them awake?" Jak sounded as cheerful as Ray. He had to keep brushing back his whiskers as he grinned.

"You can't sleep in a spacesuit anyway," Briggs pointed out. "And they haven't dared to take their suits off since Rokey turned on the sound."

"Wait another two or three hours," Lord Jak said. "Then send in Two Knife and his men to round them up. We've taken their fleet. We have them now. They are helpless in there."

Ray looked over to Rokey and said with quiet pride, "And not a shot fired."

Where the Girls Are

The same holo-fire burned in the big marble fireplace on the *Reach,* but the Hupp were gone, returned to their tree-homes. The den seemed very large and quiet now, even with the party group there: Whytock as host, restored to his starship, Ray and Rokey, Lord Jak, Captain Briggs and Sejan. Burke moved among them noiselessly, refilling wineglasses and dessert trays. With the Hupp no longer onboard the *Reach,* Whytock was once again indulging in his beloved, sweet-smelling cigars. Somehow the smoke always drifted off behind him, however, away from everyone else in the room.

"You have set off on a most impressive line of research with the Hupp," Whytock said to Sejan. "What led you to ask the question about their gender?"

"Actually, Wennofar gave me the idea," Sejan said. "When we were introduced to the Hupp onboard the *Reach,* she kept asking, 'Are you a girl-Hupp or a boy-Hupp?' After awhile, she began deliberately trying to find a girl-Hupp, and she asked me to help her."

"She's at that age," Briggs said. "She knows the change is coming, but she is still untouched by it."

"Her friends at school are older than she is by quite a bit." Sejan's big-brotherly wisdom and concern softened his words. "The Hupp are like children, and she can be the big girl around them. She likes that. They make her feel happy, I can tell."

"Her innocent curiosity has led us to a most curious fact about the Hupp," Whytock said. "This DNA data Sejan has collected is conclusive, and I am singularly impressed," Whytock continued. "There are other symbiotic peoples in the galaxy, but the Hupp have a most unusual arrangement."

"It's not really symbiosis, sir," Sejan said. He spoke politely, but he was proud of his knowledge. "The Hupp and his treehome are genetic counterparts, alternating generations, as it were."

"You've studied this quite thoroughly," Rokey said approvingly.

"As much as I can so far, yes, Your Honor. It is a most fascinating puzzle."

Briggs and Lord Jak made proud-parent faces. Whytock beamed.

"The treehomes have double the number of chromosomes," Sejan took up his account once more, obviously pleased by the adult attention. "The chromosomes themselves are identical to the Hupp chromosomes, but the Hupp have only the one set."

"So, if you double a Hupp, you get a treehome?" Whytock said. He was clearly caught up in Sejan's discovery.

Everyone laughed. Whytock looked around in surprise, then caught on and beamed.

"That's the strange part, the bit even the Hupp can't explain. In order to get another generation of Hupp, two of them sleep together," – he hesitated, aware of the nuance, and held up his hands in protest – "No, really, they just, literally, *sleep* together in the sleeping-twig appendages at the back of the main chamber. Apparently, the DNA exchange happens among the two Hupp and the tree, there in the sleeping twigs, somehow, by the physical contact. Eventually, buds form along the back wall around the sleeping twigs, and the buds grow into children. The children stay attached to the treehome wall by the tail until they get big enough to be safe in the open air, then the attachment drops off, releasing them."

Sejan had everyone's attention now, and knew it. "But no one knows where the treehomes *themselves* come from!" he said with some energy. "Wildtrees can be adopted by moving into the chamber in the trunk, and they eventually change and grow into treehomes. Nate told me that there are Hupp who live in converted wildtrees. But they don't know how the wildtrees grow, either."

Rokey had been listening most intently, remembering his direct experiences of the village grove and the Hupp people, remembering the dead face of Massay looking up from the sand. "Nate told me that the treehomes absorb the dead. The trees are their source, their home and to the tree they return."

"But where did the trees come from?" Sejan went on, absorbed in the topic. "There are so few Hupp, really, for an entire world of people, and there is such a minimal amount of dry land. How did the cycle of treehome and Hupp get started?"

"I see that you are not going to mind making a home here in the Hupp System, are you, Master Sejan?" Whytock said. His animated face showed a flash of genuine relief and pleasure. "They have a friend in you already. I'm sure you will be a great help to them as they discover themselves."

"Yes, sir," Sejan said. "This is a lot more interesting than school," – he nodded toward his father – "and my family can be together here."

"For the first time since leaving Wozur, the people of the *Tamaroan* have a real future," Lord Jak said. "We have a goal and a home, not just an ambition."

"It will take a lot of income to maintain the *Tamaroan* here," Ray said. He did not sound quite as pleased with the situation as everyone else. He had the echo of "pirates" in the back of his mind.

"Yes, it will," Whytock said smoothly, stepping in over Lord Jak's response. "And sparing no expense is my department. The *Tamaroan* and crew have been hired by the government of Hupp. As Minister of Defense and Finance of Hupp, I have directed that all income from the patents on the process for growing membrane like the Hupp's skin goes into their defense fund – a number of spacesuit manufacturer's have already bought licensing rights. That will get us started, don't you think?"

"You mentioned something about that before you went to Wozur," Rokey said. "Your research people came up with a viable process?"

"Yes!" Whytock's white smile beamed his pride. His strange, dark eyes were genuinely alight. "A remarkably profitable one, too. I checked in with them before leaving Wozur, and I'm told that the Hupp-based process runs at *one one-thousandth* the cost of current nanite-built spacesuit materials, and the final product has greater flexibility."

"That should cover quite a *lot* of expenses," Lord Jak said.

"In addition, we haven't gotten through a fraction of the material we pulled out of Richards' computers." Whytock was warming to his topic. "I intend to dismantle his black-market empire, obviously, but first I hope to sift out the several operations that *are* legitimate. He was careful to distribute his activities among a number of corporations and financial entities. Not all of his activity was illegal, odd as that may sound. That was his way of covering his truly criminal acts."

"What do you intend to do with the so-called legitimate operations?" Rokey said to Whytock.

"Oh, keep taking a profit from them, what else? Let's just say that there will be major changes in the upper echelon, but that's simply business-as-usual, isn't it? That profit will also be directed toward the maintenance of the *Tamaroan's* base of operations here, to pay for the Hupp's guardianship. I doubt most of those companies will even notice the change."

"So, Richards ends up paying for the trouble he started here?"

"He will never be able to pay for the lives he has taken," Whytock said, his demeanor and his voice serious. "I will see to it that he and his crew are tried in federal courts for their many crimes. They will be mind-wiped, I am sure, but the Hupp will never forget what was done to them."

"They'll never forget you, either, Mr. Whytock," Sejan said after the silence in the room had stretched thin. "We all played a part, but you started the process that saved their world."

"Thank you, Master Sejan. Those are kind words." His smiled had recovered. Whytock turned to Rokey. "Where will you and Captain Harris go? Now that you have played your part in their history?"

"With that hold full of fuel-cells you gave us," Rokey said, "We can go anywhere we want."

"As far away as we can get from wherever van Zandt went or is likely to be," Ray said. "It's nice to be popular, but it could be fatal if we get to be too well-known around these parts."

"We will miss you," Lord Jak said. "Both of you."

"It has been good to see furred faces again," Rokey said to them in Wozurn. "I will think of you often."

"You could stay here with us," Briggs said then. "You know you would be welcome."

"Then who would look after me?" Ray broke in with a grin.

"But do you really have to go?" Briggs said sadly.

"Yes, ma'am," Ray said, his grin sharper, his green eyes suddenly hard. "I need to buy a new coat."

As Close as the Sky

"There, you see that little group of orange lights moving across the sky?"

Seff puffed himself up higher in the branches at the top of Tree to see more clearly. "Oh, yes! I see it now. That is the *Tamaroan?*"

"Yes. Sejan tells me we will see her several times each day and night, as she passes over us in her orbit."

"So they are not far away at all?" Seff sounded awed. He was still so impressed by their adventure.

"They are no further than the radio in your chamber."

"I *like* having a radio," Seff said as he settled back into the enfolding nest of twigs and leaves. "It makes me want to think of things to say to people. I haven't figured out how to paint sound, yet. That's even more difficult than painting fog!"

"They will be wonderful paintings, Seff," Nate said fondly.

It felt so good to be home, even with the great ocean so close and the enormity of outer space and civilization out there beyond the sky. So many new things to remember, so many new memories yet to come and, at last, a chance to remember them in peace.

Tree began humming her evening song. They watched the lights of the *Tamaroan* sail across the sky and disappear behind the horizon. Then they watched the stars come out in their grand patterns.

www.ingramcontent.com/pod-product-compliance
Lightning Source LLC
Chambersburg PA
CBHW030818310726
48980CB00006B/546/J
9781592246021